Lions and Tigers and
MURDER,
Oh My

**Center Point
Large Print**

Also by Denise Swanson and available from
Center Point Large Print:

Dying for a Cupcake
Murder of an Open Book

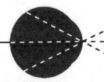

**This Large Print Book carries the
Seal of Approval of N.A.V.H.**

Lions and Tigers and

MURDER,

Oh My

A DEVERAUX'S DIME STORE MYSTERY

Denise Swanson

CENTER POINT LARGE PRINT
THORNDIKE, MAINE

This Center Point Large Print edition
is published in the year 2018 by arrangement with
The Berkley Publishing Group, an imprint of
Penguin Publishing Group, a division of
Penguin Random House LLC.

The text of this Large Print edition is unabridged.
In other aspects, this book may vary
from the original edition.
Printed in the United States of America
on permanent paper.
Set in 16-point Times New Roman type.

ISBN: 978-1-68324-688-6

Library of Congress Cataloging-in-Publication Data

Names: Swanson, Denise, author.
Title: Lions and tigers and murder, oh my :
    a Deveraux's dime store mystery / Denise Swanson.
Description: Center Point large print edition. | Thorndike, Maine :
    Center Point Large Print, 2018.
Identifiers: LCCN 2017051082 | ISBN 9781683246886 (hardcover)
Subjects: LCSH: Murder—Investigation—Fiction. | Large type books. |
    GSAFD: Mystery fiction.
Classification: LCC PS3619.W36 L56 2018 | DDC 813/.6—dc23
LC record available at https://lccn.loc.gov/2017051082

ACKNOWLEDGMENTS

A huge thank-you to Shay Connelly and Kim Greene for helping Devereaux figure out how to break up with one of her suitors. And to Shelly Franz for giving Dev the perfect example of how not to do it.

Lions and Tigers and
MURDER,
Oh My

CHAPTER 1

Shuffling slowly back from my newly completed sales exhibit, I tilted my head and studied my handiwork. It was the beginning of October, and I was experimenting with something new for my Halloween merchandising. After clearing out the area near the entrance of my shop, Devereaux's Dime Store and Gift Baskets, I had set up contrasting seasonal displays. One nice. One naughty.

On the right side, I had arranged traditional holiday products. Bright orange pumpkins adorned the shelves, colorful goblins and ghosts hung from hooks, and bags of trick or treat candy spilled temptingly from bushel baskets. The vibe was good, clean fun.

Opposite that space, I had created a sexy black-and-white fantasy. Naughty nurse and wanton witch costumes lay draped over a velvet couch. A marble-topped Victorian coffee table with a sign that read POTIONS held a selection of delectable chocolates, as well as edible body gels and flavored massage oils. And a muscular male mannequin was dressed in an abbreviated kilt and tam-o'-shanter, and not much else.

"Damn it to hell!" I blurted out. "Am I taking too much of a risk?"

Yes, I was talking to myself. I did that sometimes when I needed expert advice.

Snickering, I returned to my contemplation. Although it was true that I had become somewhat famous, or maybe infamous, for my custom-designed erotic gift baskets, I usually tucked all the wicked bits and pieces safely out of the sight of my regular shoppers. But I was tired of hiding that part of my business and had decided that Halloween was the perfect time to test the waters.

Now I was having second thoughts. Were my customers ready to be smacked in the face with the sensual darkness and guilty pleasures of my offerings? After all, I did have a teen lounge on my second floor. Would their parents be appalled at the display? But the raciness was more hinted at than overt, so really, it should be okay. Right?

While I was still vacillating between tearing down the display or leaving it up, the sleigh bells above the front door jingled. Turning my head, I saw an attractive man in his late forties or early fifties stroll inside as if he owned the place.

Hell! It was only eight a.m. and the store was supposed to be closed until noon on Mondays. Evidently, after my new tenant had arrived, I'd forgotten to turn the dead bolt. This was the first official day of the renter's lease, and having the second-story office suite occupied would take some adjustments on my part. Like remembering to lock the freaking door.

The stern expression on the face of the guy in the expensive suit who was striding toward me was a reminder as to why I hadn't previously gone public with the spicy side of my sales. This would be a good test. Should I take down the suggestive display or leave it intact?

I narrowed my eyes, squared my shoulders, and prepared to defend myself.

Although Mr. Suit seemed familiar, I didn't think he was a native of my hometown. With a population a shade over four thousand, I recognized most of the indigenous inhabitants of Shadow Bend, Missouri. However, I wasn't as up-to-date on the more recent move-ins, the ones who had built McMansions in Country Club Estates.

The new folks had relocated here from Kansas City looking for cheap land and their concept of rural living. Unfortunately for them, their fantasy didn't include the reality of smelly farm animals, slow-moving tractors, or locals who had their own idea of how the community should be run.

When the man's unblinking stare skimmed my new display, then looked me up and down with a grim air, I braced myself for battle. His lips pressed together in a harsh white line, then he puckered his mouth, and as he glanced around, he shook his head.

The guy studied the paperback bookrack, the three-stool soda fountain, and my pride and joy, the antique brass cash register, clearly unimpressed with the vintage ambience. When he turned his nose up at the glass candy case, I gave up any hope that the shop might charm him.

The kind of person who didn't appreciate fudge, truffles, and other mouthwatering confections would never be one of my shoppers. There was no way that the store would ever win him over. Nor did I want him as a customer. This meant I didn't have to be nice to him.

"We're closed until noon." I crossed my arms. "The door should have been locked."

He ignored my not-so-subtle order to leave and demanded, "Jake Del Vecchio?"

Seriously? I knew I didn't look my best dressed in jeans and a sweatshirt, but I was pretty damn sure my more than generous curves made it abundantly clear that I wasn't named Jake.

Lifting my chin, I looked down my nose and said, "No. I'm Devereaux Sinclair."

This morning before coming into work, I had meditated, used lavender calming oil, and drank green tea. Yet I still wanted to smack this guy.

"That's not what I meant, and you know it." A scowl twisted his attractive features, and his brown eyes narrowed. "The business card Chief Kincaid gave me listed this address for Jake Del Vecchio. But evidently, Chief Kincaid has sent me on yet another wild-goose chase. He's treating my concerns like they're unimportant. A big joke," Mr. Suit huffed. "Not that I'm at all surprised. I've found that isn't unusual for public officials around here."

The guy was obviously a know-it-all. I pursed my lips. The problem with people who think they know it all is that they actually never seem to know when to shut up. Looked like it was time to educate him.

"Chief Kincaid is very good at his job." I put on my best don't-mess-with-me expression, the one I'd learned when I had worked in the cutthroat investment consulting business. "A job that doesn't always get the respect it deserves." Once I was sure the guy understood me, I said, "Jake's office is on the second floor." I jerked my thumb toward the rear of the store. "Up the stairs. The first door on the left."

"And he's a private investigator?" Once again, Mr. Suit's gaze flitted around my store. "Chief Kincaid said he had been a U.S. Marshal."

"That's right. He left the marshal service due to a line-of-duty injury," I explained, curious as to why Eldridge Kincaid had fobbed off this bozo on Jake.

The chief wasn't one to recommend a citizen go to a private detective unless there was a good reason. Maybe he didn't want the police department to become involved in the matter. And if that was the situation, I was more than a little bit worried what kind of mess Jake might be getting into if he took Mr. Suit's case.

If Jake was just my tenant, I probably wouldn't care, since I'm really not the warm-and-fuzzy type. But Jake was also my boyfriend.

Okay, fine. He was one of my boyfriends. He and Dr. Noah Underwood were, as my grandma Birdie liked to say, vying for my affection.

I was physically attracted to them both, but I hadn't made up my mind which man I truly loved. Each had pros and cons, and the decision was turning out to be a lot more difficult than I had ever imagined. What I had thought would be a sprint was turning into a marathon.

On the pro side for Jake, his ex-wife, Meg, had finally moved out of the house he shared with his great-uncle Tony on the Del Vecchio ranch. On the con side, instead of returning to St. Louis, Meg had rented an apartment in Shadow Bend.

The compassionate part of me understood that after the trauma Meg had experienced six months ago, she wasn't ready to live completely on her own. The hard-hearted part of me wished she had someone other than her ex-husband to lean on.

Still, Jake had taken a couple of steps in the right direction. Meg was out of his house, and after getting his private investigation license, he rented my empty office space, saying that this way he'd be able to spend more time with me.

In addition to all that, he was encouraging me to get my own private investigator's license so that we could work cases together. I really appreciated that instead of insisting that I stop getting involved in solving crimes, he wanted me to be his partner.

For Jake, becoming a PI in Missouri had been a lot quicker and a lot easier than I had expected. With his prior law enforcement experience, all he'd had to do was submit to a background check, pass a licensing exam, meet continuing education requirements, and obtain professional liability insurance.

It would be a bit more complicated for me to get my license. Still, I was considering it because, as it turned out, I was damn good at figuring out mysteries and helping the cops put the bad guys in jail.

Even if I didn't become a PI and work for him, with Jake upstairs we were bound to see more of each other than when he'd been overwhelmed with caring for his ex and managing his uncle's ranch. Although he continued to oversee the ranch, he'd hired a couple more hands, and during this time of year they weren't quite as swamped as they were in spring and summer.

I suddenly noticed that all the time that I had been thinking about my complicated love life, Mr. Suit had remained in front of me. Why hadn't he proceeded to the second floor to find Jake?

I raised a questioning brow at him and he murmured, "Devereaux Sinclair." Wrinkling his forehead, he muttered, "Chief Kincaid mentioned you."

"Oh?"

"He said you had your finger on Shadow Bend's pulse and you knew almost everything that went on around here." Mr. Suit squinted. "He mentioned that you had been instrumental in helping him solve some of his more complicated cases."

"He did?"

Now I was really wary. The chief freely acknowledged my assistance, but to volunteer that information to a stranger was suspicious. Why was he so eager for this guy to seek help outside the police department? It wasn't as if our tiny rural community was overrun with crime and the cops were too busy to handle minor complaints.

"Yes." He stared at me appraisingly, then added, "You said the store was closed. Could you come upstairs with me to Del Vecchio's office? You may have heard something that could help."

"Why should I help you?" I raised a brow. "You've been nothing but rude and dismissive since you walked in here."

"Uh . . ." Mr. Suit blinked, then inhaled sharply and said, "Sorry. When my mind gets focused on something, I have trouble thinking of anything else, even common courtesy." He smiled and said, "I apologize."

"Accepted." Normally, I wouldn't have been so

16

forgiving, but I had the time and he'd aroused my curiosity. "Let me lock the door and I'll follow you up."

As we climbed the steps, I heard hammering. And when we got to the office, I saw that Jake had been busy decorating. The walls that he'd painted a neutral taupe now held sepia-tinted photographs of the Old West. And a deer antler hat rack was near the doorway with his Stetson hanging from the tip of one of the horns.

I hadn't been in his office since his furniture was delivered yesterday afternoon, and now I admired the rustic walnut desk and the pair of antler-and-cowhide Western chairs that he'd arranged for visitors. Jake's own seat was a massive leather throne.

It seemed as if my little lesson on manners must have made an impression on Mr. Suit, because after he perused the decor, he smiled and held out his hand to Jake. "Mr. Del Vecchio?" Jake nodded and the man introduced himself. "I'm Elliot Winston."

Jake flicked a questioning glance at me, and as always his arresting good looks totally captured my attention. I indulged myself for a few seconds and ogled the way his broad chest filled out his shirt.

But all too soon, I forced myself to meet his amused gaze and explain. "Mr. Winston invited me to join him while he talked to you. He wanted to find out if I'd heard anything about the matter he wants to discuss."

For a nanosecond, as Jake stared back at me, I could actually see the sexual attraction zinging between us. Then he blinked and it was gone.

Jake turned his scrutiny to Elliot, waving us both to the visitor chairs, and said, "And this matter is . . ."

Elliot had an aristocratic attractiveness, but Jake's rugged good looks were more to my taste. Whereas Elliot's perfectly even features and lightly tanned complexion were nice, Jake's chiseled face and his bronzed skin pulled taut over the sculpted ridge of his cheekbones were a lot sexier.

While Elliot was as lean as a runway model, the strong column of Jake's throat rose from the collar of his red plaid Western-style shirt and his broad shoulders strained the flannel fabric. I barely stopped myself from licking my lips when he smoothed his palms down his faded Levi's. The worn denim lovingly molding his leg, emphasizing his drool-worthy thighs.

"Bear with me. I need to start at the beginning." Elliot's voice snapped me out of my lust-filled reverie. He took a pamphlet from the inside pocket of his suit jacket and asked, "Are either of you aware of my plans for a wildlife park between here and Sparkville?"

"I've read about it in the newspaper," Jake answered as I nodded. He folded his six-four, well-muscled body into his desk chair and continued, "As I recall, the article in the *Banner* mentioned that there was opposition from an animal rights group and some other problems as well."

"The Animal Safety Alliance refuses to see reason." Elliot frowned.

"From what folks have been talking about in the store," I chimed in, "the owners of the land adjacent to the park aren't too thrilled about its existence, either. Your neighbors are not fans of the idea of wild animals roaming free."

"The four hundred acres is completely enclosed by reinforced electrical fences." Elliot blew out an exasperated sigh. "People need to understand the park will bring in tourists and help small businesses in the area."

Although dollar signs danced in my head, I pushed aside my greed and countered, "Isn't it immoral to breed wild animals for the sole purpose of confining them to a cage all their lives?"

"We won't be buying animals from breeders, and unless they require medical treatment, they won't be in cages." Elliot turned toward me. "The park will be a refuge, taking in animals whose owners abandoned them or who were found injured and in need of veterinary care."

"What type of animals will you have?" Jake had begun taking notes.

"Initially, there will be bison, deer, llamas, and camels," Elliot answered. "But my true passions are the big cats. Once we have the set-up in place, we'll also shelter any of those that need a home."

"How far along with the project are you?" Jake asked, a furrow forming between his dark brows. "I recall the *Banner* article said that you inherited the land, but how about financing, permits, and zoning?"

"The funding is in place." Elliot straightened the crease on his pants. "The initial capital will come from my personal accounts, donations, and investors."

"How about the legalities?" Jake asked.

"The county board meets in two weeks to consider the change of zoning needed," Elliot answered. "And during that meeting, they'll decide on the special-use permit that's required as well."

"Does it appear to you that the board will approve?" I asked.

There was no question in my mind that the county could use an economic boost. Several area factories had closed, and we were all hurting. I just wasn't sure if a wildlife park would be the answer to our economic woes or cause more problems than it was worth.

"As of now, there's one undecided vote." Elliot crossed his legs.

"Is that why you want to hire me?" Jake's tone

was harsh. "I won't provide blackmail information."

"No!" Elliot jerked as if he'd been slapped.
"I'm here about my wife."

"Are you in the process of a divorce?" Jake
asked, his striking blue eyes dimming.

Domestic dispute cases were the bread and
butter of a private investigator. Jake and I had
discussed it, and he'd told me that although he
knew he had to take those clients, he found that
kind of work distasteful. It was a shame that his
first job would be something he didn't like doing.

"Divorce?" Elliot frowned. "Not at all." His
expression unreadable, he continued, "My wife's
been kidnapped, and the police refuse to do
anything about it."

CHAPTER 2

Kidnapped? I mouthed the word to Jake and widened my eyes. I hadn't been expecting that.

"Don't you think that little nugget of information should have been the first thing you mentioned to us?" I snapped.

"Along with getting hyperfocused on whatever I'm trying to accomplish, I am also extremely linear." Elliot's gaze softened. "It's not that I don't love my wife, it's just the way my mind works." He frowned. "And Gabriella's disappearance is a direct result of my attempt to open up the wildlife park. Everything starts with my initiation of that project."

"All that aside, I find it hard to believe that Chief Kincaid refused to investigate a kidnapping." Jake's tone made it clear that he was certain the chief would never have been that negligent. "In fact, he might even call the FBI if he suspects she was taken across state lines."

"Well, he didn't." Elliot thrust out his chin. "The chief isn't convinced Gabriella was kidnapped. I'm not even sure that he believes that she's missing."

"But he did enter her information into the Missouri uniform law enforcement system and the National Crime Information Center system, correct?" Jake raised a challenging brow. "He would have also notified his officers to review her information and keep an eye out for her."

Elliot nodded reluctantly. "Kincaid may have dotted all his i's and crossed all his t's, but it was obvious he thought I was a crackpot."

"I doubt that," Jake said, then asked, "How long has she been gone?"

"I'm not sure."

"Seriously?" The disbelieving word escaped before I could stop myself.

This was Jake's first case, and I didn't want to screw things up for him. But jeez Louise! How could the guy be oh so concerned, but not have a clue as to how long his wife had been gone?

Noticing that my fingers were drumming an agitated rhythm on my thigh, I stilled them. Maybe I'd had too much coffee this morning. *Nah.* I hadn't had enough caffeine until I could thread Birdie's Singer sewing machine while it was running. And I was nowhere near that level yet.

"I . . ." Elliot's eyes clouded, and he seemed to be involved in some passionate inner deliberation. Finally, he admitted, "We had a disagreement, and I spent a night in the Sparkville Holiday Inn. It was a stupid argument, and . . ." He trailed off again, then twitched his shoulders as if unable to explain himself.

"So the last time you saw her was when?" Jake's impassive voice broke the tension.

"Saturday night around seven." Elliot blew out a forlorn breath.

"And you're just starting to worry now?" I snapped. "More than thirty-six hours later?"

"I reported her missing to the police as soon as I got home yesterday morning." Elliot scowled.

"Oh. Well, okay then," I said grudgingly.

I own up to being a smartass, but I had to remember the smart part. Otherwise, I was just an ass. And that wasn't fair to Jake.

"I'm not a moron," Elliot muttered.

It was plain to see that the guy was unhappy we were asking him questions. Questions that I was sure Chief Kincaid had already asked him. But what had he expected? That without any information other than Gabriella's name and description, Jake would saddle up and ride off to find her?

"Did you have any contact with your wife after you left your house?" Jake glanced up from his notes. "Call her or text or anything?"

"No." Elliot shook his head. Sincerity dripped from his voice as he explained, "I thought it would be best if we both cooled off. Once she had calmed down, I figured I could make her see my point of view."

"What did you and your wife fight about?" I asked, keeping my tone neutral.

Was Elliot's concern about his wife's disappearance genuine or some sort of cover-up?

I glanced at Jake, who dipped his head slightly, indicating we were on the same page.

Ignoring my question, Elliot looked at Jake and said, "I'd like you to get on this immediately. Do you have a contract for me to sign?" When Jake was silent, he pulled a sheaf of folded papers and a checkbook from his pocket. "What's your fee?"

"I need some more information before I decide whether to take your case." Jake leaned forward and folded his hands on the desktop.

"I have a copy of the report that I gave the police and her picture." Elliot pushed several pages toward Jake. "Surely that's enough to get started."

Seconds went by as he and Jake stared at each other, and when Jake didn't break the growing silence, Elliot cleared his throat and huffed, "Fine. Gabriella was concerned about the amount of money that the wildlife park required. She wanted me to get more donations before opening and not put as much of our personal funds into it."

"Did you need her signature to access the capital?" I asked.

My Spidey senses were tingling. In my prior life, before I bought the dime store, I had worked a lot of years for an investment company. Granted, that business had collapsed when the owner was arrested for fraud, but I had been a damn good financial consultant, which meant being able to read people's motivations. Maybe Elliot had gotten rid of his wife to free up his assets.

"No." Elliot barely glanced at me, focusing all his attention on Jake. "The cash is from my trust fund. It has nothing to do with Gabriella."

"Does your wife have her own income?" Jake asked, leafing through the papers Elliot had pushed toward him. "Is she employed outside the home?"

"Gabriella has credit cards and access to our joint checking account." Elliot uncrossed, then recrossed his legs. "But no outside earnings. She's been a stay-at-home mother since her first pregnancy."

Elliot appeared old enough that his children probably weren't toddlers, but I realized no one had mentioned Gabriella's age. And it certainly wasn't unheard of for a rich guy to have a much younger wife.

Many women walk out on their husbands, especially if they're fighting about money, but a lot fewer would be willing to abandon their kids. While my mother had left town the day my father was sent to prison, she hadn't just disappeared. Mom had at least dropped me at my grandmother's before taking a powder.

Although my father had finally been proven innocent and recently released from the penitentiary, and I'd more or less made peace with my mother, I still felt a twinge of pain when I thought about that awful time. Finding myself suddenly without parents, and ostracized by a town that thought my dad was a criminal, had been hard enough. But the last straw in my basket of woes had been when my high school boyfriend, Noah Underwood, deserted me.

Yes, the same Noah Underwood that I was currently dating. Back then, after my family was disgraced, Noah's mother had blackmailed him into breaking up with me. Of course, that little tidbit hadn't come to light until recently. At the time, all I knew was that the boy who had vowed to love me for all eternity had abandoned me.

Even all these years later, those memories could still bring me to tears. Clasping my hands together to stop them from shaking, I blinked the moisture from my eyes and concentrated on what Jake was saying.

"Are your children missing, too?" Concern etched deep lines next to Jake's mouth.

"No. Our oldest boy took a job offer out of the country in January." Elliot was avoiding Jake's gaze by staring over his shoulder at a picture of a silhouetted cowboy riding a horse across the plains. "Our youngest son left for a year abroad last June, and Gabriella has been at loose ends since then."

"Could she have gone to visit one of your kids?" Jake asked, his expression deadpan.

"I'm not an idiot!" Elliot yelled, his face

turning an alarming shade of red. "When I couldn't find Gabriella, I called the boys right away. Neither of them have seen or heard from her since Saturday. Besides, her passport is still in our safe at home so she couldn't have left the U.S." His complexion turned even redder. "Do you think I'm insane?"

"Take a deep breath." I patted his shoulder. "Everyone is a little crazy, but it's not a competition, so relax. Just tell us what we need to know."

Elliot harrumphed. Evidently, in his eyes my weak attempt at humor had failed.

"Any family she might be staying with?" Jake didn't seem too upset with Elliot's shouting or the fact the man looked ready to have a coronary. "How about her friends or maybe a neighbor?"

"Gabriella's folks and mine are all dead." Elliot's skin tone had gone from lobster to maroon. "And I called everyone in her cell's contact list."

"You have her phone?" I asked.

Now I really was starting to worry. Nowadays, very few modern women willingly left their cells behind. Either Gabriella had been forced to go, or she was afraid the phone could be tracked.

"It was on the kitchen counter next to her handbag." Elliot ran his fingers through his dark blond hair. "That's why I know she didn't leave of her own free will."

I had to agree with him. Women did not wander off without their purses. Odds were that Gabriella really was missing and that her absence wasn't voluntary.

"How about her clothes?" I asked. "Did she pack a bag?"

"I couldn't tell." Elliot's cheeks reddened further. "I'm not really interested in fashion, so I don't notice what she wears or what she owns."

I kept my lips zipped shut. To me, it didn't sound like Elliot was a very interested husband at all. But, hey, what did I know? It wasn't as if I'd ever been married.

Jake was silent as he read through the pages of information Elliot had provided. I tapped my nails on my thighs, impatiently waiting to hear his verdict. Would this be our, I mean his, first case?

Shoving his chair back, Jake opened the desk drawer and withdrew a single sheet of paper. He offered it to Elliot, who snatched it from Jake's hand.

"It's a standard contract," Jake said. "You agree to pay an immediate retainer of a thousand dollars. I charge fifty an hour plus expenses. Meetings, travel time, and phone conversations are also billed at that rate, so if you call me for continual updates, it will cost you." He stared into Elliot's eyes. "Not to mention, annoy me."

"Understood." Elliot stretched out his palm. "Give me a pen and I'll sign it."

"One more thing." Jake held the ballpoint just out of Elliot's reach. "As per section eight of the contract, if you fail to provide me with accurate information, I'm not responsible for unproductive investigative time. I can and will stop the investigation. In addition, any remaining portion of the retainer is forfeited."

"Of course." Elliot grabbed the pen and scrawled his name. Flipping open his checkbook, he asked, "A thousand, right?" Jake nodded, and Elliot filled in the amount. Handing the check to Jake, Elliot asked, "When can you start?"

"Right now." Jake rose to his feet. "Let's head over to your house. I want to look around and see if there are any clues." He glanced at me. "It's still a few hours until the store opens. You want to take a ride and see if you spot anything?"

"Sure." I held back a grin. "I finished my display, so I'm free, and if worse comes to worst, I can text Dad to come in and open."

When Jake and I had discussed me helping him out and the possibility of me getting my license at some future point, I had talked to my father about increasing his hours at the store. Dad had been working for me since he got out of the penitentiary, and I found that I really appreciated having him as my backup both at the shop and at home. For the first time since Dad had gone to prison, I didn't feel as if the weight of our entire family's well-being was on my shoulders.

"Do you need me there?" Elliot asked. "I have an important meeting scheduled with that undecided county board member. I can cancel if you think it would help, but if all I'm going to be doing is standing there while you poke around, I'd really like to talk to this woman again." Elliot must have noticed my shocked expression and said, "My falling to pieces isn't going to bring Gabriella back." He shrugged sheepishly. "I'm the kind of guy that does better if I keep my mind occupied, otherwise, I'll just end up sitting at home crying."

"I'm good on my own." Jake smiled. "You go ahead to your meeting."

"Great. The address is on the paperwork that I gave you, and this is for the front door." Elliot fished a key ring from his pocket, slipped off a key, and gave it to Jake. "I'll come in through the garage. Just leave it on the counter when you're done." He frowned. "Please don't think that I'm not concerned about my wife."

"No. Of course not. If that were the case, you wouldn't have hired me," Jake assured him. "It's not as if your presence would help."

Shaking Jake's hand, Elliot said, "Thanks for understanding." As he backed out of the office, he added, "Call me if you have any questions."

I studied Elliot's departing figure. Now that Jake had taken the case, the man seemed more relaxed, but there was still an aura of guilt surrounding him. Was that a normal reaction? Or was it the sign of something else? Did Elliot feel bad because he'd left his wife alone the night she went missing? Or was he the reason she was gone?

Had Elliot killed Gabriella?

CHAPTER 3

There was something about Jake's truck that always set my pulse pounding. It might have been because the first time Jake and I ever kissed was sitting inside that pickup on a cold February night, parked by a frozen pond.

That evening, despite the impending murder charge hanging over my head, it had felt like we were the only two people in the world. I had the strangest impression that I had found my home, the place I was supposed to be, in his arms. And for me, that feeling of rightness was as rare as finding a calorie-free cupcake.

Cradled against Jake's chest while we cuddled in the cab of his truck had been one of the best moments that I could ever remember. At least until his ex-wife had called and interrupted what might have been my first-ever experience with backseat sex.

Still, I think the real reason that the massive Ford F-250 gets my blood pounding is that it reeks of strength and toughness and determination. Qualities which are high on my list of must-haves for the people I allow in my life. And Jake possessed them all in spades.

There's also the fact that I'm a bit of a car fanatic. I adore that Jake keeps his truck as shiny as if it had just left the dealership. Especially since, unlike a lot of men who drive huge pickups, Jake actually uses his on a working ranch.

Jake had parked the gleaming black F-250 in front of the dime store, and as he opened the passenger side door for me, I made a mental note to tell him that in the future I'd prefer he use the private lot behind my business. There were three spaces back there, so even when Dad was working, there was room for Jake's truck, and I liked to leave the spots facing my display window open for customers.

When Jake put his hands around my waist to boost me into the gigantic truck, I remembered the one thing I didn't like about the Ford—getting into it. It was like scaling the side of a Clydesdale just to get inside the stupid cab, and my struggle to mount that sucker made me feel inadequate. Not a quality I wanted to add to my résumé.

Jake, of course, was able to swing himself in without any effort whatsoever. But he was Paul Bunyan tall and Wolverine strong, and I was more like the superhero's weak sidekick. Or worse yet, the helpless girlfriend. And helplessness was yet another feeling I didn't enjoy.

I couldn't do anything about my lack of height, and anyway, five-six was average for a woman, but I kept vowing to start lifting weights. Still, Jake claimed he liked me soft and cuddly, and he *had* stopped teasing me about my difficulty with climbing into his pickup, so for now, I'd skip the visit to the gym.

As Jake slid behind the wheel and buckled his seat belt, he said, "Okay with you if we stop and talk to Chief Kincaid first?" I nodded, and he turned the key in the ignition. "I'd like to hear what he has to say about Elliot Winston and his missing wife."

"It is odd that the chief doesn't seem to want to investigate."

"Exactly." Jake slapped the steering wheel. "There's definitely something funny going on."

I smiled at the glint of excitement in Jake's eyes and said, "Being on a case truly oils your rifle, doesn't it?"

"Yep." Jake reached over and squeezed my thigh. "But it's investigating with you that really turns me on."

"Aw." I was too choked up to say anything more and gazed out the windshield.

Shadow Bend's business district was situated around a town square. The PD was located between the hardware store and the dry cleaner, all of which were only a couple of blocks from my shop. Normally, we'd just walk over, but since we were on our way to the Winston house, Jake drove the short distance and parked in front of the station in one of the five spaces reserved for police visitors.

As we approached the square cinder block building with its front window bars and overall crushing atmosphere, I forced myself to take a calming breath. I had developed a sort of weird claustrophobia during my father's imprisonment, and the police station's structure reminded me of the penitentiary where Dad had been incarcerated.

Now that my father was free, my paranoia was easing up, but my chest still tightened uncomfortably as Jake ushered me inside. I was so intent on overcoming my aversion to entering the PD that I was almost run over by a woman shouting obscenities over her shoulder as she pushed past me and rushed outside.

I suppose someone cursing isn't all that unusual for a police station. After all, most folks aren't happy to be there. But this enraged individual was one of my best friends, Poppy Kincaid, and the person she was screaming at was her father, the chief of police.

Running after Poppy, I caught her just as she yanked open the door of her Hummer. Her white-blond curls looked as if she had run her hands through them until they surrounded her head like a silver tumbleweed, her amethyst eyes were teary, and her slim body shook with rage.

I grabbed her hand before she could get inside the SUV and asked, "What happened?"

It was no secret that Poppy and her father didn't

get along. They had been on the outs for years. He was the epitome of law and order, and she was the town bad girl. Poppy was the type of woman who would see your sarcasm and raise you a heaping helping of sass. Not a characteristic her strict chief of police dad appreciated.

Still, they'd tolerated each other until last Christmas. Something had happened during the holidays that had shoved their relationship from passable to explosive. And I was afraid that whatever had occurred today had caused it to detonate beyond repair.

"Mr. Holier-Than-Thou Chief of Police told me that unless I straightened up, I was going to hell," Poppy ground out between clenched teeth.

"And?" I knew that couldn't be all that had set off my friend.

"I told him it was too late for me to change, so that at this point, my only choice is to go big or go home."

"That must have gone over well." Chief Kincaid was not known for his sense of humor. "What happened after you said that?"

"He told me not to blaspheme, and I called him stupid." Poppy's smile was forced.

"You didn't." I exhaled loudly. The chief would not have taken that well.

"Hey," Poppy said, twitching her slender shoulders. "I'm sorry I hurt his feelings, but I thought he already knew."

"Seriously, Poppy?" I gripped her hand. "Why do you two do this to each other?"

"I can't talk now." She drew in a shaky breath. "I'll text you later, and we can find a time to meet up at the bar for a drink."

"In the state you're in, I don't think you should be alone."

"No worries." Jerking her fingers from my grasp, she slammed the door, fired up the engine, and backed onto the street. Squealing her tires, she roared away, daring the cops to stop her.

As I reentered the PD, Jake stood waiting in the lobby. He raised a brow, and I shook my head, indicating that I had no idea what had just happened. Jake shrugged and marched up the short flight of concrete stairs that led to the rest of the station. As I joined him at the front desk, he introduced us to the dispatcher and told her that we needed to speak to the chief.

I was relieved to see that Miss Perky Boobs wasn't on duty. In the past, she had made it clear that anytime I was out of the picture, she'd be happy to take Jake for a ride—and not on Mister Ed. Or even if I still was in the picture, and he wanted to start up something on the side, she was up for a good gallop.

Hell! I was pretty damn sure if he showed the slightest bit of interest, she'd do him in the squad room with the whole police force watching.

Luckily, instead of Nympho Barbie, the woman

working today looked more like Mother Goose, which saved me from the possibility of an assault charge. She smiled at us both, then put down her knitting, picked up the telephone, and buzzed Chief Kincaid.

When he answered, she said, "You have visitors." She listened to his response, then said, "Jake Del Vecchio and Deveraux Sinclair." She nodded to the receiver, then replaced it on the base, and said to us, "He'll see you now."

When we entered his office, the chief was sitting behind his desk. He motioned for us to close the door and take a seat. The only indication that he'd just had an altercation with his daughter was the slight ruddiness of his smoothly shaved cheeks and the pain in his steely blue eyes.

Eldridge Kincaid was as unruffled as if he'd just had a refreshing night's sleep, rather than a screaming match with his only child. I had long speculated that he had multiple uniforms stashed in his private bathroom, and that if the one he was wearing got the slightest hint of a crease, he immediately changed into a freshly ironed alternative. Now I wondered if he also had a big bottle of Valium back there, too. Or maybe a salt lick of Xanax.

As soon as we sat down, the chief looked at Jake and said, "I take it Elliot Winston has hired you."

"He did." Jake nodded.

Glancing at me, the chief raised a brow. "I

didn't realize you were part of Del Vecchio Private Investigations. Who's minding the store?"

"It doesn't open until noon." I didn't bother to address the first part of his comment.

"Right." The chief's expression was amused, but it sobered as he turned back to Jake. "What do you think of your first client?"

"Interesting." Jake crossed his legs, balancing his cowboy boot on his knee. "I appreciate the referral, but why aren't you handling the case?"

I studied Chief Kincaid. Local law enforcement can get defensive when federal agencies like the U.S. Marshals stick their nose in hometown police business, and even though Jake was retired from the service, cops weren't usually too fond of private investigators, either. So I wasn't too sure how the chief felt about Jake or vice versa.

I knew that I was in Chief Kincaid's good graces, because he saw me as a positive influence on his wild daughter. However, Jake was a whole other matter. While the chief had sent him a client, I wasn't too sure that he'd done Jake any favors, and I watched carefully as Chief Kincaid opened his center drawer, withdrew a file, and flipped open the folder.

"Oh, we're looking into his missing wife, all right." The chief's voice was dry as he riffled through a stack of papers, then slid one from the pile. "But Mr. Winston wasn't happy with the direction of our investigation."

Hmm. Elliot Winston had given us the impression that the police weren't doing anything. In my previous profession as an investment consultant, discovering that a client had lied to you was a red flag. Judging from Jake's scowl, obviously a PI felt the same way.

"And what direction is that?" Jake asked, his expression once again impassive.

"Either Mrs. Winston left voluntarily, fearing that her husband might harm her," Chief Kincaid said as he tented his fingers and rested his chin on them, "or Mr. Winston killed her, disposed of the body, and is trying to cover up the crime by playing the concerned spouse."

I bit back a million questions and fought to maintain as deadpan an expression as Jake's. I knew there was more to this story, but the chief wasn't someone you could rush. He would proceed at his own pace, no matter what we said or did.

"What makes you believe that Gabriella Winston wasn't abducted?" Jake asked, withdrawing a small notebook and pen from the breast pocket of his shirt. "The Winstons have money. Even if there's been no contact so far, there still could be a ransom demand."

"I wouldn't be surprised if Winston receives a ransom note." The corner of Chief Kincaid's lips twitched upward. "I just don't think it will be from the alleged kidnapper."

"Have you arranged to have the Winstons' phones monitored?" Jake asked.

"They don't have a landline." The chief sighed. "We've put a trace on both Mr. and Mrs. Winston's cells, but I doubt the ransom demand will come by phone."

"Because you think that Winston will be behind it, and he's aware of the measures you have in place," Jake said. He paused a few seconds and added, "Plus, having someone make the call would involve securing an accomplice who could then blackmail Elliot Wilson."

"Precisely."

The chief definitely knew something we didn't know. The question was—would he share that information? Despite my best friend's issues with her father, I admired Eldridge Kincaid. I respected his determination to do the best possible job for the people of Shadow Bend, which was why I was sure there was more to this situation.

However, it seemed as though we were at an impasse. Evidently Chief Kincaid didn't fully trust us. Jake and the chief stared at each other, the silence getting thicker and thicker, until I was ready to say something just to end it.

Finally, as if coming to a decision, Chief Kincaid took a stack of pictures from the back of the folder, handed them to Jake, and said, "These are photos of the Winstons' kitchen and living room."

So the police had been to the Winston house and brought in a crime scene team to gather evidence. Another thing Elliot Winston had failed to mention.

As Jake examined the snapshots, I leaned over his arm so I could see them, too. The family room was trashed, and the kitchen floor had a trail of blood drops leading from the counter to the back door.

I glanced at Jake. His brow was wrinkled, and he repeatedly flipped back and forth between the pictures. What did he see that I didn't?

No longer able to control my curiosity, I said, "Okay. I give up. What?"

Jake laid out half a dozen photos of the family room on the top of the chief's desk and swept his hand across the array. "See how all the furniture, lamps, and so on are flung around the room?" I nodded, and he continued. "But the walls are pristine. There isn't one scuff mark on the paint."

"Ah." I blew out a breath. Why hadn't I noticed that?

"Also, the throw rugs are in place, and none of the artwork is damaged."

"Right."

"Plus, see this big couch?" Jake pointed. "It's upended. However, that type of sofa would be too heavy just to shove over. Someone would have to lift it."

"Which means?" I asked.

Jake glanced at the chief and said, "The scene was set up to look like there had been a struggle."

"That was my tech's conclusion." Chief Kincaid nodded. "And I agree. According to the husband, their housekeeping service had been there on Saturday afternoon, and beyond the two housekeepers and the Winstons, there were no other fingerprints and no trace of anyone else in the family room or kitchen."

"In that case," I mused, "either Gabriella Winston did this so she could get away from her husband, or Elliot Winston killed her and did this to make the authorities think his wife was kidnapped, not dead."

CHAPTER 4

Gusts of wind battered Jake's pickup as we made the ten-minute drive west of town to the Winstons' house. Although it was warm inside the cab, the gloomy weather outside made me shiver. Clouds rolled across the ashen sky and rain threatened the horizon.

I hoped the incoming storm didn't strip the trees of their colorful leaves. The foliage had just reached its peak, and the leaf peepers who visited the area would be disappointed. And if the day-trippers were unhappy, they didn't stick around to shop in my store.

Rousing myself from my meteorological musings, I turned to Jake, who had been silent since we left the police station. "Now that you've heard what Chief Kincaid had to say about Gabriella Winston's alleged kidnapping, what do you think about it?"

"One thing in Elliot Winston's favor is that there was no record of domestic violence complaints against him." Jake kept a tight grip on the wheel as the wind continued to buffet the high-profile truck.

"Understatement much?" I teased. "In that case, it's also a positive that they didn't find a body or any severed limbs around."

"You are just a little ray of sunshine, aren't you, sugar?" Jake's blue eyes twinkled. "Maybe I should start calling you *sunny*."

"Not going to happen." I shook my head, hiding my smile. "Unless you want me to come up with a pet name for you. And, believe me"—I shot him a warning glare—"you won't like where my imagination goes, sugar britches."

"Gotcha." Jake's tone was indulgent, then became serious. "I sure hope Gabriella just got fed up with her husband's obsession with the wildlife park and moved on to greener pastures."

"If not, the alternatives don't bode well for her." I shuddered. Frowning, I asked, "Did you find Elliot Winston's demeanor odd? For someone who claims to love his wife, he certainly doesn't seem to put his concern for her ahead of his other interests."

"The intel guy on my team was like him." Jake shook his head. "Bruce adored his wife and children, but you would have never guessed it by his behavior. He wasn't good with social cues and didn't pick up on facial expressions at all. A lot of his emotional responses were inappropriate, because he was so single-minded and preoccupied with finishing whatever task he was working on." Jake smiled. "But when push came to shove, he would do anything, give up anything, for his family."

"Hmm." I considered Jake's words. I'd known

people like that, too. Elliot may be a little eccentric, but he'd involved both the police and Jake, which, in my opinion, bought him the benefit of the doubt. Not everyone showed their love in the same way, and I wasn't sure that I wouldn't do exactly what Elliot had done. Except, instead of getting help, I'd investigate on my own. But I sure wouldn't sit around crying and wringing my hands. I'd carry on as normally as possible until I was damn sure there were no other options.

As we turned into Country Club Estates, the smooth pavement of the development's streets was a marked contrast to the patched blacktop of the county road. It was as if we had entered an entirely different world. Huge homes with fancy fountains and circular driveways, surrounded by immaculate lawns and lavish landscaping, lined the neighborhood. Not a single leaf marred the velvety grass, which was quite a feat, considering the amount of trees in the area. There had to be a whole bevy of gardeners on duty at all times in order to maintain that kind of perfection.

When Country Club Estates was first being built, out of curiosity and sheer boredom, Gran and I had taken a drive through the development. But I'd had no reason to visit since then. It wasn't as if I could afford any of these houses.

Pointing, Jake said, "The Winstons' place is the next street over."

Most of the lots were either on the golf course,

the lake, or nestled into the wooded areas. The Winstons' property had the best of all three. It abutted the golf course, had dense stands of trees on either side, and was across from the lake. Definitely the preeminent location of the entire development. Which probably meant it was also the most expensive.

As Jake pulled into the Winstons' driveway, I stared at the brick McMansion. It had to be over five thousand square feet. The front was a bit underwhelming, but from the glimpse I'd gotten from the road, the back of the house was the real showstopper.

After Jake helped me down from the truck, I looked around. We were facing the four-car garage, and I nodded at it. "I know the chief said that Gabriella's car was still here, but did he indicate whether the Winstons had any other vehicles, and, if so, were they AWOL?"

"Not that I recall." Jake frowned. "I'll have to check, but my guess is that if one were missing, Kincaid would have mentioned it."

"Well, we don't have taxis or bus service in Shadow Bend, so if Gabriella is in hiding, someone picked her up." I trailed Jake up the cobblestone walkway. The leaves of the surrounding trees rustled loudly, and I could hear the faint barking of a dog somewhere across the street. "The chief said that none of the neighbors saw anything, right?"

"Yep. With lots this big and the way the landscaping is designed for privacy, I wouldn't necessarily expect any witnesses." Jake glanced around. "But I'm surprised there're no security cameras."

"People who move to small towns want to believe they're safe and don't need surveillance equipment." I waited while Jake inserted the key in the door. "Some of the customers in my store who are new to the area brag about not even locking up anymore."

"Terrific," Jake grunted. "Why don't they just put a ROB ME sign in the front yard?"

I chuckled, then as Jake and I walked into the house, I gulped. "Wow!"

From the small entryway I could see down a hallway that ended in floor-to-ceiling windows. Even with the overcast weather, the gorgeous patio and in-ground pool were inviting, and the open concept made the already spacious interior feel enormous.

As an investment consultant, I had often visited clients who lived like this. But it had been quite a while, and I'd forgotten the luxury in which the truly wealthy surrounded themselves.

A little voice in my head whispered temptingly that if I married Noah, I could live like this, too. Noah would build me the house of my dreams, fill it with anything I desired, and be happy to do it.

Shoving that avaricious thought out of my head, I followed Jake through the corridor and turned left into a combination of dining area, kitchen, and family room. It appeared that someone, probably the same housekeeping service the Winstons regularly employed, had cleaned up the chaos we'd seen in the crime scene photos, as well as any mess the forensic techs had created.

Stepping farther into the space, I was surprised that there were no family pictures or keepsakes on display. There were paintings and artwork, but no trophies or memorabilia of any kind.

And although on either side of the towering stacked stone fireplace there was a pair of built-in shelves containing objets d'art, there wasn't a single book anywhere. *Heck!* I didn't even see a magazine. Didn't these people read at all?

I made a mental note to check for an e-reader or tablet, then explored the kitchen and found the door leading outside. This was the exit that the purported kidnapper had used to remove Gabriella from the house. As I turned the knob and pushed, I winced at the loud creaking noise. Either the Winstons didn't use this door much or didn't care that it sounded like the lid of Dracula's casket opening.

After noting that there was a sidewalk lined with motion sensor lights that went toward the back of the house, I turned to Jake, who was pacing off the area, and said, "Is it okay if I look around the rest of the place? I need to get a picture in my head."

"Sure." Jake tore off a few sheets for himself, then handed me his legal pad and said, "Draw the floor plan and note anything that strikes you as odd."

Leaving Jake examining the scene of the crime, I crossed over to the other side of the house. The formal living room was painted Tiffany blue and decorated in gray and white, with an ornate crystal chandelier hanging from the high ceiling. It seemed more like a furniture showroom than a space that was ever used.

I made a rough sketch and moved on to the master suite. It took up the remaining area on this side of downstairs and was accessed through a short hallway.

A massive bathroom was on my left as I walked down the corridor, and a walk-in closet that was stuffed to the gills was on my right. Sticking my head inside the closet, I could understand why Elliot had no way of knowing if any of Gabriella's massive wardrobe was missing. A few items wouldn't leave much of a gap among the closely packed hangers or in the stuffed-to-the-gills built-in drawers.

The color scheme of gray, white, and blue continued from the living room, but the bedroom was definitely not for display purposes only. The king-size mattress resting on a sleek platform was unmade, women's clothes were tossed on a white leather and chrome chaise lounge, and the floor was littered with discarded shoes.

I wrinkled my brow. There was something off here. What was it? I wandered over to the dressing table. The top was covered with expensive brands of makeup, perfume, and lotion. And a heavy silver frame held a photo of a beautiful ebony-haired woman with big cornflower blue eyes. She was sitting on a thronelike chair, wearing a satisfied smile.

Hmm. I recognized Gabriella from the picture Elliot had given to Jake. Picking up the photograph, I examined it, looking for a clue as to the missing woman's personality. Diamonds dripped from her ears, throat, and wrists. Gabriella could support an impoverished village for a year with what she'd paid for the dress and jewelry alone. Throw in the shoes, and she could add reopening Shadow Bend's library to her charitable endeavors.

Still, that wasn't what was bothering me. I walked over to the bed. Only one pillow bore the imprint of a head. The other was perfectly fluffed and smooth. Opening the drawers of the armoire, I saw only women's clothing, and the same had been true for the closet. In fact, there was no evidence that Elliot Winston ever set foot in this room.

As I pondered that little fact, I noticed a door.

Another closet? Opening it, I walked into an adjoining bedroom. This one was as masculine as the other was feminine. It was decorated in leather and wood, and although not as large as the master, still a good size. As was its connecting bathroom.

A quick check of the walk-in closet and chest of drawers, and I was convinced that this was where Elliot laid his weary head while his wife occupied the master suite all alone.

Moving on to the second floor, I discovered four more bedrooms. Two obviously belonged to the sons, and here I found the snapshots, keepsakes, and books lacking in the rest of the house.

The third bedroom was clearly for guests, and the remaining one was being used as an office. Unfortunately for my inner snoop, there was nothing lying around, all the drawers in the desk and file cabinet were locked, and there was no laptop or tablet present.

Downstairs, I located the laundry room, which opened onto the garage. Peeking into the cavernous space, I noted that only one vehicle was parked there, along with a snowmobile, a Jet Ski, and an ATV.

The laundry room contained the usual appliances, a quartz counter with a sink, and a wall of built-in cabinets. Everything was immaculate, and I recalled that Chief Kincaid had said that the cleaning crew had been through the house Saturday afternoon. From the state of her room, Gabriella must have tried on several outfits, then taken a nap after the housekeeping service departed. Either that or the cleaners weren't allowed in the master suite for some reason.

As I made my way back through the hallway, I inhaled deeply. The only scent was the lemony odor of furniture wax. There wasn't a single hint of food or a pet or anything personal in the air.

Having learned only that Gabriella and Elliot Winston had separate bedrooms and that their housekeeping service did an excellent job, I went in search of Jake. He wasn't where I had left him, but the open kitchen door provided a clue as to his whereabouts.

I found him in the backyard, his shoulders hunched against the wind, speaking into his cell phone. "So there were no missing vehicles." He paused to listen, then asked, "How about credit cards?" He nodded and said, "No? Okay. Have the companies alert you if there's any new activity, and let me know if anyone contacts you."

When Jake disconnected, I guessed: "Elliot Winston?"

"Uh-huh." Jake scanned the area, a frown marring his handsome face. "You almost couldn't pick a better setup to snatch someone." He gestured to either side of the property. "Gabriella could have been taken out through the woods, or if the guy could maneuver her across the street and had a boat available, he'd have her trapped." Jake scratched his jaw and narrowed his eyes. "All the kidnapper needed was to have a car waiting at another location, and he'd be home free."

"Yeah." I nodded toward the golf course. "I suppose a struggling or unconscious woman in a cart would draw too much attention."

"Unless she just appeared drunk." Jake shrugged. "Plus, we're still not exactly sure when the abduction took place. If it was Saturday night after Winston left, no one would have been on the golf course to notice, but if it was Sunday morning before he got home, the course would have been crowded with golfers."

"There was a party at the country club Saturday evening, and no one mentioned seeing anything odd that night," I said, not adding that I had attended the dinner dance with Noah. "So the golf course might still have been risky if she was taken on Saturday. The kidnapper would have had to have left his getaway car in the parking lot and been willing to take the chance that someone might see him stuffing her into it."

"Good point."

Jake shot me a look that said he was well aware of how I had acquired my insider knowledge of the party, and why I had left that tidbit out. It wasn't as if I were attempting to hide that I had gone out with Noah, I just tried not to rub either guy's nose in the fact that I dated both of them. Something that I needed to stop doing soon.

I glanced at my watch. It was eleven thirty, and the dime store opened at noon. I either had to call my dad into work or get back there myself.

"What's your next move?" I asked, trying to schedule the rest of my day.

"Let's head to the office," Jake said. "Meet me in the driveway. I have to lock the doors and leave the key on the counter."

I nodded and walked around the house. The wind had turned colder, and a few raindrops fell on my face.

A couple of seconds later, Jake hurried out the front door, aiming his key fob at the truck. He helped me into the cab, wiped the moisture from my cheek, and gave me a sweet kiss before jogging around the hood and sliding behind the wheel.

As he reversed out of the driveway, he said, "I need to start phoning nearby motels and restaurants. If Gabriella Winston is hiding out, she doesn't have identification or credit cards, so she probably wasn't able to go too far, and she has to eat."

"Unless she had help," I reminded him. "She's a gorgeous woman, and about the only interesting fact that I came up with when I searched the house was that the Winstons don't appear to sleep together."

"Can you ask around and find out if there's any talk of an affair?" Jake stepped on the gas, then added, "For either of the Winstons."

"Sure." I belatedly buckled my seat belt. "After that scene at the police station, I need to check on Poppy anyway. I'll call Boone and arrange to meet them both for a drink after I close the store. If anyone would have heard any rumors, it would be the two of them. Boone keeps on top of things like that, and Poppy didn't name her bar Gossip Central for nothing."

Boone was my other BFF and one of three lawyers in Shadow Bend. Poppy owned the most popular hangout in the county, and she made sure that if there was any juicy scandal around, she was the first to know. Not only did she have the local grapevine, she had also bugged the booths in her club.

"You know"—Jake entwined his fingers with mine—"I'm really glad I got a PI license. It feels good to be on a case again, but the best part is spending time with you." He brushed his lips over my knuckles. "And I love that I can pop downstairs and we can have a quick lunch together, or at the end of the day we can grab a bite to eat before going home."

"Me, too," I whispered. The more I saw Jake,

the more I realized how much I liked him as well as lusted after him. "It's great that Meg and your uncle don't seem to need you as much as before."

"It is a relief." Jake blew out a long breath. He was silent for a moment, then asked, "Hey, did I tell you that Meg got a job?"

"Isn't she still a marshal?" I asked, forcing myself not to frown.

I wasn't happy to hear that Jake's ex was settling in Shadow Bend. I had thought her stay here would be temporary. Just until she was completely recovered from the trauma of being held by a serial killer.

"She says she needs something to do until she's strong enough to go back to the service." Jake glanced at me, a crease of worry in between his eyes. "Does it bother you she's staying in town?"

"Not at all," I lied, then pasted a smile on my face and asked, "Where's she working?"

Jake's wicked grin reminded me a lot of my grandmother's cat Banshee right after the nasty feline had destroyed the last remaining set of La Perla underwear that I owned. After I kissed my days of earning a six-figure salary as a financial consultant good-bye, I shopped for my undies at Target rather than Nordstrom.

"You'll never guess," Jake drawled.

"Brewfully Yours or the bakery?"

"Nope and nope."

"Little's Tea Room?"

"Uh-uh." He shook his head, his eyes twinkling. "I'm stumped."

I was pretty sure if she was working for one of my friends, they would have given me a heads-up, which eliminated the local B & B, Gossip Central, and Forever Used, the upscale consignment shop.

"Underwood's clinic." Jake's smile was toothy. "She's Dr. Dweeb's new receptionist."

"Oh." I kept my expression only mildly interested. "That's great."

I wasn't sure how I felt about Meg working for Noah. On one hand, since the two men disliked each other, it would keep her far away from Jake. On the other hand, I didn't trust her and figured she had to have some reason for taking a job with the other guy I was dating. I just couldn't figure out what.

However, what worried me even more was that I had to wonder why Noah hadn't told me about his new employee. Not that he was required to clear his hiring choices with me, but a warning would have been nice.

Was this another instance of the distance I felt he kept between us? He was open about his physical desires, but his emotions were often as tightly sealed as a Ziploc bag.

CHAPTER 5

Puddles shimmered on the blacktop in the noon brightness as Noah Underwood drove to work. It had been cloudy all morning, but after a brief shower the sun had finally come out. The TV meteorologist had promised that it would start to climb back into the sixties, and the afternoon was supposed to be one of the beautiful autumn days that made this part of Missouri famous.

Noah certainly hoped so. The recent temperature swings and unusual pressure fronts that had moved through the area the past month had been hard on everyone's health. And since he and his staff at the Underwood Clinic were the ones who had to deal with the illnesses that it brought, the weather had been especially tough on them.

Although Noah had always wanted to be a small-town doctor, he hadn't fully understood the reality of the profession until his practice had been in business for a while. After completing a combined B.A. and M.D., he'd done a three-year residency in family medicine, then returned to Shadow Bend and opened the Underwood Clinic. It had just celebrated its fourth birthday in September.

One of the factors that compensated Noah

for the intense days and administrative hassles was his five-minute trip to work. When Dev talked about her old job and driving an hour or more into Kansas City every day, he was truly grateful that he'd never had to make that kind of commute. He'd probably have ended up shooting someone, and that wouldn't do his kindly doctor image any good.

After easing his taiga green Jaguar into a parking spot in the employee lot, he let himself in the building's rear entrance. It was twelve fifty when he entered the clinic, and as he walked to his office, he could hear the voice of his head nurse, Eunice Vogel, coming from the check-in desk. Her words were indistinguishable, but her tone made it clear that she was upset.

Eunice's daughter Madison had been his receptionist since he'd opened his practice, but she'd recently eloped with her high school sweetheart. Her new husband was a corporal in the army and stationed in Fort Benning, so she now lived in Columbus, Georgia.

Noah was still a bit perturbed that Madison hadn't given him any notice before quitting and moving away, but Eunice was livid that she been deprived of throwing a big, fancy wedding for her daughter. The temporary receptionists they'd had filling in until they could hire someone for the full-time position had all quit after a few weeks working with Eunice. Not that he'd been sorry to see them go. None of them had been able to figure out the patient scheduling software. Had Elexus found someone new?

Elexus Rodriguez, the newly minted physician Noah had recently lured into a partnership, had volunteered to take on some of the administrative responsibilities. Monday through Saturday she and Noah alternated covering the two shifts—seven a.m. to one p.m. and one p.m. to six p.m., although when the place was really busy, their shifts often overlapped. But with the clinic closed on Sunday, at least they both had the day off.

When Elexus had offered to hire the new receptionist, Noah had been thrilled. He hated interviewing potential staff and was uncomfortable dealing with personnel issues. Elexus had no such concerns dealing with their workforce.

If it *was* the new receptionist with whom Eunice was angry, Noah hoped Elexus would handle the matter before he officially went on duty. With that in mind, Noah slipped into his office and closed the door. He switched on his computer, typed in his password, and opened up the list of the afternoon's appointments.

He liked to review the day's patients and take a couple of minutes to prepare himself if there were any possibility of a serious ailment coming at him. For the most part, he treated acute problems and managed chronic medical conditions. Anything more severe was referred to a specialist, and emergencies were transported by ambulance to the county hospital. But there was always that one individual who didn't reveal the extent of his or her illness until all hell was about to break loose.

Today's schedule looked fairly typical, starting with Donald McGowan's drug and alcohol screening. Mac was the golf pro at the local country club, and after some issues with substance abuse that had endangered club members, his employers had negotiated the monthly tests. Mac had sought help with his addictions and was more than willing to pee into a cup in order to keep his job.

In a metropolitan or suburban setting, Mac would go to a facility that specialized in drug and alcohol checks. But in rural Missouri his only nearby options were the county hospital, which was forty minutes away, or Noah's practice. Mac chose the clinic.

His only requests were that he deal directly with a doctor rather than a physician assistant or nurse or tech and that the doctor personally send the specimen to the lab and review the results. Because Mac seemed like a nice guy and the country club was willing to pay for the service, Noah accommodated him.

After reviewing the rest of the afternoon's appointments, Noah shut down his laptop, put on his white lab coat, and left his office. As he walked from the examination and office area into the waiting room, he saw Eunice facing the reception desk. The petite blonde's shoulders were rigid and she was shouting.

Stepping around the nurse, he came to an abrupt halt and closed his eyes. When he opened them and looked again, the woman perched behind the check-in counter was still Jake Del Vecchio's ex-wife, Meg. What in the hell was she doing there? She was a U.S. Marshal, for crying out loud.

Granted, she was on medical leave, but why would she have taken a job as a receptionist? That had to be way too tame for her, not to mention severely underutilizing her abilities, since it was unlikely she'd have to take down any criminals or escort a drug king to prison while working in Noah's practice.

Instead of wearing the pale pink smock the clinic provided, Meg had on a dark turtleneck and black blazer. She didn't appear as gaunt as she had when Noah had met her in September, and the long red hair framing her beautiful face had regained its luster.

Pulling him out of his thoughts, Eunice clutched Noah's arm and demanded, "Doctor, please instruct our new employee on proper dress for the clinic." The wiry middle-aged nurse glared. "She won't listen to me."

Meg's pretty green eyes sparkled as she gazed

at Noah and said, "You can't really expect a grown woman to wear something decorated with kittens and puppies. Especially if it's the color of a baby's ass."

"Language," Eunice snapped. "We do not curse in this practice, and as I've been telling you all day, we wear pastels to make the patients comfortable." She scowled, wrinkles bracketing her lips. "Why can't you just do as you're told?"

"Because I don't take orders from petty tyrants." Meg leaned forward, clearly ready to go a couple more rounds with the older woman.

"Eunice"—Noah decided he'd better step in before his nurse and new receptionist came to blows—"Can you get my first appointment settled in an examination room while I sort this out with Ms. . . ."

"Del Vecchio," Meg supplied. At Noah's raised brows, she added, "Hey, Jake was soooo insistent that I take his name, I saw no reason to go to all the trouble to change it back after the divorce."

"I can certainly get your patient ready for you, Doctor," Eunice said sweetly, patting her short hair. "But even nurses can't fix stupid." She shot Meg a death stare and added, "Although we *can* sedate it."

"I'm busy." Meg fluttered her fingers at Eunice. "And you're ugly." Pitching her voice into ditzy-blonde range, she added, "Have a totally awesome day."

As the nurse stalked into the waiting room, she stage-whispered, "Doctor, you need to get rid of the Wicked Witch of the Chest before I toss a urine sample at her and she melts."

Noah hid his grin. Meg did indeed have rather large breasts for her slender frame. And he couldn't help noticing how well the thin knit of her sweater molded to those enticing curves.

Damn it! What was he doing ogling the receptionist? Shaking his head, he said, "What color smock would you like?" Although he couldn't believe he had to deal with this kind of bullcrap, Noah kept his tone mild.

"Black." Meg crossed her arms. "If I have to, dark navy. I don't do colors."

"You do if you want this job." Noah clenched his jaw. "Clinic policy mandates soft colors. Right now you look as if you should be working in a funeral home rather than a medical clinic."

Meg's cheeks turned red and her thick dark lashes closed. Her glossy pink lips moved, and it was clear she was counting. Finally, she took a deep breath, unclenched her fists, and looked at him.

"Blue or green," Meg muttered between clenched teeth. "No prints."

"Fine. There should be a smock like that in the storeroom. Find it, put it on, and stop antagonizing Eunice."

"She's an asshole." Meg's lips made a moue

of distaste. "Or maybe she just has rectal-cranial inversion and you need to do some surgery."

Noah swallowed a chuckle, turned to go, then couldn't stop himself from asking, "Why are you working here?"

"None of your fu—" Meg bit off the word, then said, "Freaking business. Dr. R hired me. Check with her if you have any questions."

"I certainly plan to do that." Noah wondered why the woman irritated him so much. He routinely dealt with difficult patients without getting annoyed. "I take it this is just temporary?"

"Look," Meg said, then stopped.

She pulled her hair into a ponytail, fastening it with an elastic band from her pocket, and Noah frowned, missing the sleek curtain enveloping her shoulders.

"Yes?" he asked.

"I know you and Jake are in some kind of pissing war over that woman you're both so gaga over, but I promise you I can do this job." Meg shot him an impish grin. "Besides. Look at it this way—the longer I'm around, the more chance there is that Dev will blow her cool, have a big fight with Jake, and you'll win by default."

"So you want your ex-husband back?" Noah asked, strangely disappointed.

"God, no." Meg laughed. "The only good thing between Jake and me was the sex, and that burned out real quick. I was an idiot to marry him."

"But you don't mind ruining his chances with another woman?"

"Nope." Meg shrugged. "If my mere presence can come between them, I'm doing him a favor. Better now than after a couple of kids."

"That's pretty harsh. Don't you believe in second chances and true love overcoming all?" Noah asked, a disturbing thought niggling in the back of his mind. He'd allowed his mother to break up his relationship with Dev. Granted, he'd been a teenager, but . . .

Suddenly all expression was wiped from Meg's face and she said, "Are you seeing patients today, Doctor? Or just giving me a hard time?"

Before he could answer, the phone rang and Meg answered. She listened, then quickly handed him the receiver and said, "You'd better take this."

"Doctor?" A frantic voice blared in Noah's ear. "I caught my two-year-old eating ants. Should I bring him to the emergency room?"

"That's probably not necessary." Noah frowned. "Just keep an eye on him."

"Yeah. Okay." The man paused. "I gave him insect poisoning to kill the ants, so I figured there was no real problem."

"Call nine-one-one immediately!" Noah yelled. "Take the can of poison with you."

Noah disconnected so the man could call for the ambulance. He'd thought he'd heard everything, but his patients continued to astound him.

As he thought about the call, Meg gestured for him to leave and said, "Are you just going to stand there all day? Some of us would like to keep on schedule."

Without another word, Noah walked away. What had happened? They'd gotten past the smock issue and they'd been having a decent conversation. Then suddenly, just before the phone rang, some kind of switch had flipped and Meg had resumed her snotty persona. What had triggered her change?

Shrugging, Noah headed for the corridor leading to the examination rooms, but before he went through the door, Yale Gordon, the physician assistant, rushed up to him and said, "Hey, Doc. We've got trouble. You gotta see this."

"What's up?" Noah followed the PA into the waiting room and stared at the steady stream of people filing through the entrance, heading toward the check-in desk.

Generally, there were three patients scheduled per hour—one each for the doctor and the PA, and one being prepped by the nurse.

Yale grimaced. "Apparently, there was some sort of leak at the Yager aerosol factory. A few workers were taken to the hospital by ambulance, but the foreman loaded the rest on a company bus and brought them here."

"What are the symptoms?" Noah asked, studying the folks lined up at the desk.

Several were scratching their arms and necks while others were coughing and rubbing their eyes.

"Diarrhea and headaches mostly," the PA reported. "The man leaning against the wall is complaining of chest tightness and shortness of breath."

"Why didn't the EMTs take him?" Noah asked. "He should be at the hospital."

"Until a few minutes ago, he was asymptomatic." Yale shrugged. "Do you want to see him first?"

"Yes." Noah nodded. "Put him in exam one. Then check if Elexus is still around. Also ask whatever first-shift staff hasn't left yet to stay."

"Will do."

Noah did a quick head count, then mentally scanned the list he'd just looked at in his office. "In the meantime, I'll have Ms. Del Vecchio reschedule as many of today's appointments as we can."

"I'll let everyone know." Yale hurried away.

It took the rest of the afternoon, but after triaging the waiting patients, Noah, Elexus, and Yale managed to treat all the factory workers, as well as the regularly booked folks who couldn't be postponed. The factory workers all responded well to medication, and only one other man had to be sent to the hospital.

It was a quarter to seven when Noah watched the last patient leave. Most of the first-shift staff who had hung around to help went home at five with Elexus, and Noah had told Yale to go soon afterward.

As Noah took off his white jacket, he realized he'd never seen Donald McGowan. Maybe Mac had decided to allow a tech to draw his blood this time rather than wait around. Noah wrinkled his brow. At least he hoped that was what happened. It would be a shame if the golf pro hadn't shown up because he was abusing alcohol and drugs again.

CHAPTER 6

When Jake and I got back to town, I showed him his new official parking spot in the lot behind my building. I could tell by the way that his cheek creased that he thought I was being a bit controlling, but smart man that he was, he didn't say a word.

As we walked across the gravel to the rear entrance, I was glad that the wind had died down to a pleasant breeze, the cold drizzle had stopped, and the sun was peeking out from behind the clouds. It would be a nice afternoon, which should help business.

Mondays were tricky. Most of the week, early afternoon—between lunch and school dismissal—was usually slow. Sometimes I didn't see a single customer in the afternoon until three o'clock when the teens came in for their snacks. But on Mondays, because the store had been closed for the past forty-four hours, there was always a chance that it would be crowded.

Jake and I entered through the back room. It was a few minutes before twelve, and he immediately headed upstairs to make some calls in his quest to locate the lovely Mrs. Winston. For me, it was time to return my attention to the dime store.

After putting my purse in my desk, I locked it, then opened the safe and retrieved the money drawer. Even though most customers nowadays used credit cards, there were still a lot of folks that preferred cash. Which required me to keep a good supply of small-denomination currency available to make change.

I went out front, turned on all the lights, and prepared to open up the store. When I bought the place from the Thornbee twins, who at the age of ninety-one had decided to sell the five-and-dime and retire, I kept as much of the vintage feel as I could.

The sisters' only other offer had come from a pharmacy chain, and because their grandfather had built the dime store when Shadow Bend was no more than a stagecoach stop, they accepted my much lower bid. Their sole condition was that I retain the original charm of the place. And I was more than happy to meet that demand.

Owning a small-town dime store rather than working as a financial consultant had lowered my income level from being able to buy whatever I wanted to some months barely being able to pay for my health insurance. However, I never regretted my decision, because it had allowed me the freedom to care for my grandmother.

A little over two years ago, I had noticed that Gran had begun to have some memory issues. I discussed my concerns with her doctor, and after several months of observation, medication, and journaling, he informed me that in order to be safe in her own home, Birdie needed me to be around more.

At that moment, I knew I had to find an alternative way to earn a living. And when I heard that Thornbee's was for sale, I made my decision. As soon as the dime store purchase was finalized, I handed in my two weeks' notice at Stramp Investments.

Soon afterward, my boss, Ronald Stramp, was arrested. Some people thought I'd resigned from my job because I found out that he was a crook, and that he'd paid for my silence. But I'd been as surprised as the rest of the world when his Ponzi scheme was revealed.

Stramp maintained he wasn't guilty. Ironically, my father also claimed he had been set up and was innocent of both manslaughter and bank embezzlement. The difference was that my dad really had been framed. Stramp hadn't. But no one believed either of them.

However, while my father had spent thirteen years behind bars before proof of his innocence came to light, the jury at my boss's trial acquitted him. Predictably, the people Stramp had bamboozled out of millions were incensed that he didn't go to jail. And just as predictably, most people blamed me for his freedom.

Sadly, because I hadn't been aware of Stramp's

scam, I hadn't been able to testify about his scheme. It killed me that my ignorance allowed him to get away with his crime, but it was almost worse that I had been so dumb that I'd never noticed what he was doing.

My only defense was that Stramp was an extremely secretive and clever man. Both of which he proved by disappearing the minute his trial was over. And he'd taken his ill-gotten gains with him. All efforts to recover the money he'd conned from hundreds of individuals had failed. There were civil suits pending, but no defendant to sue.

A rapping on the dime store's glass door brought me back from the past, and I hastily unlocked the entrance. There were several shoppers waiting for me to let them in, and I stepped aside to avoid the stampede.

I wasn't sure why they were in such a hurry. Maybe they were running errands on their lunch hour. But their reasons didn't matter. As I moved behind the checkout counter, I enjoyed the excited voices.

The cheerful hubbub wasn't muffled by any acoustical tile or cork matting. Instead, the old tin ceiling and hardwood floors resonated with clicking heels, laughter, and the wonderful sound of people socializing.

When I'd bought the place, I'd also purchased the adjoining building and knocked out the shared wall. That one renovation had doubled the store's interior. Then recently, when the owner of a mega successful cupcake company decided to hold a baking contest in Shadow Bend and use my second floor for the event, that area had been remodeled, too.

In addition to Jake's office suite, I used the added space as a teen lounge where the after-school crowd could hang out. Provided, of course, they bought their drinks and munchies from my soda fountain.

Working steadily, I helped shoppers find items, cleaned up messes created when people rummaged through my carefully arranged stacks of merchandise, and, my favorite, rang up purchases on the old brass cash register. Its distinctive *ding*ing always made me smile.

At one o'clock, my student clerk, Taryn Wenzel, showed up. On the recommendation of Mrs. Zeigler, the high school principal, I had hired him from the vocational education program. After losing my two previous clerks—one to college and one for less auspicious reasons—I'd had to take on a couple of new staff members. My father was filling one vacancy, and Taryn the second.

I had no idea why he was in voc-ed, since he'd made it clear he'd be attending the University of Central Missouri's software engineering program when he graduated. When I asked, he mumbled something about planning to own his own company and wanting practical experience in running a small business.

I hadn't pursued the matter because, frankly, I didn't care. As long as he did what he was told and didn't steal from me, I was a happy camper.

After stowing his belongings in the back room, Taryn came up to the counter, and once I'd handed a woman her purchases, he said, "Hi, Dev. Do you want me to set up for the knitting group?"

The Knittie Gritties, a knitting club that met at my shop every Monday afternoon at two, was one of several groups for whom I provided meeting space. In exchange, they bought the materials for their projects, refreshments, and any other bits and pieces that caught their eye from me.

"That would be great," I answered distractedly. "Put out the usual chairs."

I was keeping an eye on a group of women examining my racy Halloween offering. They'd been giggling, which I hoped meant they were intrigued rather than offended. So far no one had objected to the erotic half of my display, but the day was young.

"Why are you staring at those ladies?" Taryn tilted his head, and his wire-rimmed glasses slipped down his nose. "Are they shoplifting?"

"No." I didn't want to explain my concern to a sixteen-year-old.

"Then why are you frowning and biting your thumbnail?" Taryn was a keen observer. "Why don't you just go over and ask what they're doing?"

"Because I don't want to bite the hand that—"

"Looks dirty," Taryn finished for me.

If it were someone else who said that, I'd think they were making a joke, but Taryn had no sense of humor. Or at least none that I'd been able to find, so I nodded my agreement.

"Do you want me to go over there?" Taryn offered, and when I shook my head, he stared at me for a moment, then shrugged and asked, "Are you opening the teen lounge today?"

"Yes. I told the kids a week, and it ended on Saturday."

Although I allowed Taryn to handle the lounge, I popped up there at irregular intervals to keep an eye on the group. On one of my stealth visits, I'd caught some of the popular kids tormenting a chubby freshman girl and had closed the room for seven days as a punishment. Beyond not wrecking the joint, I didn't have many rules for the kids. But any kind of bullying was a crash-and-burn offense.

"Shall I set up the drink and snack bar up there?" Taryn asked.

"Do the crafters first, then the teens," I instructed. "Will you be okay handling the lounge or do you want me to do it?"

"I can do it." Taryn pushed up his glasses. "They'll be on their best behavior after you closed the space. None of them ever thought you'd go through with it, but now they know you will."

"That's right," I said, then having not learned from my previous attempt at using a cliché around Taryn, I foolishly added, "Once bitten, twice—"

"The stitches." Taryn frowned.

"Good to know," I said solemnly, then glanced at my watch. "You better get a move on. The knitters will be here in half an hour."

I hid a smile as he scurried away. The teens hadn't expected me to enforce the consequences of breaking my rules. But what they didn't realize is that I had no maternal instinct, which meant I didn't feel sorry for them, and I couldn't care less if they got mad at me. After all, it wasn't as if there was any other place in town that would allow them to hang out like I did.

While Taryn got things ready for the crafters, I continued to serve customers. By one forty-five, the rush was dying down, and when the first of the Knittie Gritties arrived, I was able to accompany them to the craft alcove.

For the scrapbookers, quilters, and sewers, I set up long worktables, but when the knitters, crocheters, and needlepointers held their meetings, I had Taryn haul out the comfy chairs and ottomans. They appreciated the coziness, and a relaxed shopper is more in the mood to spend his or her hard-earned money.

When the group had first started meeting at my store, I'd expected the stereotypical blue-haired old ladies. But my narrow-mindedness had taken a hit when the ages ranged from early twenties to nearly ninety. And my biases were totally shot down when one of the members had turned out to be male. I was slowly learning how my preconceived notions about people were often entirely off base.

Normally, I didn't hang around during the club's meeting, but today I wanted to pump them for any gossip about Gabriella and Elliot Winston. With that goal in mind, I took the chair next to Irene Johnson.

Irene was a tall, solidly built woman, with a stoic air and calloused hands. She kept house for several individuals in town, including Noah, and I hoped she might know which service the Winstons had hired.

Irene and I chatted for a few minutes, then I asked her, "Do you know who cleans for Elliot and Gabriella Winston?"

"I heard they hired that fancy new company that just opened up in Sparkville." Irene rummaged in her knitting bag. "Diamond Discreet."

"Do you know anyone around here who works for that business?" I asked.

"Uh-uh." Irene shook her head. "Diamond Discreet only uses people from the city and not too many of them speak much English. DD claims they can't risk us locals gossiping about their clients."

"That's discriminatory." I narrowed my eyes. "Maybe those of you who have applied and been turned down should sue Diamond Discreet. I'm sure Boone St. Onge would handle the case and take his fee from the settlement."

It frosted me when money that should be spent in Shadow Bend went into Kansas City instead. But it was hard to convince people that they could get the same items or services cheaper and/or better in town.

"Nah." Irene grinned. "I make way more as an independent contractor."

"Good to know." I patted her hand and said, "Nice chatting. Have fun. I'd better go see if anyone needs anything. Oh, just FYI, I've got your favorites—maple oat pecan scones today. And they go fast."

Getting up, I wandered over to where Vivian Yager sat with her lap covered by a half-finished sweater. She was an attractive woman in her late forties, the founder of the Knittie Gritties, and the owner of Curl Up and Dye. I particularly wanted to talk to her, because her beauty shop was a hotbed of gossip.

Vivian personified all that I loved about living in a small town. Her sparkling personality and a heartfelt smile welcomed everyone, and she was quick to offer help to anyone in need. Her original little group of knitters had grown from less than a handful to over a dozen, and she welcomed the new additions as if they were old friends.

I pulled up an ottoman next to her chair and said, "How're you doing with the ghost tour?"

Vivian was an active member of the chamber of commerce and was the head of the committee organizing the Halloween weekend activities. Instead of the usual cheesy haunted house, she and her group had found area locations that were supposedly frequented by spirits.

"It's suffered a devastating blow." Vivian screwed up her face. "We've been trying to get permission from the owner of the Malone house to use it. That spooky place would be our star attraction. But the city council is alleging that it's structurally unsound and won't allow us to include it."

"Because of that fire a few months ago?" I guessed, recalling the article in the town paper. "I thought it only damaged the basement."

"That's what the first inspector concluded, but the mayor hired an independent guy, and he said that smoke and water affected the whole place." Vivian made quotes in the air and added, "Worsening the derelict condition the building was already in." Vivian ran her finger over the embroidered daisy pattern on her knitting bag. "Not that his report was a surprise. The mayor wants the house torn down."

"Why?" I asked.

"Hizzoner has some sort of scheme going for the land around it." Vivian made a face. "He wants that acreage, and it will be cheaper without the building."

I tried to remember what I knew about the house. It was on the road that ran behind my family's property. If you cut across the field, it was an easy walk between the two. When I was a teenager and wanted to sneak out at night, I'd have my friends pick me up at the end of the Malones' driveway.

"Who owns it?" I asked.

It hadn't been occupied since Roberta Malone died in a fire my freshman year of college. And as far as I could tell, there hadn't been much upkeep in all that time.

"That's part of the problem." Vivian clanked shut the round metal handles of her bag. "We'd like to get our own inspector in to refute the mayor's, but we need the owner's permission. Hizzoner didn't need it, because he was acting on behalf of the city and public safety."

"Right," I sneered.

Vivian grinned and continued, "Riyad Oberkircher handles the taxes and such on the house, but he's telling us that due to client-attorney privilege, he can't divulge the identity of the owner." She reached up and smoothed her short ash-blond hair, then sighed. "The records still show Roberta Malone on the deed."

86

"But didn't Roberta Malone die in the previous fire?"

"Yep." Vivian slipped the point protectors off her needles. "Rumor has it that fire was set by the jealous wife of Roberta's married lover, and now Roberta haunts the place looking for revenge. There have been a lot of reports of strange lights and noises. Which is why the house is the perfect ending for our tour."

"Yikes!" It was silly, but I wasn't a big fan of disturbing things that went bump in the night. I thought awhile, then said, "Wait a minute. Maybe the present-day owner is a descendant of Roberta and she has the same name as her relative. A distant cousin or something."

"Maybe. But if so, she doesn't want to be found." Vivian shrugged. "When the wife of the propane delivery man told me that he fills the tank at the Malone house about once a year and it's hooked to a generator, I was almost convinced that someone was living there. Unfortunately, the bill goes to the lawyer, and Riyad claims that the generator is used to keep the furnace running in the winter, so the pipes don't freeze. And he says the lights are on timers to discourage burglars."

"Sure," I said, snickering. "Because no one around here knows the place is empty."

"Exactly."

"It sure would be a shame to just tear down

such a cool old house," I mused. "I think it's the only nineteen hundreds French Colonial in Shadow Bend."

"It would." Vivian's knitting needles clicked in a soothing rhythm. "There's a beautiful mural on the staircase wall, and the dining room has a gorgeous hand-painted and jeweled ceiling." She tsked. "Four generations of Malones lived there. Think of all the fancy parties that old house has seen. All the wheeling and dealing."

"Oh?"

"Don't you remember?" Vivian gave me a strange look. "Roberta's father was Shadow Bend's mayor for over thirty years."

"Right. I'd forgotten that." I nodded, then brought the conversation around to my intended subject before Vivian had sidetracked me with the Malone house controversy. "Do you know Gabriella and Elliot Winston?"

"Elliot spoke to the chamber of commerce." Vivian didn't question why I was asking about the couple. This was a small town. Eventually most residents came up for discussion. "It was one of the meetings you didn't make."

"What did you think of him?"

"He was enthusiastic." Vivian's tone was neutral. "But I'm not sure about his wildlife park. I suppose it *might* help the town economy, but who can say?"

"True. It's really hard to figure out what's a

good idea and what isn't," I agreed. "Did his wife accompany him to the meeting?"

"No." Vivian shook her head. "Apparently, she's against him opening the park."

"Really?" I pasted a surprised expression on my face. "Why do you say that?"

"My nephew Vaughn is dating Muffy Morgan, and she's Gabriella's BFF." Vivian raised a brow. "Muffy mentioned that Gabriella was so upset about how much money Elliot is sinking into that place, she consulted a lawyer."

"About a divorce?" I asked.

"Muffy didn't say." Vivian shrugged. "Just that Gabriella wanted to see if there was any way to protect her share of the marital assets."

"Seems prudent." I stood. "I guess I'd better get back to work. Do you or your group need anything?"

After Vivian assured me they were all set, I returned to the front of the store. I sent Jake a quick text about Gabriella and the lawyer, then got to work.

The after-school crowd would be in soon, and I had to make sure the soda fountain was fully stocked and ready for the onslaught. Taryn would handle drinks, as well as the other snacks upstairs, but it was still warm enough that a lot of the kids would want ice cream. And I'd found out the hard way that making hungry teenagers wait in line was never a good thing.

As I made sundaes, milk shakes, and banana splits, I thought about what Vivian had told me about Gabriella. Did Elliot know about the lawyer? Because if he did, that might have given him a motive to murder his wife.

CHAPTER 7

It was five fifty and the Knittie Gritties were long gone, as were Taryn and the teenagers. The only ones left in the store were a couple of last-minute shoppers wandering the aisles and Jake, who had just come down from his office and taken a seat at the soda fountain.

I poured him a cup of coffee and nudged a plate of leftover pastries in his direction. When he grabbed a bear claw and devoured it in two bites, I grinned. Another plus in having him around was that he could eat the surplus treats before I ended up stuffing them into my mouth. I hated seeing food go to waste, and I couldn't sell day-old baked goods, so they often ended up in my stomach—and on my hips.

Watching him demolish a chocolate chip scone, I wondered how, eating the way he did, he kept his stomach so flat. It was probably the hard ranch work, wrestling bales of hay and five-hundred-pound calves, while my daily exercise mostly consisted of stocking shelves and scooping ice cream. But I had a sneaking suspicion that Jake's metabolism might be way better than mine, too.

When the final customers headed toward the front counter, I scooted over to the cash register and rang up their orders. After bagging their selections, I walked with them to the door, said good-bye, turned the lock, and flipped on the neon CLOSED sign.

Although it had only been a half day, we'd been busy nearly every single second, and I was pooped. Returning to the soda fountain, I picked up the pot and emptied the remaining coffee into my mug. After dumping in some fake sugar and creamer, I dropped onto the stool next to Jake and blew out a tired sigh.

After taking an energy-enhancing sip, I asked, "Any progress with the Winston case?"

"Nothing so far." Jake frowned. "I'm heading out to show Gabriella's picture to some of the places that sounded the most promising on the phone, but I'm not holding my breath that anyone will recognize her."

I made a sympathetic sound, then asked, "Will you be talking to Gabriella's best friend, Muffy Morgan? Did you see my text saying that Muffy told her boyfriend's aunt that Gabriella had consulted an attorney to stop Elliot from pouring all their money into the wildlife park?"

"Yep." Jake narrowed his eyes. "I need to stop by Winston's house later and see if he knew about it."

"Do you think he'll tell you the truth?"

"Hard to say. That's why I want to ask him in person, so I can see his reaction." Jake set his empty cup on the counter and reached for the last pastry. "You still planning to see Poppy and Boone tonight?"

"Uh-huh." I rolled my shoulders, trying to loosen the tense muscles. "We're meeting at seven for tacos and margaritas."

Generally, when the three of us wanted to have a long heart-to-heart, we got together at Poppy's bar. But because she'd been acting so strangely lately, I phoned Boone to plan our strategy. I told him about the scene between Poppy and her father at the police station and suggested we have dinner at the Mexican restaurant near the highway instead of at Gossip Central.

Boone agreed and said he'd speak to Poppy and that he'd drag her to the restaurant if necessary. We both knew she preferred to stay at her club so she could keep a close eye on the business. But Gossip Central was closed on Monday night, so she didn't have that excuse.

Jake broke in to my thoughts about my BFFs and asked, "How's your grandmother doing?" As he spoke, he got up, stood behind me, and started massaging my neck. "Birdie and Tony seem to be seeing a lot of each other. I hear they're taking a senior bus trip to a play in Kansas City tonight."

Tony Del Vecchio was Jake's great-uncle and Gran's teenage sweetheart. Because Tony was a year older than Birdie, he graduated from high school first. When she'd refused to marry him until she got her diploma, he'd enlisted in the marines. That impulsive decision had resulted in Tony fighting in the Korean War and going MIA just before it ended.

While I had been growing up, Gran and Tony had avoided each other. Even after both their spouses died, they hadn't reconnected, which was odd, since Tony had purchased all the land Gran had sold off, and our properties shared a border. Only after I'd been accused of murder and Gran had been forced to ask for help to clear my name, had they started seeing each other again.

I knew their decades-long estrangement had something to do with her marrying my grandfather so soon after Tony went missing. However, she'd always refused to tell me the reason for her hasty wedding.

In the past, I hadn't wanted to upset her by attempting to pry the information out of her. But it might be time to get those facts on the table and clear the air.

Although I was happy that she and Tony had rekindled their friendship and were dating after all those years, it worried me that there might be a secret between them that could ruin their happiness. Plus, if I ended up with Jake, a problem between his uncle and my grandmother was bound to mean that he and I would be on opposite sides, which would be detrimental to our relationship, too.

I realized I had been lost in both the wonderful

feeling of Jake's fingers kneading out the knots in my muscles and my musings, so I quickly said, "Gran is doing amazingly well. Between my father getting out of prison and moving back home and Tony courting her, Gran's memory has made a nearly miraculous improvement."

"That's terrific." Jake moved his hands from my neck to my back and continued the massage. "What does Birdie's doctor have to say about that?"

"She says she's never seen anything like it." In order to enjoy Jake's attentions more fully, I leaned my forearms on the counter and rested my head on them. "Her theory is that Gran's problems were due to stress and loneliness rather than true dementia."

"That takes a lot of pressure off of you." Jake kissed my nape, sending a pleasurable shiver down my spine. "You don't have to worry so much about getting home as soon as you can or her being alone."

"Thank goodness." I turned to face Jake. "Is Tony still having chest pains?"

"Not in the last month." Jake leaned his forehead against mine, and I enjoyed staring into his gorgeous blue eyes. "The cardiologist didn't find any indications of heart problems, so he thinks it was a pulled muscle.

"Since both our elderly relatives are doing so well"—Jake's lips brushed my ear, sending another delightful tingle through my body—"I was thinking maybe we could get away for a weekend."

My pulse raced. I wanted to spend an uninterrupted two days with him. I really did. But was it a good idea? I'd told myself that it would be too slutty to sleep with either Noah or Jake until I committed to one of them. Being alone with Jake might be too tempting to resist the chemistry between us.

I didn't answer Jake. Although my libido was begging me to make a decision and end my bedroom drought, I just wasn't sure which guy was the right choice.

Frustrated with myself, I got up, went in the back room to grab stock for the paperback spinner rack, and started to fill in the empty slots. Jake silently watched me until I finished, then waited for me to close up the store.

As he and I walked out to the parking lot together, he glided his hand under my ponytail, cupped my neck, and slid his other palm up my inner arm. My nerve endings fired, and I leaned in and closed my eyes.

His lips skimmed mine in a barely there kiss and my mouth opened, wanting more. Jake took my invitation, and I tasted coffee and cinnamon. I pressed against his hard length. His hands abandoned my arm and neck to gather me closer, turning the kiss from sweet to wild.

After what felt like both a nanosecond and an eternity, Jake pulled back. I couldn't stop the small sound of protest from escaping my lips, and he kissed my forehead before releasing me.

"Text me which weekend works for you, and I'll make reservations." Jake gave me an unyielding stare.

"I haven't said that I'd go."

"You haven't said you wouldn't, either."

"Fine." I raised a brow. "I'll let you know my answer when you pick me up Saturday night for our date."

Jake nodded, got into his truck, and drove away.

As I slid into my Z4 and headed to the Mexican restaurant, I exhaled loudly as if I'd been holding my breath. Had I just agreed to decide between Noah and Jake by the end of the week? And what would Jake do if I still couldn't choose?

Mexilicious had been open only a few months, and neither Poppy nor Boone had eaten there yet. I'd been there once with Jake and was looking forward to their homemade tortilla chips and salsa.

The restaurant was in a large building located at the end of a small strip mall that also boasted a dentist's office, a pet boutique, a nail salon, and a chiropractic clinic. The outside of the eatery was nothing special, but when customers walked through the front door, they had a pleasant surprise.

The interior was bright, with a contemporary feel to the colors and furniture. The cork flooring was pieced together in an Aztec-like pattern with glass and pebble tiles scattered throughout. Wheat grasses grew in oval-shaped planters that hung on the walls, and black-and-white photographs of Mexico completed the decor.

Since I was the first of our little group to arrive, I requested a table in the back corner and waited for my friends. Boone was usually on time, but prying Poppy away from Gossip Central might take a while. Even though the bar was closed today, she'd have a million excuses to do just one more thing before she left.

Settling in to wait, I ordered a basket of tortilla chips and a Diet Coke. Although I really wanted a margarita, I'd wait to have it until my friends arrived.

The diners were a mixture of Shadow Benders and people off the interstate. Most of the locals in the place stopped by to chat with me, and I had to turn down several persistent offers of company. Small-town folks didn't like seeing anyone eating alone, and they were determined to rectify that situation whether I was willing or not.

Twenty-five minutes went by, and I had polished off nearly all the chips, before Boone and Poppy finally strolled through the door.

Poppy had a mutinous expression on her beautiful face, and Boone's smile wasn't as wide as usual. Clearly, they'd had a tiff.

I waved them over to me, and when Boone took the chair next to mine, he hissed, "She's in a mood."

His bright white teeth contrasted with his bronze complexion. He claimed that his skin was naturally that color, but Poppy and I knew differently. We probably should have tried to talk him out of using the covert tanning bed he kept in his back bedroom, but we both had equally unhealthy addictions.

Mine was coffee and Poppy's was men that were no good for her. She had the more interesting bad habit, but in the long run, mine was probably less dangerous. A racing pulse versus none at all.

Poppy assured us she was careful, but it seemed as if the guys she dated were getting wilder and wilder. I was afraid one of them might really hurt her. And I didn't mean emotionally.

Glaring at Boone, Poppy plopped down facing me and snapped, "Why couldn't we have met at Gossip Central like we always do?"

"Because we're in a rut." I motioned for the server. "You hardly ever leave that place anymore."

"Why would I have to go anywhere else?" Poppy pursed her lips. "I have everything I need. Internet, take-out delivery, and BOB."

"Bob?" Boone asked.

"Battery-operated boyfriend," I explained as the waitress arrived, then seeing Boone's mouth open, I shot him a quelling glance, turned to the server, and said, "A pitcher of margaritas and another basket of chips, please."

"We are *not* in a rut." Poppy was like a tiger with a gazelle in its jaws, refusing to release the notion she might be wrong. "It's just that I need to be at the bar in case there's a delivery or something." She glanced around, frowned at several men who dared to smile at her, and said, "Besides, it's more private."

"We're not discussing state secrets." Boone paused as the waitress returned with our drink and appetizer order. He thanked her then looked at me and raised a brow. "Are we?"

"Of course not." I picked up the pitcher and poured, hoping tequila would help everyone relax. Booze may not solve problems, but then again neither does water, so we might as well indulge. I shoved a glass in front of each of my friends and said, "Try the tortilla chips and salsa. They're both homemade."

Boone reached for the basket, but Poppy concentrated on her margarita.

Figuring it would be best to approach Poppy's issue after she'd had a couple of drinks, I said, "Jake got his first PI client today."

If this were a different type of case, I wouldn't be able to talk about it to my friends. But considering there had been a police report, which would end up in the community news section of the *Banner* on Wednesday, Jake wasn't as concerned about confidentiality as he was about me pumping my pals for information about the missing woman.

Boone barely took time to swallow what he was chewing before squealing, "Tell us everything!"

"Do either of you know Elliot and Gabriella Winston?" I asked.

"In a way." Boone's hazel eyes crinkled. "But I can't say how."

Immediately, I flashed back to what Vivian Yager had said about Elliot's wife going to an attorney to protect her share of the marital assets.

"Because Gabriella is your client," I said. With only a trio of lawyers in town, there was a one-out-of-three chance she'd gone to Boone.

"How did you . . ." Boone's mouth clamped shut. He crossed his arms and shook his head. "I can neither confirm nor deny that statement."

"You just did." Poppy snorted, her mood apparently improved by Boone's discomfort.

"Did not." Boone sneered.

"You two need to grow up." I shook my head. Sometimes it felt as if I were the only adult in our group.

"I may behave myself in public." Boone smirked. "But I'm never growing up."

"I suppose that would be asking a lot," I said, chuckling.

Boone smiled, then said, "Why are you asking about the Winstons?"

"Gabriella is missing." I took a sip of my drink. "Depending on whose theory you believe, she's either been kidnapped, left Elliot of her own free will, or her husband killed her and hid the body."

"Wow! Just wow." Boone straightened. "Although I can't say why I think so, I'm pretty sure the first option is the only viable one."

"Why?" Poppy's voice rose. "Because no one gives up on their marriage?" She glanced at me, then skewered Boone with a look. "Name one couple any of us knows personally who have been together for more than five years and are still in love."

We'd had this conversation before, and I was glad Poppy was talking to Boone instead of me, because I still couldn't come up with an example. Certainly no one in my immediate family. My mom was hunting for husband number five, and I wasn't convinced my grandparents had ever been truly in love. They'd loved each other, but I wasn't sure if they'd been *in* love.

Although Poppy's parents had celebrated their thirty-sixth anniversary in June, it would be hard to claim that Mr. and Mrs. Kincaid still had any passion for each other, especially since the chief seemed to spend every waking moment at the police station.

Then there was Boone's family. His parents

were still married and even lived together, but the only time in the past twenty-five years his folks had spoken to each other was when Boone had been arrested for murder. Once he was cleared of the charge, Mr. and Mrs. St. Onge had gone back to communicating through e-mails and texts.

When Boone was silent, I said, "Uh, guys. Can we get back to the case?"

Poppy and Boone apologized in unison, but before we could get on track, the server came to take our dinner orders. Once the food had been negotiated, it took me a second to remember where we were.

"Okay, then." I refocused and looked at Poppy. "Do you know the Winstons?"

"Elliot is the one trying to open that wildlife park outside of town. He occasionally has meetings at Gossip Central," Poppy answered. "And Gabriella was in the bar once with a bunch of women from the country club for a bachelorette party."

"Did you pick up any interesting tidbits when they were there?" I asked.

"Elliot is willing to do just about anything to get that park up and running." Poppy made a face. "He was even flirting with that woman on the county board who looks like she's about a hundred years old."

"Dolly Clover?" Boone asked. "She's actually fairly young, in her fifties, but she just doesn't do anything to try to make herself attractive."

"Good to know." I raised a brow, then turned to Poppy and asked, "Besides trying to sweet-talk Dolly, did Elliot do anything that was suspicious?"

"No." Poppy rolled her eyes. "But he's got a one-track mind."

"About the park?"

"Definitely. With him it's all"—Poppy put her hands to her cheeks and singsonged—"lions and tigers and bears, oh my!"

"How about Gabriella?" I asked Poppy, glancing at Boone, who clearly was dying to join the conversation but bound by lawyer-client confidentiality, he had to bite his tongue.

"Gabriella seemed to like both booze and men," Poppy answered. "She said her philosophy was that if she was stuck with lemons—i.e., her animal-obsessed husband—she'd order a lemon drop martini and pick up a hot guy."

"Well, it was a bachelorette party," I reminded her.

"True." Poppy smiled meanly. "But none of the other women left with the male stripper."

CHAPTER 8

Jake had struck out at the first motel. Neither the desk clerk nor the maid had recognized Gabriella Winston's picture. As he drove to the next place on his list, his thoughts turned to his last words to Devereaux.

Everything inside of him had screamed that he insist that they make firm plans for their weekend alone. Instead, he'd gritted his teeth and accepted that she wasn't ready to commit. At least she'd agreed to give him an answer about the getaway by Saturday. And although there had still been some uncertainty in those pretty blue-green eyes of hers, there also had been a flicker of desire and a flash of acceptance that it was time to make a choice.

She needed to decide between him and Dr. Dull. Jake had been patient for nearly eight months, and his tolerance had almost reached its limit. Each evening she spent with Underwood was torture for Jake. The idea of another man's hands on her lush hips or his mouth on hers was enough to drive Jake over the edge.

He'd actually found himself reaching for his gun a few times before getting himself under control. Jake snorted. What had he thought he was going to do? Shoot his competition?

Unfortunately, whenever he'd told Devereaux it was him or Underwood, she had stuck out her cute little chin and repeated the word *no* until he finally gave up. When he pushed, she had always said that she understood if he couldn't wait for her, but she just wasn't certain yet.

At least after this afternoon's conversation, it had seemed as if she would finally make a decision. Too bad he wasn't totally certain that he would be Deveraux's pick.

Jake's breath hitched and his heart gave an agonizing squeeze at the picture of her walking down the aisle toward Underwood. He rubbed his eyes, trying to banish that image from his mind.

He was so lost in thought, worried that Devereaux would return to her first love rather than choose him, that he missed the crossroad for the next motel. He adjusted his Stetson, made a three-point turn, and headed his truck back toward the junction.

Jake suddenly smiled, realizing that he had an advantage on Underwood. He knew that the finish line was in sight. The good doctor still thought they were in the middle of the race.

He grinned and gripped the steering wheel tighter. Actually, he had two advantages. While Dr. Dweeb was across town working in his clinic, Jake's office was in the same building as the dime store. He would be able to spend time with Dev every single day this week. And when she made her choice, he'd be the one who was front and center in her mind, as well as, with any luck, in her heart.

This was one of the major reasons why he'd rented that particular space. After he'd nearly wrecked things with Devereaux by having his ex-wife living with him for the past few months, Jake had vowed to put Dev ahead of everything else in his life. Underwood still hadn't grasped that necessity.

Jake's smile widened. He loved Deveraux, and down deep he truly believed she loved him. Dr. Dumbass was only an old habit that Dev needed to break. And Jake was just the man to help her do it.

Whistling, he pulled his pickup into the motel's lot. He parked, then for a moment he leaned back and imagined that Deveraux was in his arms. He loved the feel of her soft curves and the smell of her fiery, yet sweet perfume. It floated around her like a hint of their future, which would definitely contain both sugar and spice.

As Jake got out of the cab and strolled into the tiny office, he reluctantly set aside his daydreams of the feisty cinnamon-haired woman he hoped would one day share his bed, his name, and his life, and concentrated on the case. There was something off about Gabriella Winston's disappearance, but before he could work on any other angle, he needed to follow normal procedure for a missing person.

Being on the private side of law enforcement felt a little strange. He'd never thought about quitting the marshal service and settling down in Shadow Bend. But after he'd been injured, he'd finally spent enough time with his great-uncle to see that Tony needed help on the ranch. And then he'd met Deveraux, who had shown him that there was something more in life than the adrenaline rush of chasing bad guys.

A year ago, if someone had asked Jake if he would ever become a rancher or a private investigator, he would have said no effing way. *Hell!* Eight months ago, his fondest desire was to heal enough to get back to hunting down the perps.

But that was before he kissed Devereaux. No woman had ever affected him the way she had. All of a sudden, being a marshal didn't seem as wonderful if it meant spending time away from her.

Jake had wanted to be a U.S. Marshal since he was twelve years old. In sixth grade, one of his teachers had shown the class a documentary about them, and Jake had been fascinated. However, when he'd realized that his uncle wasn't getting any younger and neither was he, suddenly, leaving the marshal service hadn't seemed so far-fetched.

Once he admitted that his leg would never be a hundred percent again, he knew it was time to do something else. And the possibility of starting a life with Deveraux had clinched the deal.

A faint rustling from the room behind the motel's check-in counter jerked Jake's attention to the present. The bell over the door had jingled when he'd entered the office, and he'd been standing there a good five minutes. Why hadn't anyone come out to see what he wanted?

"Anybody there?" Jake yelled, resting his hand on his weapon.

Thankfully, Missouri allowed concealed carry. He obtained a permit at the same time he'd applied for his PI license. Now he was glad he had.

Was there something hinky going down? Jake called out again, and when there was no answer, he eased behind the counter. Flattening himself against the wall, he took a quick look into the room.

A fluffy white cat was perched on a newspaper spread across the lap of an elderly man sleeping on a beat-up recliner. The feline glared at Jake, then jumped to the floor and disappeared.

Jake smiled at his own paranoia and cleared his throat until the man woke up. The guy stared at Jake, then used the lever to lower the footrest and stood.

Smoothing a hand over the few strands of hair on his head, the guy said, "Can I help you?"

"Sorry to disturb you." Jake stayed by the

room's entrance, not wanting to invade the man's living quarters. "Are you the manager?"

"Owner," the guy grunted, walked toward Jake, and held out his hand. "Dill Dorland."

"Jake Del Vecchio." Jake shook hands. "I'm a private investigator."

"What can I do you for?" Dill's faded brown eyes held a spark of interest.

"I'm looking for this woman." Jake gave the guy Gabriella's picture. "Is she a guest here?"

"Let me get my specs." Dill rummaged in the recliner's side pocket until he found a pair of wire-rimmed glasses, then perched them on his snub nose and peered at the snapshot. "She's not staying here." He thrust the print back at Jake. "Why do you want her?"

"Could she be staying with another guest?" Jake asked, ignoring the old man's question. "May I show the photo to your housekeeping staff?"

"You already did." Dill grinned, revealing several missing teeth. "I'm the chief cook and bottle washer. Only other person around here is my wife."

"Could I speak to her?" Jake wondered if the guy was drawing the conversation out because he was cantankerous or just bored.

"Tootie!" Dill yelled toward the door opposite from where Jake stood. Then when a woman the size and shape of a gun safe emerged, the old man said, "This is the boss."

"Ma'am." Jake tipped his Stetson, then held out the picture. "Have you seen this person?"

Tootie studied the photo, pursed her lips, and wrinkled her brow. "She kinda looks like that lady that was here a while back." She turned to her husband. "The one I told you about that was real put out that we didn't have room service and claimed she was allergic to foam pillows."

"I don't recall anything about room service and pillows." Dill shrugged at Jake. "The ball and chain here complains that I never listen to her. Or something like that . . ."

"Fine." Tootie whacked her husband's arm and said, "The woman with the all the fancy jewelry. You remember her?" Dill nodded, and Tootie said to Jake, "I'm pretty sure this is that lady."

Dill crowded next to his wife, scrutinized the snapshot, and said, "Iffen it's the one I'm thinking you mean, her hair was a different color and a lot shorter."

"Idjit!" Tootie thumped her husband's shoulder again, and this time the smack was so hard he stumbled back and had to grab a nearby table to steady himself. "She was wearing a wig."

"When was she here?" Jake broke in before Dill's wife did the guy bodily harm.

"It was right around the time there was all that talk about aliens." Tootie nodded to herself. "I remember she saw the headline in the county paper when she was checking in and cracked up."

"That's right." Dill scratched his crotch. "You made me carry her suitcase for her, and she got a call while we were walking to her room. She was hooting and hollering with whoever was on the line about the Martians invading Shadow Bend. She was saying that if her husband was in town, he'd jump on the ET bandwagon and waste even more of their money hunting creatures from outer space."

"How long did she stay here?" Jake asked, taking out his notebook.

"Just the one night." Tootie folded her arms. "And she left a mess."

"A mess how?" Jake raised a brow. Considering the clientele this place had to attract, Gabriella must have really destroyed the room.

"Well," Tootie tittered. "We have our share of guests who come here for some loving, but this lady must have really liked it rough."

"Could she have been assaulted? Lots of women don't report sexual abuse." Jake frowned. "Did you see her when she checked out?"

"Yep. I did." Dill rolled his eyes. "She called for me to put her suitcase in her car. She didn't have a mark on her and seemed in a real good mood." He winked. "If you know what I mean."

"What kind of car did she have?" Jake asked, flipping through his notes to check what Gabriella drove.

"A snazzy red sports car." Dill sucked in his cheeks. "I don't know the make or model."

Jake noted that Gabriella drove a red Lexus RC 350 coupe.

"Did you see the person who joined her in her room?" Jake asked.

Both Tootie and Dill shook their heads.

"Did you notice any strange vehicles in your parking lot that day?"

"There was that bright green one." Dill dug in his ear as if searching for buried treasure. "Did you see it, Tootie?"

"Yep. I sure did. It looked like a metallic lima bean." The woman shot an impatient glare at Jake. "And no, I don't know what kind of car it was."

After a few more questions, Jake thanked the couple for their time and walked out to his truck. He sat in the cab for a few minutes, digesting what he'd learned and deciding on his next move. Did Elliot know his wife was cheating on him? Had Gabriella run away with her lover or been killed by her husband for having an affair?

Either way, he needed to talk to his client before he did anything else.

It had been twilight when Jake arrived at the motel, but had gotten darker while he'd been inside. As he drove toward Country Club Estates, a plastic sack blew across the blacktop, and he noticed that the wind was picking up and it was drizzling again. October's weather was turning out to be as unpredictable as a rabid squirrel guarding a bird feeder.

Twenty minutes later he pulled into the Winstons' driveway. There were no lights shining from upstairs or the front windows, but when he walked around the side, he saw patches of illumination on the back lawn. Jake checked his watch. It was almost eight o'clock. Elliot must be relaxing in the family room.

Before returning to the front door, Jake stood still and listened. Beyond the sound of rustling leaves, the property was silent. He took a deep breath. There was a faint whiff of smoke. He glanced upward. No telltale white fumes from the Winstons' chimney. It must be someone nearby who had their fireplace going.

A sudden gust of wind lifted the brim of Jake's hat. He pulled it down, hurried around front, and rang the bell. Either Elliot was expecting someone or the man was a sprinter, because within seconds the door swung open.

At the sight of Jake, his eyes widened and said, "Did you find her?"

"Not yet." Jake watched his client's reaction carefully as he said, "But I do have some information about your wife's activity before she went missing."

"Oh. Well then, you better come in." Elliot gestured for Jake to follow him and walked down the hall and into the kitchen. After waving Jake to a stool, he said, "I was just having something to eat. Can I get you a bowl of chili and a beer?"

Jake hesitated for a second, but he hadn't had anything but the dime store's leftover pastries for supper. And maybe having a meal together would make Winston open up about his wife and their true relationship.

"Sounds good." Jake smiled.

He was surprised that a guy like Elliot Winston was eating something so down-home. And he'd have pegged the guy for a wine drinker rather than knocking back a few brews.

A long counter ran the length of the room, and Jake took a seat on one of its stools. Stacks of papers littered the otherwise pristine quartz surface, and it was clear that Winston had been working as he ate.

As Elliot dished up dinner, Jake glanced at the scattered pages. A few had columns of numbers, but the rest were from various wildlife groups. One letter implored Winston to take a lion and a tiger that had been rescued from an abusive circus act.

"Here you go." Elliot handed Jake a bottle of Fat Tire amber ale and slid a steaming bowl in front of him.

"Thanks." Jake took a taste and nodded his appreciation.

"This is my mother's secret recipe, but Gabriella hates the smell of chili, so I rarely get to make it." His chin dipped to his chest. "I sure wish she was here to complain about it."

"I'm sure you do." Jake patted his arm. "Glad to see you're eating. In a situation like this, lots of folks would forget to take care of themselves, which doesn't help anyone."

"I eat when I'm depressed." Elliot stuck a finger in his waistband. "My pants are already feeling too tight."

"Exercise is good for depression."

"Yeah, maybe." Elliot shrugged, then asked, "So what did you find out?"

"I've been showing your wife's picture around at various businesses in the area, and one owner recognized her." Jake took a swig of the malty liquid, swallowed, looked Winston in the eye, and then added, "It was a small motel just outside of Sparkville."

"You're sure it was her that they saw?" Elliot's Adam's apple bobbed when Jake nodded. "And they said she had stayed there?"

"Yes. She wore a wig, but they described her vehicle, and she wasn't alone." Jake ate another spoonful of chili to allow Winston to process the implications of what he'd been told, then said, "It was in early September."

"I was out of town on business the first two weeks of last month." Elliot's shoulders slumped. "Gabriella was supposed to go with me. She likes shopping in New York. But at the last minute she said she thought she was getting a cold and canceled."

"Sorry, man." Jake wasn't sure what else he could say, and he had to ask, "You didn't have any hint that your wife was having an affair?"

"I knew she was restless." Elliot leaned his head in his hands. "Even though I let her build this ridiculously large and elaborate house, she wasn't happy living in Shadow Bend. Or the Midwest, for that matter."

"Where did you live before?" Jake asked, then ate more chili. He hadn't realized he was so hungry.

"Los Angeles."

"When did you move here?"

"I inherited the land outside of town five years ago, and we bought this property then." Elliot snatched up his beer and drained the half-full bottle. "I thought it would be a good place for the boys to go to high school. Our oldest was running with the wrong crowd in L.A., and I wanted to get the kids into a more wholesome environment. It took a little over eleven months to build the house, and we moved in as soon as it was ready."

"Did Mrs. Winston object to coming to Shadow Bend?" Jake asked.

"Not at first." Elliot scrubbed his fist over his eyes. "The country club set was excited to have someone from California among them, and she liked being a big fish in a small pond."

"Did she spend a lot of time at the club?" Jake took another drink.

Elliot looked down for a long moment, then said, "I guess so." His expression was regretful. "I don't really know. Once I got the idea of using the land I inherited to open up a wildlife park, I . . . I wasn't around much." He shook his head "This is all my fault. I knew Gabriella was unhappy. She's always required a lot of attention."

"Maybe you should have noticed," Jake said slowly. "But the only ones who are at fault for cheating are the people screwing around."

Elliot didn't appear convinced. He stood, went to the fridge, and came back with two more beers. When Jake shook his head, Elliot shrugged and returned one bottle to the refrigerator.

"There's something else." Jake hated to have to hit the guy with another blow, but it had to be done. "Your wife consulted an attorney to see if there was a way to stop you from using your money for the wildlife park."

"I know." Elliot's voice was raw. "I saw the papers, but since the lawyer concluded that she had no recourse, I didn't say anything to her. Maybe that was a mistake."

Jake nodded, and as the men silently finished their meal, he studied Winston. Either he was a darn good actor or he'd had no idea that his wife had been seeing another guy.

"Did you find out anything else?" Elliot asked, then hurriedly chugged the remaining beer in his bottle as if he couldn't bear to hear the answer.

"Not yet." Jake flipped open his notebook and asked, "Do you know anyone that drives a small bright green car?"

"Not that I can think of." Elliot got up, grabbed his and Jake's bowls, and put them in the sink. "Was that what Gabriella's lover drove?"

"Maybe." Jake picked up the empty beer bottles, and when Winston slid open one of the lower cabinets to reveal the two trash bins built into it, Jake tossed them into the recycle container. "I'd better get going."

"Okay." Elliot followed Jake out of the kitchen and down the hall toward the foyer.

As Jake neared the door, he spotted something on the floor. He bent down and scooped up an envelope. *ELLIOT WINSTON* was on the front. There was no return address or postage stamp.

He handed it to Winston, who tore it open, slid out a single piece of paper, and unfolded it. He scanned the contents and gasped. Then gave it to Jake.

Typed in the center of the page were the words: *IT WILL COST YOU A MILLION DOLLARS IN UNMARKED BILLS TO SEE YOUR WIFE ALIVE AGAIN. YOU'LL BE NOTIFIED WHERE TO LEAVE THE MONEY. YOU HAVE TWO DAYS. DO NOT INVOLVE THE POLICE.*

CHAPTER 9

Poppy, Boone, and I had finished our dinners and were contemplating the dessert menu. Since Boone and I had to drive home, we'd both stopped drinking after our second margarita. Leftovers weren't a problem, though, because Poppy had been happy to finish off the pitcher by herself.

As we ate, we'd continued to talk about Gabriella's disappearance. Boone wasn't able to contribute much because of the whole lawyer-client privilege issue, and since the Winstons didn't hang out at her bar, Poppy just plain didn't know anything more about the couple.

After we'd run out of gossip about Elliot and his wife, we turned to what was going on in our own lives. I updated my BFFs about Gran and Tony, my father taking on added responsibilities at the dime store, and Jake's inviting me to go away for the weekend—which my friends encouraged.

Once we'd finished discussing my love life, I turned to Poppy and Boone and asked, "Do either of you know a good electrician? The lights in the employee restroom keep flickering, and I'm afraid either Jake or my father is going to electrocute himself trying to fix them."

"I'll get ahold of my handyman," Poppy offered

"If he's available, I'll text you when he can fit you into his schedule."

My repair problems settled, Boone obsessed over the Halloween weekend activities. He was on the chamber of commerce committee that was organizing the event, and he was even more upset than Vivian at not being able to nail down the Malone house.

As Boone continued about the house, he said, "Whenever I drive past the place I feel someone watching me, and I swear that I've seen a curtain twitch more than once."

Boone's preoccupation with the house led us into reminiscing about our high school adventures. Whenever Gran grounded me, I'd go out my window, cross the field between our two houses, and meet my friends in the Malones' driveway.

"Dev"—Poppy poked my arm—"do you remember the time that Roberta Malone ushered you into her inner sanctum via a shotgun aimed at your heart?"

"How could I forget?" I shook my head. "Miss Roberta made me sit and talk to her for what seemed like hours. She wanted to know all about my life and future plans. Finally, just before she let me leave, she told me not to make the same mistakes as her. She warned me that the man I welcomed into my heart and into my bed needed to be willing to put me first. At the time, I thought she was a lunatic. But now that I remember her advice, I may need to consider it a little more seriously in the very near future."

"Yeah, right." Poppy snorted, then quickly changed the subject. "Did I tell you that business is booming at the club? I had to hire more servers and a bouncer for Friday and Saturday nights. The customers tend to get a little rowdier on the weekends." She winked. "And I sure don't want to have to call in the cops."

During dinner, I hadn't broached the subject of what was bugging Poppy. But now that she was nice and lubricated, and had mentioned the police, I considered how to tackle the topic. Should I go head-on or edge into it?

Before I could come up with an idea, the server appeared at our table to take our dessert order. We all went with the flan. Boone and I asked for a cup of decaf, but Poppy ordered an Irish coffee. She was definitely imbibing more heavily than usual, and I needed to find out why.

Once we had our dessert and drinks, I screwed up my courage, turned to Poppy, and asked, "What happened between you and your dad this morning?"

"I told you." Poppy didn't meet my gaze. "Just the usual crap."

Refusing to be put off, I persisted. "You said your dad told you that unless you straightened up, you were going to hell." I narrowed my eyes. "What triggered that sage piece of advice?"

"He found out where I got the financing for the bar." Poppy squirmed.

"Shit on a shingle!" Boone blurted out, then covered his mouth. "How did that happen?"

Boone didn't like to curse, and although Poppy and I had promised him not to use the F-word anymore, if any occasion called for it, this one did. Poppy had gotten the money for her club from her father's older brother. A guy Chief Kincaid hadn't spoken to in forty years.

Blackie Kincaid lived in Nevada and owned the High Tail Inn brothel. Being the bad girl that she was, Poppy had defied her father's decree that no one in the family have any contact with his brother and had gotten in touch with her uncle when she was in college.

Having no children of his own, Blackie had practically adopted Poppy. And when she decided to open Gossip Central, he'd been thrilled to lend her the cash interest-free. He'd wanted just to give her the money, but she turned down his generous offer. In another six months or so, she'd finish paying off the loan.

"Dad wouldn't tell me how he found out about Uncle Blackie bankrolling the bar's start-up," Poppy huffed. "But I think he must have used some of his law enforcement contacts to investigate me, which is so totally heinous, I can't even wrap my mind around it."

"Honey, you have no idea how much data the

government has on all of us. Or how easy it is to discover that info if you know where to look." Boone wrinkled his nose. "Your father wouldn't have had to pull any strings. All he'd have to do is take a stroll through the Internet."

Boone was a bit of a conspiracy theorist. I knew I had to stop him before he started in on how the Freemasons control and manipulate the government. Or something equally as outrageous.

Hastily redirecting the conversation, I asked, "What did your dad want you to do? The money's already spent, and you've almost repaid it."

"Who the eff knows what Chief Holier-Than-Thou wants?" Poppy mixed the whipped cream into her Irish coffee and took a healthy sip of the steaming liquid.

"He didn't say?" Boone patted the swath of tawny-gold hair that rested on his forehead. "That doesn't sound like the chief. He doesn't usually make you guess. He just tells you to your face what he wants you to do."

I flinched. Boone challenging Poppy's perception of her dad wouldn't end well.

"You always take his side." Poppy poked out her lower lip. "You're supposed to be my best friend and support me no matter what."

"Damn it all to hell!" Boone glared, possibly because he'd just sworn again. "We do support you. But you need to get over this feud with your father. Agree to disagree."

"Don't you think that I've tried that?" Poppy cried. "He keeps picking at me. Wanting me to change and settle down and be . . . Iris."

"Ouch!" I made a sympathetic face and squeezed my BFF's fingers.

Poppy's sister had been the good girl of the family. She'd been a freshman in college studying to be a kindergarten teacher when she died in a car accident fifteen years ago.

"'Ouch' is right." Boone winced in sympathy and covered Poppy's and my hands with his.

"So what did your dad want you to do?" I asked.

I knew the chief had made some kind of outrageous demand or Poppy wouldn't have been as riled up as she was when I saw her. Had he ordered her to get a teacher's certificate and work with five-year-olds?

"Close the bar," Poppy muttered. "Go to grad school and get my psych degree."

I cringed. My guess had been close.

"Oh." Boone frowned, then used his thumb to smooth the line between his brows and asked cautiously, "Any possibility of that?"

"Not an icicle's chance in hell." Poppy crossed her arms. "Dad can't understand that I'm happy. I like running a business and I'm good at it. I make a great living and it's fun. I like the rush of the bar on a Saturday night when things are really jumping."

"Did you ever tell your dad that?" I asked. "I mean, really explain, not yell."

"He doesn't listen to me or my mother. He never has." Poppy's lips pinched together. "He only hears what he wants to hear."

"Have you tried when you're both calm?" I asked. "Rather than in the heat of the moment?"

The chief had always listened to me. He didn't always do what I wanted, but he'd always heard me out. Surely, he could do the same for his own daughter.

As if reading my mind, Boone shot me an unreadable look. "Maybe Dev could go with you as a sort of intermediary." He shrugged innocently. "I mean, she and the chief seem to work well together in solving crimes."

"Well . . ." Poppy's expression was speculative. "Do you really think it would help?" She looked down, playing with her napkin. "I mean, I'm not the wild child he thinks I am and . . . and . . ."

"And you'd like to stop fighting with your dad," Boone finished for her.

She nodded, and Boone whipped out his cell. "Why don't we schedule a meeting right now?"

"No!" Poppy and I shouted simultaneously, then she said, "I don't like planning things like that ahead of time."

"Why?" Boone held his phone at the ready.

"Because if you do," Poppy smirked, "the word

premeditated gets tossed around in front of the judge."

I chuckled, and before Boone could pursue the matter, I said, "Let's think this over a little. There's no need to rush into anything."

I wasn't sure what I was afraid of. Maybe that I'd lose my good relationship with the chief, as well as damage my friendship with Poppy. Whatever it was, I wanted time to consider the idea before I agreed to act as a mediator for the Kincaid family.

Boone reluctantly put his phone back in his pocket, and I breathed a sigh of relief.

The three of us sat in silence finishing our desserts and drinks until I remembered a conversation that I'd had with Poppy a month or so ago. Was this about more than her father?

Licking the last of the flan off my spoon, I asked, "Is there another reason you want to improve your bad-girl rep?"

Poppy's hand jerked, splashing her drink, and she said, "I don't know what you mean."

"Like, maybe the guy you told me about?" I smiled slowly. "The one who isn't your type and is too different for even a fling?"

"No." Poppy's gorgeous heart-shaped face turned as red as the bottle of hot sauce sitting on the table. "Not really. And, like I said, he's in love with someone else, so it wouldn't matter what I did."

"And why am I just hearing about this now?" Boone crossed his arms.

"It's not important." Poppy tried to shrug off the whole conversation.

"Doubtful." Boone ticked off the facts. "First, you never blush. Second, your motto is that if the man isn't married, then he's available. And third, you've never cared about differences before. In fact, you always say you like having nothing in common because there's no possibility of becoming emotionally involved."

"Which is exactly why this guy can't be on my radar." Poppy slumped. "Just thinking about him makes me doubt myself too much."

"Sweetie." I slid my chair over and put my arm around her shoulders. "You're amazing. Any man would be lucky to have you. We can always improve, but that doesn't mean we aren't great the way we are."

"Tell us who he is." Boone leaned across the table and took Poppy's hands. "We really can't make any informed suggestions without knowing."

I saw the unhappy set of Poppy's face and noticed a flash of guilt before she said, "I can't. It would just cause trouble."

Shoving aside the flicker of alarm, I ignored the idea that had popped into my head. If I didn't think about it, it would go away. Right?

"Now I'm intrigued." Boone's grin was wolfish. "Who is this guy?"

"Let it go, Boone!" Poppy snapped, her voice cracking suspiciously.

Oh. My. God! Was Poppy on the verge of tears? The only time I had ever seen my friend cry was at her sister's funeral. Certainly not over a man.

"We'll talk about it another time," I said. Poppy was beginning to worry me.

"No, we won't." Poppy's expression was stubborn. "Just drop it. I'm sticking to men who are like this Irish coffee. Hot, fueled by alcohol, and able to keep me up all night."

"Fine." Boone's nostrils flared. "But I thought we were best friends."

Shoot! The last thing I wanted was for my two BFFs to fight.

Searching my mind for a change of subject, I spotted a good-looking blond guy tapping his foot impatiently at the take-out counter. When he saw me looking at him, he flashed a grin and I nodded. He looked vaguely familiar, but I couldn't figure out where I'd seen him.

"Do either of you know who that is?" I moved my chin slightly in the man's direction. "I feel like I should know him."

"That's Mac McGowan." Boone's eyes brightened at the prospect of good gossip. "Mac's the golf pro at the country club. Although maybe not for long; I heard they were thinking of firing him."

"Why's that?" Poppy asked, evidently happy for the distraction.

"He hit the trifecta of sins." Boone dissolved into what could only be described as a fit of giggles. "At least, sins for the hired help."

"Which are?" Poppy asked, peevishly drumming a fingernail on the tabletop.

"One, he got caught doing coke in the locker room," Boone said, sticking a finger in the air and nearly wiggling with glee. "Two"—his ring finger joined his pinkie—"he came to work drunk."

"And three?" Poppy's bloodred nails were hitting the table in double time.

"Patience is a virtue," I admonished, snickering at her eagerness.

"And three"—Boone raised a third finger—"he got caught naked in the hot tub with the club president's wife."

When Boone paused dramatically, I asked, "Why in the world would McGowan do something like that? He had to know there was a decent chance that he'd be caught."

"It's the drugs," Poppy said. "Part of the high is not having to think about what's right and wrong. Just doing what feels good at the moment."

Boone frowned at our interruption and said, "Even worse than being discovered nude with a married woman, there was another lady present."

"Who?" Poppy squealed. Her thirst for gossip was second only to Boone's.

"No one knows." Boone's lip curled. "She

managed to get away without anyone seeing her face. All they could say was that she had a great body."

"And by great, you mean a hundred pounds soaking wet, right?" I asked with a sarcastic edge to my voice that I couldn't hide.

It had taken me years to become comfortable with my curvier-than-acceptable figure, and I was no longer jealous of the size 00s, but it was still a little annoying that everyone thought less was more.

Poppy and Boone looked at each other uncomfortably until I blew out a breath and said, "Sorry. Sometimes societal expectations still get to me." I frowned. "Women will never achieve true equality until they can appear in public bald and with a beer belly, and still feel attractive."

Poppy ignored my feminist rant, punched me lightly in the arm, and said, "You have beautiful hair." She leaned forward and touched my ponytail. "A lot of women pay big bucks to get this cinnamon gold color you have naturally, but you scrape it back instead of showing it off."

This was the same thing she said to me on a semiregular basis. I should just tell her why I opted for a ponytail. But I didn't, because I didn't want her pity. Since I'd given up the big bucks of the financial industry, I'd had to forgo the luxury of having my hair cut by someone who knew how to handle the thickness and the curls. I'd tried Vivian Yager's beauty salon, but even she admitted that my unruly mane was a challenge.

Taking my silence as a green light to join in the let's-critique-Dev session, Boone said, "Not to mention your gorgeous eyes. Do you realize people wear aquamarine contacts so their eyes will look like yours? But you do nothing to emphasize them."

Again, good makeup was expensive, and I was allergic to most of the drugstore brands. I didn't waste the pricey cosmetics on everyday situations. *Jeez.* You would think they'd never seen me looking good.

"Not to mention how you dress." Boone's gaze wandered over my jeans and sweatshirt. "I saw the cutest outfit in *Glamour*. It would be perfect for you. Let me get it for you as a Halloween gift."

"Forget it." I crossed my arms. "I've vowed not to wear any clothing modeled by a woman who weighs less than Gran's cat."

"Fine." Poppy leaned back, suddenly deflated. "But you have two hot guys who love you. Who cares what other people think about your body type?"

"True." That shrill alarm sounded in my head again. Since when did someone as gorgeous as Poppy look so unhappy at the thought of the men in my life? In all the years we'd been friends, she'd never exhibited one iota of jealousy before.

Something was definitely up. Something I didn't want to even think about. I hoped I was wrong, but I had a feeling that I wasn't.

Time to end this evening before one of us revealed something we'd all regret. None of us were ready to deal with what I feared might be exposed.

I quickly stood and said, "I'd better hit the restroom before I take off."

"Good idea." Boone rose and glanced around. "Where are they?"

"Near the entrance." I looked down at Poppy. "How about you?"

"Nah." She grabbed the check. "I'll pay and meet you guys up front."

Boone got out his wallet, and I dug through my purse. We each gave Poppy enough cash to cover our share of the bill, then made our way toward the bathrooms. As we neared the door, I glanced out and saw Mac McGowan juggling a tower of take-out containers as he fumbled with his keys. He saw me watching him and scowled, then quickly got into a small bright green car and drove away.

Boone followed my gaze and snickered. "Is Mac driving an avocado?"

"Sure looks like it."

I was a bit of a car snob, and the tiny vehicle just seemed wrong for such an athletic guy. Granted, he wasn't super tall or bulked up, but it still seemed an odd choice for him.

Shrugging, I went into the ladies' room. To each his own.

But why had he glared at me? Did he think I was coming on to him because he'd seen me looking at him earlier? *Nah.* A guy like that would probably expect all women to be interested in him. Which made his frown all the more puzzling.

CHAPTER 10

It was barely nine thirty when I said good-bye to Poppy and Boone, got in my car, and headed home. It was unusual for our friends' night out to end so early. Typically, our get-togethers lasted long past the witching hour. Of course, we were normally at Gossip Central, and no one there minded if we monopolized a table for an entire evening. At Mexilicious, it wouldn't have been fair to the server to stay much longer.

And, although I'd never admit it out loud, I wanted to get home and check on Dad. Even though Gran was on her big date with Tony in Kansas City, she would have fixed Dad something to microwave for his dinner, so the actual food wasn't an issue, but I felt guilty that he might have been lonely eating the meal all by himself.

I had sent Dad a text telling him I would meet up with my BFFs, so he wouldn't have expected me for supper. Still, I worried about his state of mind. I hoped there was a good movie on TV or a *MythBusters* marathon. He loved that program.

Since getting out of prison, Dad had stuck close to the house. At the best of times, he'd never been one to socialize much, and the years of unjust incarceration had made him even less inclined to seek the company of others.

One reason was just Dad's natural introverted nature. But a bigger cause was that even though the real criminal had finally confessed to everything—the bank embezzlement, planting the controlled substance in my father's glove box, and drugging him—Dad had still been the one behind the wheel when the vehicle hit and killed an innocent young woman. And not everyone had welcomed him home.

Unfortunately, some of the townspeople didn't care that my father had been roofied. They felt he'd committed vehicular manslaughter and so should have served the rest of his sentence. And they made their displeasure known.

It certainly helped that Chief Kincaid had stood by Dad's side. They'd been friends before my father's wrongful conviction, and the chief had openly resumed that friendship when he was freed. Which was a big reason that although I was uneasy about mediating the feud between Chief Kincaid and his daughter, I would do my best for them.

With that virtuous thought, I pulled into the lane that led to my grandmother's place. The house was located at the edge of town on the ten remaining acres of the property my ancestors had settled in the eighteen sixties. I had lived with my grandmother there since I was sixteen when Mom had dropped me like an unwanted kitten on Gran's front porch.

Before my grandfather died, back when the Sinclairs had been prosperous landowners, the hired hand had lived in an apartment above the garage. But when Dad got out of prison, he'd moved into that space, and now three generations of Sinclairs occupied the old homestead. It was a bit too cozy when any of us wanted privacy, but mostly it was nice to be close to what little kin I had left.

Due to premature deaths, several generations of only children, and entire families packing up and moving away, Birdie, Dad, and I were the last Sinclairs in Shadow Bend. When my grandfather died sixteen years ago, Gran had refused to accept her son's financial help.

Instead, she started selling off the land surrounding the house to pay taxes and support herself. And later on, once legal fees had exhausted my father's savings, Gran had to support me on that money as well. By the time I'd begun to earn a hefty salary and could provide for us both, it was too late. My heritage had vanished piece by piece. Which is why I prized the acres we had remaining.

As I maneuvered my car through the deep shadows of the white fir and blue spruce lining either side of the lane, I felt myself relax. There was something about driving down this familiar lane that lifted my spirits and eased all my worries. It was the only spot where my gerbilon-an-exercise-wheel mind calmed down and allowed me to unwind.

Although I couldn't see the small apple orchard or the duck pond as I passed them, I knew they were there and wondered if the fall weather would allow us to hold one more picnic before it got too cold. Or maybe we could have an autumn bonfire with hot cider from our own fruit. Gran could make her famous potato salad, and we could roast hot dogs and make s'mores.

When I got to the end of the lane, I saw that Dad's apartment was lit up like downtown Kansas City. Should I go up and say hi?

Although I really wanted to make sure he hadn't been too lonely at dinner, we were still adjusting to living in such close quarters. And, sadly, I wasn't comfortable enough with our relationship yet just to stop by for a nightcap or a father-daughter chat.

After twelve years apart and only a few months together, we continued to tiptoe around each other. Having been a teenager when he was sent to prison, neither of us knew how to treat the other now that I was adult. It was an odd situation for us to be in. We were getting a bit more at ease with each other every day, but neither of us was entirely sure how to act. And my being his employer didn't help matters.

Dad's Grand Cherokee was in my usual spot, so I parked on the concrete pad off to the side.

I didn't want him to have to move my car if he needed to leave before me in the morning. Turning off the engine, I grabbed my purse from the passenger seat and got out.

The halogen light mounted on the garage illuminated the area, and, patting the hood of my BMW, I examined the shiny sapphire black finish for any dirt or scratches. I loved my Z4. It was one of the few luxuries of my old life that I hadn't sold. I'd kept the expensive sports car, knowing that chances were mighty slim on my being able to afford a vehicle like that ever again. I'd rationalized that I'd never get what the car was worth and hung on to it with both hands.

As I dragged myself away from my precious BMW, I heard a noise and saw movement on the outside steps leading to my father's apartment. Dad must have seen me pull in and was coming down to talk.

Before I could move out of the shadows, a feminine voice said, "Dinner was wonderful, Kern. But you should have let me drive myself here. Now you have to take me back into town."

Shoot! Should I reveal myself or stay where I was until they left? Would Dad be self-conscious coming face-to-face with his daughter after entertaining a woman in his apartment? There was no reason to be embarrassed. It wasn't as if I'd walked in on them in bed, and I was glad he'd had a date.

Wanting to know the identity of the woman who had spent the evening with my father, I edged a little closer. She was in her late forties or early fifties and was very pretty. My dad stood a few steps above her on the staircase, and when she looked up at him, I saw her dark blond hair brush the shoulders of her red sweater.

Dad moved down to her and laid his hand lightly on her generously curved hips. Her navy slacks and scarlet peep-toed pumps looked expensive, as did the purse hanging from her shoulder.

I chewed on the end of my ponytail. She looked familiar, but I couldn't place her.

"Nonsense. A gentleman always escorts a lady to and from a date."

My father's voice held a happy note that made my heart lift. He'd been quiet since my mother had breezed in and out of town. He missed his ex-wife and had probably hoped Yvette would stick around after losing her husband. Knowing Dad wanted Mom to stay in Shadow Bend, I'd felt guilty that I was relieved when she left.

"I had a wonderful time, Kern." The woman sighed. "That might have been the most delicious fried chicken that I've had in my entire life. And I know for a fact that was the best apple pie I've ever eaten. I'm certainly glad you stopped into my shop to admire the painting in the window."

Ah! That was where I'd seen her. She'd opened

up A Pretty Picture on the town square. There'd been quite a bit of talk at the last chamber of commerce meeting about the place. Opinions were split about fifty-fifty as to whether an art gallery, even one that offered painting lessons and art supplies, could earn enough money to survive in Shadow Bend.

As she and Dad stepped off the stairs, I realized how silly it was to be hiding, moved into the light, and greeted them.

My father's emerald green eyes beamed, and he said, "Dev, I'm glad you got home in time to meet my new friend Catherine Bennet. Catherine, this is my daughter, Deveraux Sinclair. She owns the dime store across the square from your shop."

I extended my hand and said, "Nice to meet you. I've been admiring what you've done to the entrance of your building. Very classy."

"Thanks." Catherine smiled. "And I love the vintage feel of your exterior."

After a few more minutes chatting about our businesses, I said, "I'll let you two get going. I need to make a call before it gets too late."

We said our good-byes, and I watched them get into Dad's Cherokee. Although my father had been away for thirteen years, he hadn't changed that much. He was still tall and lean, with a military-like posture. Yes, his auburn hair was woven with silver strands and there were lines in his face that hadn't been there before his incarceration, but prison hadn't altered his personality. It hadn't hardened him or drained the kindness from his soul.

I waved as Dad and Catherine drove away, then unlocked the front door and stepped into the foyer. Pausing, I enjoyed the rare treat of having the house all to myself. I stood, reveling in the absolute quiet. No voices, no television, no sound whatsoever.

Suddenly, the silence was shattered by a god-awful yowl that reminded me that I wasn't truly alone. Rushing into the living room, I found Banshee, my grandmother's belligerent Siamese, sitting on the cat tree staring out of the picture window toward the rear of our property. His tail was twitching, and he looked ready to pounce on whatever he saw outside.

Afraid of his sharp teeth and nasty claws, I cautiously moved forward to see what had gotten him into such a lather. Generally, only Gran's presence could induce Banshee to move— well, her and the sound of a can of Fancy Feast being popped open. He slept twenty-three out of twenty-four hours and used the remaining sixty minutes to eat, visit his litter box, and harass me.

When I had moved in with Gran, Banshee made it known in no uncertain terms that he disliked the new human in his kingdom. He destroyed any property of mine left unattended, peed on my bed, and took great delight in scratching any part of me that he could reach.

Lucky for me, the Siamese was so intent on whatever had disturbed his beauty rest that as I gazed out the window he seemed unaware of my presence. I didn't see anything moving in the space illuminated by the outside light. However, the area out by the old barn was in total darkness, so a whole pack of wolves could have been frolicking under the moon, and I would have been none the wiser.

I peered into the shadows for several seconds, but other than a few leaves blowing across the driveway, everything was quiet. If there had been any creatures stirring out there, they were long gone. Maybe a small branch had smacked into the glass, startling the cat. The wind had picked up again and the trees around us were all old.

Or, it was only a few weeks until Halloween. It could be that things that went bump in the night were getting an early start on the holiday.

Chuckling, I glanced at Banshee. The Siamese had turned his back to the window and was using a front paw to clean his ears. Snubbing me, he curled up on the carpeted platform and closed his eyes.

Thankful that he hadn't bitten me while I was distracted, I let sleeping cats lie. Before heading into my bedroom, I detoured into the kitchen and took a bottle of water from the refrigerator. I hadn't had that much to drink, but it was always a good idea to hydrate after consuming alcohol. I didn't have time for a morning hangover.

After changing into my nightshirt and securing my hair on top of my head, I stretched out on my bed and dug my cell out of my purse. I was shocked to see that I had missed a couple of calls and texts. Somehow, I'd managed to turn the ringer to vibrate, and since the phone had been in my bag, I hadn't felt it shaking.

Now that I thought of it, it was odd that it had been silent all night. There was usually some sort of notification coming through.

Both Noah and Jake had been trying to get ahold of me. The men both asked me via texts to return their calls as soon as possible.

It was getting late, so instead of immediately dialing either guy, I listened to my voice mail. Noah wanted to pick me up tomorrow after the store closed and take me to dinner. He had something to tell me. My guess was that the something he wanted to share was Meg's employment.

I sent him a quick text agreeing to the date, and then after a few swipes I heard Jake's voice. "Dev, Winston received a ransom demand while I was at his place. I phoned Chief Kincaid, and he's meeting us at the police station. I'll fill you in tomorrow."

I sent Jake a reply saying I'd heard his message and had some information about Gabriella's activities before she'd been kidnapped.

As I scrubbed my face and smoothed cream

over my skin, I thought about Jake's news. Did a ransom demand mean that Gabriella really was a kidnap victim? Or was it just another ruse?

Crawling under the covers, I closed my eyes. It had been a long day and I was tired. A lengthy fifteen minutes later, I sighed. I usually was asleep before I could finish my prayers. Why was I still awake?

Flipping the pillow to the cool side, I threw off the covers, turned over, and rested my hand under my cheek. What was bothering me?

Was it something to do with Gabriella? I rewound everything I learned about the missing woman. Nope! There wasn't anything there.

Next, I thought about Gran. It was a relief that she was doing so well, almost a miracle, and I was happy she was seeing so much of Tony. I needed to find out why she'd married so quickly after he was reported MIA, but that wasn't what was interfering with my sleep.

Was it concern for my father that was keeping me awake? I was thrilled that my mother's departure hadn't seemed to upset him. At least, not very much. He appeared content working at the store, and his being my employee hadn't been as awkward as I had feared.

Was it his evening with Catherine that worried me? I examined my conscience. No. I was pleased he was dating, and she seemed like a nice woman.

Then why wasn't I in dreamland? Frustrated, I

rolled onto my back and stared upward, watching a fly on the ceiling. I knew the cause of my insomnia, but didn't want to think about the problem.

It was Jake and Noah. When Jake had suggested a weekend away, the gauntlet had been thrown down. It was time for me to make a choice, and I was torn. Actually, that was an understatement of epic proportions. I felt like a cat sitting equidistant between two cans of tuna. They both would be delicious, but how did I decide which one would be the tastiest?

For years, the men I'd dated had been nice, but none of them had made me even consider a long-term relationship. However, now there were two guys who caused me to tingle. Jake was more exciting, but Noah was a known quantity. Jake represented change, but I had loved Noah for years. So why was I still hesitating?

Poppy was sure that if I slept with them both, their performance in the sack would be the deciding factor. In theory, I liked that idea, but when I thought about it, it felt sleazy to have sex with a man before I was committed to him. I had never been a one-night-stand sort of girl.

Boone's suggestion was even worse. He thought that the reason I couldn't choose was that neither guy was the one for me. I tried on that notion. The thought of dating someone else made me queasy.

I didn't want to blow an opportunity for love. I was sure that I was meant to spend the rest of my life with either Jake or Noah. I wanted a chance at the brass ring of happiness. And the only thing between that shiny circle and me was me.

Finally, about quarter after twelve, I heard the front door open and Gran's voice saying good night. There was a low murmur, and I assumed Tony, being the gentleman that he was, had walked her inside. He'd driven them in his truck to the church parking lot, the rendezvous point for the senior bus group, and was doubtlessly ending their date on a traditional note.

Thinking about their relationship gave me an idea. I needed something dramatic to force my decision. A situation where both Noah and Jake needed me. Whichever guy I instinctively went toward would be the one I really loved.

CHAPTER 11

Tuesday was not starting out well. It was eight fifty-five when I pulled into the dime store parking lot. And by the time I got inside, put away my purse, hung up the outfit I'd brought from home to change into for my date with Noah, and grabbed the cash drawer from the safe, it was after nine.

I had wanted to get to work early in order to have a chance to talk to Jake before opening up, but I had slept in. Then, when I finally woke up, Gran had insisted I eat breakfast before leaving.

It had been impossible to turn down her buttermilk pancakes with warm maple syrup and crispy bacon. While I ate, Gran had rhapsodized about her trip to the casino with Tony. Both the penny slot machines and her beau had been hot. She'd won a hundred and five dollars, nabbed the last piece of chocolate cream pie at the buffet, and gotten a sizzling kiss from her boyfriend. Altogether, a very successful date.

When I'd edged the topic toward why she'd married my grandfather so soon after Tony went MIA, she'd stopped talking. However, she did say that she'd grown to love grandpa—*grown* being the operative word—so I had an opening for my next try at the subject.

Flipping on the lights as I hurried through the store, I found my high school helper, Taryn, waiting for me when I unlocked the front door. He glanced pointedly at his watch, making sure that I was aware that he knew I was late, and then marched past me with a muttered hello.

Ignoring Taryn's pique, I greeted him and the two women who crowded in after him with a cheery good-morning. Taryn headed to the storage room to stow his backpack, and the ladies both beelined to the paperback bookrack.

It was the first Tuesday of the month, which meant a new crop of cozy mysteries were coming out. Although the books had arrived last week, after reading a writer's blog on the importance of initial sales, I always waited until their official debut date to display them. It was a closely guarded secret that I'd managed to get my store qualified to report my sales to the *New York Times* and I wanted all the authors to have an equal chance to make the prestigious best seller list.

With my first customers of the day selecting their monthly reads, I carried the cash drawer to the register. A few minutes later, when Taryn joined me, I asked him to set up for the Scrapbooking Scalawags.

The group met at my store every other Tuesday morning at ten. They preserved their memories while enjoying lively conversation and tasty treats, which I provided for a small charge.

On my way into the store, I had stopped at the bakery—another reason I had been running behind—and picked up a cookie platter. The assorted pumpkin, praline, butterscotch, and butter pecan delights made my mouth water. And the buttercream-frosted sugar cookies shaped like acorns, leaves, and scarecrows were beyond cute.

In addition to the refreshments, I also had an enticing display of scrapbooking materials. The basics like cardstock, adhesive dots, art pens, et cetera, were in their normal aisle. However, I'd arranged a variety of fall-themed rubber stamps, craft punches, stencils, and embellishments, including stickers, chipboard elements in various shapes, fabric, beads, sequins, and ribbon smack-dab in front of the craft alcove.

As I had hoped, the tantalizing merchandise proved difficult for the scrapbookers to resist, and I did a brisk business ringing up their purchases. Between the Scalawags and my regular customers, both my clerk and I were kept as busy as Poppy's bartender on a Saturday night.

It was a shame that I didn't have time to quiz the scrapbookers about Gabriella. But from what I'd seen at her house, she really wasn't the type to arrange pictures and keepsakes artfully on the page of an album. Even in her bedroom, the only visible memento had been her own photo.

By the time Taryn left for school at twelve thirty, he looked exhausted. I hoped he'd have a chance to catch his breath while he ate lunch and would be able to concentrate in his afternoon classes. I felt bad for the poor kid, but if he truly wanted to know what owning his own business would be like, this type of experience was invaluable.

In the next half hour, the store emptied out. At twelve fifty-five, when my father, carrying my afternoon bakery order, arrived for his shift, I was making a sundae for my only remaining customer.

The woman's curly white hair was fastened to the top of her head. It matched her fluffy white sweater and the equally fluffy white anklets on her feet. She reminded me of a poodle, and when I presented her with the strawberry-covered ice cream, I casually leaned forward. I was dying to see if she also had a fluffy white tail.

Handing me the white bakery box, my father captured my gaze and raised his eyebrow in mock disapproval. I smiled sheepishly and gave a tiny shrug. After stashing the goodies, I made sure that Ms. Poodle didn't need anything, moved out from behind the counter, and followed Dad into the back room.

As he hung up his Windbreaker and hat, I said, "When you get a chance, please set up the craft alcove for the Quilting Queens."

The quilting group usually met on the opposite Tuesdays from the scrapbookers, but something had come up and they'd asked to use the space today. It meant rearranging the furniture and getting a second round of refreshments from the bakery, but the quilters spent a lot of money on supplies, so I couldn't refuse them.

Especially since I'd recently gotten a great deal on bundles of precut autumn fabric. Once I'd checked on Ms. Poodle and fulfilled her request for a glass of water, I swapped the scrapbook material display for the quilting fabric and threads. When I was finished with that, I restocked and straightened the rest of the store shelves.

The woman at the soda fountain finally finished her treat and left, so after letting Dad know where I was going, I made a quick pit stop in the back. The necessities taken care of, I refastened my ponytail, put on a little lip gloss, then headed upstairs to talk to Jake.

I could hear his voice as I neared his office. Although he didn't sound angry, his tone wasn't exactly happy, either. The door was open, but I knocked lightly on the wood anyway. He flashed me a smile and gestured for me to come in and take a seat.

As he continued to talk on the phone, Jake rolled his eyes. "No. Really. I'm only looking for the one lady." He listened, then said, "While I appreciate your help, there's really no need to call every time a lone woman checks into your motel."

After a few more uh-huhs, Jake hung up, grinned at me, and said, "It's great when folks are helpful, but the ones who are helpful *and* bored can be a problem. Dill Dorland from the Halfway Inn has called me six times already. Who knew that many single women checked into the place?"

"Considering that motel's reputation"—I giggled—"quite a few."

"Ah." Jake's cheeks creased. "I kind of wondered if that was the case."

"The rent-by-the-hour rates should have been your first clue," I teased.

"Since I wasn't there for a room, I didn't inquire about the price." Jake leaned forward, lowered his sexy voice, and murmured, "I promise we'll go somewhere much nicer for our weekend getaway."

"If I agree to go." I crossed my legs and let my foot swing back and forth.

Jake frowned, then nodded and asked, "Busy day in the store?"

"Surprisingly so." I smiled. "But a brisk business day is a good thing."

Jake had come downstairs several times during the morning to see if we could talk, but I'd always been surrounded by shoppers. It was a relief that he hadn't demanded my attention or gotten angry that I didn't have time for him. Instead, he'd just waved and returned to his office. It boded well for our relationship.

"I'm glad the store is doing so well." Jake picked up a pen and threaded it between his fingers. "I know how you agonize about that."

"Thanks. I do worry." I appreciated how he always listened to my concerns. "Anyway, there's a bit of a lull now, so I should be okay until the quilters arrive." I straightened. "Bring me up to speed."

"After you left to meet Poppy and Boone, I started showing Gabriella's picture around at various motels and restaurants in about a twenty-mile radius," Jake said. "I figured if she'd left of her own free will, she couldn't get too far without her purse or vehicle."

"Unless someone picked her up," I said slowly. "Or if she'd been organizing this for a while and had a car and cash stashed somewhere."

"True." Jake wrinkled his brow. "But it's best to work on one theory until it's exhausted, then move on to the next. And the easiest one to eliminate would be that Gabriella left on the spur of the moment because of her fight with Elliot about the wildlife park."

"Okay." I nodded. "I can see your point. You were working under the assumption that she might have gotten a buddy to take her somewhere nearby, hoping to make her husband worry about her. Then after he'd suffered for a few days, she'd go home."

"Yep. If she were truly leaving Winston, she'd

157

probably be back in L.A." Jake tossed the pen in the air and caught it. "Today, I'd planned to visit the people that Winston listed as her friends."

"But the ransom note that Elliot received last night changed your mind," I guessed.

"That and what I found out from my new pals Dill and Tootie Dorland." Jake grinned. "Although Gabriella hadn't been at the Halfway Inn recently, she had spent the night there a month or so ago."

"Seriously?" I barely stopped myself from squealing. "I take it she wasn't alone."

"She was by herself when she checked in." Jake's blue eyes twinkled. "But from the state she left the room in, Dill and Tootie are certain she spent the night with an extremely active companion."

"Well, that certainly adds a twist to the situation." I thought about all Jake had told me, then asked, "Did either of your new besties notice what kind of vehicle Gabriella's lover drove?"

"Unfortunately, neither of them are car buffs or particularly observant." Jake curled his lips. "All Dill and Tootie could tell me was that the vehicle was bright green and resembled a lima bean."

Why did that description ring a bell? I replayed the last twenty-four hours. I'd seen a vehicle like that somewhere recently.

"Mac McGowan!" I shouted. "The golf pro from the country club."

"What about him?" Jake shot me a puzzled glance, then it clicked and he said, "This McGowan drives a car that looks like a lima bean?"

"I'd say more of a lime." I wrinkled my nose. "But it reminds Boone of an avocado. So some sort of green fruit or veggie."

"Gabriella and the golf pro." Jake shook his head. "It's almost too cliché."

"Clichés are clichés for a reason," I said.

"Uh-huh." It was clear Jake was lost in thought. Finally, he said, "If it weren't for the ransom note, I'd wonder if Gabriella just got tired of her husband and ran off with this McGowan guy."

"That and the fact that Mac was at Mexilicious last night." I crossed my arms. "He was getting takeout, which is how I saw his car."

"Still." Jake tossed the pen again. "I definitely need to talk to the guy."

"Boone had some interesting gossip about Mac." I looked at the ceiling, trying to remember the conversation.

"Yes?" Jake made a go-on gesture with his hand.

"It seems Mac has been a very naughty boy," I teased, then when Jake growled, I continued, "First he got caught snorting coke in the locker room, then he came to work plastered, and the pièce de résistance . . ." I paused, waiting for Jake to growl again. His deep rumble sent enjoyable chills up my spine, and I hid my shiver when he fulfilled my silent wish. Smiling, I said, "Mac was discovered in the hot tub with the club president's wife and another woman."

"Isn't the help allowed to use the facilities?" Jake's tone conveyed that he wasn't impressed. "Breaking that rule doesn't seem too awful."

"All three of them were stark naked." I leaned back in my chair, the better to enjoy the startled look on Jake's handsome face.

"Was Gabriella the second woman in the tub?" Jake finally asked.

"I don't know," I admitted. "The lady got away before her identity was revealed."

"So Gabriella was sharing him with at least one other woman, maybe two," Jake said thoughtfully. "Would she run away with a guy she was willing to share? Give up her marriage and her lifestyle?"

"From the little that I know about her, I'd have to say no." I yawned and stretched. My restless night was starting to get to me. "And I learned one more interesting tidbit about Gabriella."

"Oh?"

"Poppy told me about this bachelorette party Gabriella attended at Gossip Central."

I yawned again, and Jake got up, walked over to the coffeemaker he'd set up on a table against the far wall, and poured me a cup of the life-giving brew. Once he'd handed me two packets

160

of sweetener and a little tub of creamer along with a stirrer, he returned to his seat.

After adding the condiments, I took a cautious sip and said, "Evidently, after the party was over, Gabriella was seen leaving with the male stripper."

"Did Poppy know who the stripper was?" Jake asked. When I shook my head, he sighed. "Shit. I wonder if it could have been McGowan."

"I doubt it. It would be too weird if the local golf pro also worked as a stripper." Frowning, I considered what Poppy had said, then shook my head. "I'm not sure if Poppy knew Mac before last night or not." I dug my cell from my pocket. "Let me check."

I texted her and almost immediately she answered: STRIPPER WASN'T MAC.

"Great," Jake groaned. "Like we needed someone else to add to the mix."

"Yeah," I agreed morosely. A couple of minutes went by, then I said, "I almost forgot. Although he couldn't confirm it, I think Boone was the attorney that Gabriella consulted."

"Too bad there's no way to find out the details." Jake's jaw clenched. "A lawyer won't break confidentiality no matter what."

"Right. But I got the impression Gabriella wasn't looking for a divorce, just some sort of restraining order regarding their money."

"When I questioned Winston about that, he said

he knew about Gabriella's attempts to get her hands on the money." Jake scratched his chin. "He claims to have seen a letter stating that she didn't have any legal recourse because Winston was using cash from his trust fund and Gabriella had no rights to that money."

"Interesting." I rubbed my temples. My lack of sleep was giving me a headache. "Tell me about the ransom."

"The note demanded a million dollars and gave Winston two days to get the money together," Jake reported.

"I know the guy is rich, but can he put together that kind of moola so quickly?"

"Winston says he can." Jake nodded. "But it'll have to come from the capital he set aside for the wildlife park, and he won't be able to take more from his trust fund for another year."

"Where's the ransom supposed to be dropped off?"

"The kidnapper will let Winston know later."

"I was sure surprised to get your message." I shook my head. "I would have sworn Gabriella hadn't really been kidnapped."

"It was fortunate that I was at Winston's house when the note arrived." Jake pinched the bridge of his nose. "Otherwise, I'm not entirely sure he would have shown it to me. And I'm positive he wouldn't have given it to the cops."

"Really?" I frowned. "You don't think Elliot

would tell you and the police about the note? It proves that his wife was really abducted."

"You'd figure that to be his first reaction." Jake rose from behind his desk. "But either he's a better actor than I'd guess or he really is more worried about Gabriella than himself."

"So you're convinced that he isn't behind her disappearance?"

"Not one hundred percent." Jake sat on the edge of the desk. "But if he is, he has to have a partner. Because the note wasn't by the door when I arrived, and it showed up while I was with him."

"No way he could have dropped it as you preceded him down the hallway?"

"Nope. I followed him, not the other way around." Jake rubbed his chin. "And I could swear he was truly shocked when I told him about his wife having an affair."

CHAPTER 12

When Noah realized that there was no one scheduled after his four forty-five patient, he instructed Meg not to put anyone in the day's last appointment slot. Normally, he would have had her squeeze someone in, but today was special. He had a date with Dev, and he didn't want to be late.

Almost giddy with the unexpected freedom, by five thirty he was out of his white doctor's jacket, in his car, and on his way home to walk Lucky, his Chihuahua. Noah had inherited the little dog after his fiancée had been murdered. After discovering that his bride-to-be had been lying to him about almost everything, Noah viewed the pup as a constant reminder that he needed to keep up his guard around those of the female persuasion.

That is, all women except Dev. Although she may not always tell him what he wanted to hear, he could count on her to be honest. Painful as the truth might be at times, she never deceived him.

Which is why it was odd that late yesterday, Noah had had the weirdest notion that Dev was keeping something from him, and he needed to see her right away. They'd had plans to go to a Sunday matinee of *The Book of Mormon* in Kansas City, but a little voice told him that waiting until the weekend would be a serious mistake.

Noah wasn't sure if his sudden compulsion to be with Dev sooner rather than later had anything to do with Meg being his newest employee or because Del Vecchio was now Dev's tenant and was around her all the time. But if there was something nudging Noah's subconscious into action, he didn't intend to ignore his gut instinct.

Especially since, if he had his way, he'd spend every night with her, not just the once a week their busy schedules usually allowed. Whatever the reason, Noah had been relieved when she texted her acceptance to his dinner invitation and looked forward to their date.

Pulling into his driveway, Noah glanced at the dashboard clock. He had twenty minutes before he had to head to the dime store. He wanted to be on time for their romantic tryst. Tonight had to be perfect.

Jumping out of his Jag, Noah hurried into the house. Lucky met him in the entryway, pirouetting and barking his excitement. He swiftly attached the Chihuahua's leash and led him down the sidewalk. They'd do a quick lap around the block, then head home.

Although Noah's upscale development boasted a beautifully maintained dog park where the neighborhood pets could run free and socialize, he never brought Lucky there unless he was sure there would be only a few other animals present. Because the Chihuahua was so small, he'd found that if they were there when there were too many of the larger breeds, he couldn't safely let Lucky off his lead.

As the tiny dog inspected every lamppost and fire hydrant, Noah reviewed his plan for the evening. He'd made reservations for one of the private window alcoves at the Manor, the best restaurant between Shadow Bend and Kansas City. The building was located on a man-made lake, and the way the twinkling stars reflected on the navy blue water was beautiful in the dark. The perfect backdrop for an intimate tête-à-tête.

The Manor attracted diners from all over, catering to an affluent clientele looking for an exquisite fine-dining experience or an elaborate party. He and Dev had eaten at the restaurant once before, but they'd been interrogating a suspect in a murder, not on a romantic date.

Unfortunately, before that part of the evening could begin, he had to figure out how to bring up the fact that Del Vecchio's ex-wife was Noah's newest employee. It would help if he had any idea whether Dev would be upset with the news or didn't really care. Elexus had claimed that there were no other viable applicants for the position and had insisted on keeping Meg as their receptionist.

Noah was still contemplating how to tell Dev

about Meg, when he heard an unfamiliar female voice call, "Doctor, wait up."

He cringed. Too many of the divorced, and sometimes still married, neighborhood women had targeted him as their next husband. Another good reason to get a ring on Dev's finger as fast as possible. He was tired of feeling like prey every time he went for a walk or mowed his lawn.

Turning, Noah forced a pleasant smile and said, "Can I help you?"

The woman hurrying toward him was a gorgeous brunette wearing a short black golf skirt and a formfitting striped top. Her sparkling white athletic shoes flashed as she darted up to him.

"Hi, I'm your new neighbor." She held out her hand. "Muffy Morgan."

"Noah Underwood." Noah reluctantly grasped her slim fingers and shook.

"I know who you are." Muffy's silvery laughter sounded phony and scraped his nerves. "All the ladies around here have pointed you out and warned me off."

"Oh." What the hell was he supposed to say to something like that? Ignoring her innuendo, he said, "I wasn't aware that any of the houses on this street were for sale."

"I couldn't afford a dog house in this neighborhood." Muffy snickered, then stepped back when Lucky growled at her. "I'm living with Vaughn Yager."

168

"Vaughn's a great guy." Noah relaxed. He might be comfortably well-off, but Yager was a billionaire. No way would Muffy risk a sure thing with him to pursue Noah. "Vaughn and I went to school together."

"He mentioned that." Muffy nodded. "It seems like everyone in this neighborhood has known each other since they were in diapers."

"I suppose that's true for this particular part of town," Noah agreed.

His subdivision was one of the first established in the area. In the nineteen fifties, the wealthy residents of Shadow Bend who wanted to live in newer and larger houses than they could find in the city limits had purchased the half-acre lots and built custom homes.

Most still lived in them or had passed them on to their children or other younger family members. It was rare for someone who hadn't grown up in the town to buy a place in this neighborhood. A few years ago, Vaughn had pounced when a house was put up for sale. Rumor had it that he'd paid well over the asking price.

"It's a little hard to fit in when I've only been here ten months and everyone else has known each other for so long." Muffy sighed. "My friend Gabriella and I talk about that a lot. She's been here four years, and she says the locals still treat her like an outsider."

"That's a shame," Noah murmured. He hated

the townspeople's us-versus-them mentality. "But at least you've made friends with some of the other new folks."

"Yeah." Muffy brightened, then her lips drooped. "But Gabriella lives over in Country Club Estates. She and her husband have this awesome modern house. I wish Vaughn would build there."

"Is he considering moving?" Noah asked, watching Lucky take care of business near a tree and reminding himself to pick it up before he left.

Noah hadn't heard that Yager was in the market for a new place. He doubted that the prosperous factory owner would give up the cachet of living in this subdivision, especially after he'd completely renovated the sixty-year-old residence.

"No." Muffy blew out an exasperated breath. "Just wishful thinking on my part." She shrugged. "It would be wonderful to be closer to Gabriella, but off the record, I don't think she'll be living there too long anyway."

"Oh." Noah didn't know Gabriella so didn't really care, but to be polite he asked, "Are your friend and her husband planning to move?"

"I think the only part of her husband Gabriella will take with her will be his money." Muffy giggled, then wrinkled her nose and said, "Although, a while back she had been gaining a little weight, and I sort of wondered if she might be pregnant. But she was a little old for that, so I didn't ask her."

"Of course not." Noah had learned that unless he could actually see the baby emerging right that minute, suggesting a woman looked pregnant was a good way to have his face slapped.

"And it was a good thing I never said anything, because Gabriella took up golf and lost the pudge."

"I see." Noah covertly glanced at his watch.

"Anyway"—Muffy shook her head—"Vaughn and I are having a party this Saturday, and I wanted to invite you."

"Thanks," Noah said. "I'll have to check my schedule." He quickly cleaned up after Lucky, then edged down the sidewalk until he was standing by his driveway. When Muffy followed him, he said, "Sorry, I've got to get going. I'm picking up my girlfriend at six."

"Devereaux Sinclair, right?" Muffy swept her long brown hair over her shoulder and petted it as if it were alive. "You should bring her Saturday." Muffy smiled toothily. "It might get the message across to the neighborhood ladies that you're off the market." She winked and walked away, then turned and said, "Of course, that plan could backfire and just bring out their competitive spirit."

Noah's conversation with Muffy had cost him precious minutes, and he swiftly filled Lucky's food and water bowls, washed his hands, and ran a comb through his hair. After checking that he had his keys and wallet, he rushed to his car. Backing onto the street, he threw the ignition into drive and pressed the gas pedal to the floor. If he wanted to be on time, he'd have to risk a speeding ticket.

When he pulled into a parking spot in front of the dime store, Dev was waiting on the step. She wore a pretty dark blue-green sweater that matched her eyes and slim-fitting black slacks that showed off her curves. Suddenly hot, he powered down the window and listened to her sexy ankle-high heeled boots click on the pavement as she hurried toward him.

Before he could tear his gaze from Dev and get out of the Jag to open the door for her, she slid into the passenger seat.

"You look beautiful," Noah said, leaning over and pressing his lips to her soft cheek. "I hope you're hungry. We have reservations at the Manor."

"Starving." Dev's smile warmed his heart. "You look great, too. I love a guy in a crisply pressed Oxford shirt with the sleeves rolled up."

"It would have been crisper if I'd had time to change." Noah's smile was rueful. "It took me longer to take care of Lucky than I planned."

"I also like a guy who's a bit rumpled," Dev teased. "So, win-win."

"How are your dad and grandmother?" Noah asked as he put the car in reverse.

"They're both doing well." Dev buckled her seat belt. "Dad had a date last night with the owner of the new art gallery. She seems nice."

"That's great."

Noah liked Kern Sinclair, and he hoped the feeling was mutual. It was too bad that Dev's grandmother despised him. He'd been working hard to win her over, but hadn't made much noticeable progress. Would she soften toward him if he sent her flowers? Probably not. Birdie Sinclair wasn't someone he could impress with trite gifts.

"How's Nadine's treatment going?" Dev asked. She scrunched up her cute nose and added, "I imagine rehab is a struggle for someone like her."

"Mother wasn't happy when I gave her the ultimatum." Noah winced at the memory of his mom's tantrum when he'd performed the intervention. "But I found a facility that's upscale enough to make her comfortable with the surroundings, and the doctors say she's making progress with her alcohol addiction and her anorexia. Her psychiatrist believes depression is at the root of both problems."

"It's wonderful that you got her help when you did." Dev patted his thigh. "You're a good son."

Noah snuck a peek at Dev. Her words had been positive, but something in her tone didn't feel right. What was he missing?

173

Shoving the nibble of worry from his mind, Noah said, "It seems that Shadow Bend has had its share of people needing mental health assistance." He stared at the road as the Jaguar ate up the miles between town and the restaurant. This was his opening. He slid a quick glance at Dev, then said, "Speaking of that, you'll never guess who Elexus hired to replace Madison."

"Meg." Dev's mouth was pressed in a straight line.

Noah grimaced. He should have known someone would have told Dev about Meg. Del Vecchio's ex working for the Underwood Clinic was probably the hottest gossip in town.

"Yeah." He hurriedly explained, "I had no idea until I walked in yesterday and found her at the reception desk arguing with Eunice."

"Is it a permanent job or is she just filling in?" Dev asked.

"I'm not sure." Noah glanced at Dev's unhappy expression. "I forgot to ask Elexus about that."

"Oh." Dev was silent for several seconds. When she next spoke, her casual tone didn't fool Noah for one second. "What's Meg's last name nowadays?" When Noah raised his brows, her cheeks reddened and she said hastily, "I never heard what she was going by, and I'm curious."

"Del Vecchio." Noah hid his smile. That should put Deputy Dawg behind the eight ball. He added, "When I asked, Meg said that since Jake had been so insistent she take his name, she was keeping it."

When Dev didn't comment, Noah reached over and took her hand. He'd let her stew on that little tidbit until they got to the restaurant. But this was his night with her, and he wouldn't allow Del Vecchio to get in the way.

Dusk made the passing scenery seem almost unreal. As he drove across a creek trickling lazily over dark gray rocks, it reminded him of what his life had been like without Dev. A slow movement forward, but lacking any zest or sparkle. Whatever happened between them, he couldn't allow himself to go back to that apathetic state.

A stubble-studded field indicated that the fall harvest was nearly complete. And the trio of deer munching the stray corncobs that the combine had missed made him think of his last patient of the day. An unfortunate fellow who had shot off the big toe of his right foot while trying to bag a wild turkey. The first bloody wound made it official. Hunting season had begun.

As Noah turned into the Manor's long driveway and pulled up in front of the imposing brick building, he noticed a large bus with animals painted on the side in the parking lot. "Looks like there's a party going on."

Dev's brow puckered. "I just hope it doesn't turn into a rowdy group of drunks."

"Me, too." Noah gave his car keys to a valet,

took Dev's hand, and guided her up one of the twin marble staircases that led to the Manor's grand entrance. As he opened the door for her, he said, "Shoot! I asked for one of the private alcoves, but unfortunately they're near the banquet wing."

"Oh, well. Can't win 'em all." Dev shrugged, then as she and Noah stepped into the stunning lobby, she stopped him and said, "Just a minute. Last time I was here, I didn't get a chance to take a good look at these Thomas Moser chairs. The craftsmanship is amazing."

"It certainly is." Noah smiled indulgently. Dev's appreciation for the finer things in life was definitely a plus on his side of the ledger. He'd bet Del Vecchio didn't know a Moser from a discount special. And didn't care. "Take your time."

Noah watched as Dev moved over to a sideboard displaying a collection of Murano glass and raptly studied the contents. After several minutes, she sighed happily and returned to his side.

Twining her fingers with his, she said, "Thanks for waiting. The colors are exquisite, and they seem to change as you look at them."

"No problem." Noah kissed her forehead. "Ready to go to our table?"

Dev nodded, and Noah made eye contact with the hostess who had been waiting for them.

The striking woman dressed in an expensive black wrap dress and red high heels immediately approached him and said, "Dr. Underwood, follow me."

She led them to an area separated from the other patrons by a heavy curtain. The table for two was set with sparkling crystal and silver and faced a floor-to-ceiling window with a view of the lake.

The hostess put her hand on Noah's shoulder and purred, "I hope this is satisfactory, Dr. Underwood."

He subtly removed her fingers and slid his arm around Dev. "Perfect. Thank you, Anne."

The hostess lingered as Noah pulled out a chair for Dev. Before he could figure out how to get rid of the woman without being a jerk, a raucous burst of laughter shattered the restaurant's quiet atmosphere and two middle-aged men stumbled through the curtain. The hostess immediately pushed them back out.

When she returned a few seconds later with menus, she said, "I apologize, Dr. Underwood. The party in our banquet room seems to be getting out of hand. I'll make certain you won't be disturbed again."

"Thank you, Anne." Noah frowned. "I hope none of those guests will be driving."

"No need to worry about that." The woman shook her head. "When he booked the event,

Mr. Winston assured us that he would arrange transportation to and from the Manor for *all* his guests. No exceptions."

"That's a relief." Noah smiled. When the hostess didn't leave, he added, "Is there something else?"

"No, Doctor." The woman's face reddened and she sighed. "I'll send your server in with the champagne and hors d'oeuvres you requested."

Noah nodded, then turned to Dev to make a comment about drunk drivers, but stopped when he noticed her expression. Her gorgeous blue-green eyes were focused inward. What the hell had put that frown on her pretty face?

CHAPTER 13

I watched the poor besotted hostess leave the alcove. If she'd been a puppy, her tail would have been dragging on the ground. Typically, I was amused at the adoration Noah inspired in other women. Tonight, it felt a little as if the lead eagle statue I'd just used in one of my gift baskets was sitting on my chest and clawing at my self-confidence.

If Noah and I ended up married, how often would I have to watch females throw themselves at his feet? And what if there came a time that he couldn't resist? Jake might be panty-melting hot, but he wasn't also the town doctor *and* Shadow Bend's golden boy. It was interesting that so many of the positives in Noah's column—attractive, rich, popular—were also the biggest negatives.

Forcing myself to relax, I teased, "So much for my pledge not to drink this evening. You know I can never resist champagne."

"Why were you abstaining?" Noah sat in the chair next to me and took my hand. "Are you worried that you're drinking too much?"

"Not really." I blew out a breath. "When I was working as an investment consultant, alcohol was a huge part of the job. There were always dinners and parties and meeting for cocktails. Once I quit that, I recognized how much I liked not living that way."

"I can see that." Noah's thumb stroked my knuckles. "During my internship and residency, when we were off duty, my friends and I hit the booze pretty hard. While you're overindulging, it's difficult to grasp how much it influences your life."

"Exactly." I eased my fingers from Noah's and reached for a glass of water. "And last night with Poppy and Noah, I realized that those old habits were coming back, so I promised myself to be more aware."

"I understand," Noah said. "Would you like me to cancel the champagne?"

"It's okay." I smiled. "I'll just stick to Diet Coke after that."

"Deal." Noah leaned toward me, his stunning gray eyes softening as he brushed his mouth against mine.

I closed my eyes. His lips were soft and warm and oh so familiar.

Before Noah or I could deepen the kiss, a thirtysomething man strode through the curtain. He carried a silver bucket containing a bottle and seemed to miss Noah's frustrated expression.

"Dr. Underwood." The man walked toward us and placed the wine stand next to the table. "Anne told me that you and your guest experienced a rude interruption to your evening, so I wanted to apologize in person."

He held out his hand, and Noah stood. "Don't worry about it." The men shook hands, then Noah introduced me, "Adrian, this is my girlfriend, Devereaux Sinclair. Dev, this is Adrian Ryker. He owns the Manor."

I tensed. Noah hadn't introduced me as his girlfriend since high school. What was up with that?

"A pleasure to meet you, Ms. Sinclair." Adrian gave a slight bow.

He was only about five foot six, my own height, but his commanding presence made him seem much taller. His white-blond hair was short and spiked. He wore a close-fitting suit made out of shimmery gray fabric and a black shirt with a polka-dot collar.

"You, too." I smiled. "I've only eaten here once before, but the food was fabulous. And I really admire your decor. Your lobby is beautiful."

"Thank you."

"How did you decide to open a restaurant out here in the boondocks?" I was curious how a man as sophisticated as Adrian ended up in the country.

Something in Adrian's blue eyes flickered before he said, "I owned a restaurant in Manhattan, but New York can be so . . . convoluted. I decided I preferred the peace and quiet to the complications."

I smiled. "Shadow Bend certainly has its own share of tricky situations."

"I'm sure it does." Adrian's lips twitched in amusement. "Dr. Underwood has been a frequent guest, but this must be a special occasion."

"Why is that?" I raised a brow. Were we still talking about complications?

"Because of the champagne, of course." Adrian took the frosted golden bottle from the wine stand and tore off the foil. "No one orders the 2005 Louis Roederer Cristal Brut for a regular Tuesday night dinner."

Since I didn't know what to say, I kept quiet and nodded pleasantly.

Noah returned to his chair, moved it a fraction of an inch closer to me, and laced our fingers together. "Any evening with Dev is a special one."

He shot a look at Adrian, and the restaurant owner nodded slightly, then popped the cork. After pouring the sparkling wine into crystal flutes, he returned the bottle to the stand and backed away.

Adrian paused at the curtains and said, "Dr. Underwood. Ms. Sinclair. Please don't hesitate to let me know if there's anything I can do to make your experience at the Manor more enjoyable."

"Thank you, Adrian. We will." Noah's tone was businesslike and his expression was impassive. Once the restaurant owner left, Noah muttered,

"I suppose a little privacy would be too much to hope for."

I hid my smile and took a sip of the champagne. I could taste a hint of apples, peaches, and a tiny bit of mandarin orange. The sweet, delicate flavor was delicious, and I murmured my approval.

Noah clinked glasses with me and said, "To us. Present and future."

My heart thudded. What did he mean? Before I could come up with a response, a server appeared and placed a plate of appetizers between us.

She gestured to the rectangular dish and said, "Dr. Underwood, you indicated to chef that you were in the mood for something new."

"I did." Noah's tiny sigh was lost on the server. "What do we have here?"

"Well," the young woman huffed, "although I told Chef that a man like you would probably prefer a meatless offering, he insisted on doing miniature sirloin ruffle en brioche coin with caramelized red onions and horseradish cream."

"That sounds great. I love a good steak." Noah winked at me and said, "*Vegetarian* is an old Cherokee word for *bad hunter*."

The server seemed disappointed at Noah's response, and she was far less enthusiastic as she pointed to the far end of the plate and said, "Here we have shrimp wrapped in bacon and roasted with a Cajun spice." Indicating the center, she added, "And wild mushroom and camembert tarts."

"It looks delicious, Mitzi." Noah dismissed the young woman. "Thanks."

"Super." Mitzi's bubbly personality returned, and, ignoring me, she leaned against Noah's arm, presumably to adjust the dish, and said, "We aim to please."

I was tempted to pull her away from Noah, but instead took a deep breath and told myself to chill. I really didn't like this side of me. It made no sense at all. I was asking Noah and Jake not to be possessive of me, which meant I had no right to be jealous of them.

Strangely enough, although I wasn't happy when women flirted with Jake, it didn't bother me as much. Was it because I cared about him less?

I didn't think so.

Maybe it was because he found it humorous, and it felt as if we were sharing a joke. Whereas Noah seemed to take the adulation as his due. While he never responded in kind, he also didn't shut them down, at least not completely.

Mitzi finally left us alone, and we spent the next several minutes reviewing the menu as we nibbled on the hors d'oeuvres. Unlike our last meal here, I didn't plan on picking up the check. And even though I was prepared for the prices, I still gulped a little when I saw the amounts.

Pushing the cost out of my mind, I concentrated on what Noah was telling me about his search for a third physician. He wanted to expand his clinic's hours and he already had too many patients for just him and Elexus to handle. When Mitzi returned to see if we were ready to order, he seemed resigned to the interruptions, and I could see why he hadn't attempted a more personal topic of conversation.

I asked for the Canadian trout filet with chive risotto, and Noah decided on rack of lamb with spring vegetables and a basil Dijon emulsion. I hoped that I could talk him into sharing one of the chops.

Once Mitzi left, Noah took a sip of his champagne, and his tone casual, but his gaze intense, said, "How is it having Del Vecchio for a tenant?"

"Fine." I paused, trying to gauge Noah's reaction. "He has his first case."

"Already?" Noah didn't seem happy at the news. "That was quick."

"I suppose it was." Popping a mushroom tart in my mouth, I chewed slowly and considered how much to tell Noah. After I swallowed, I said, "Actually, Chief Kincaid referred the client to Jake. The chief also suggested that I might be able to help out."

"Why would he do that?" Noah's gaze was flinty. "Doesn't Chief Kincaid realize that involving you could put you in danger?"

I opened my mouth to tell Noah what I

185

thought of his chauvinistic comment, but then reconsidered, leaned back, and said casually, "I guess the chief assumes that I can take care of myself."

"What does Del Vecchio think about you assisting with the investigation?" Noah's tone made his opinion of the matter clear.

"Jake is happy for my help." I swigged the remaining champagne in my glass. "In fact, he's suggested that I get my PI license."

"Is he insane?" Noah's broad shoulders stiffened and his voice cracked. "How can he be so reckless with your safety? That just proves he doesn't care as much for you as I do."

Noah's attitude had me fuming, but I forced myself to consider where he was coming from. He and Jake lived in two very different worlds. Noah was used to being responsible for his patients, taking care of and preventing bad things from happening to them.

And although Jake was protective, he'd been around many women in law enforcement, including his ex-wife. Meg had actually been his boss. Jake also understood that I enjoyed the intellectual puzzle. And that after so many years in the high-stakes realm of investment consulting, I craved the adrenaline rush of taking a chance and going all in to achieve a victory.

There was no way that I would ever convince Noah that I wanted and needed the excitement of solving the occasional crime, so I said, "Since we'll never see eye to eye on this, let's just agree to disagree and enjoy our dinner."

Noah opened his mouth, but he was interrupted by the server, who placed our salads in front of us and asked, "Would you like fresh-ground pepper?" We both nodded, and when she was finished twisting the long wooden mill, she said, "Is there anything else I can get for you right now?"

"No, thank you." Noah blew out an exasperated breath, then when the waitress left, he said, "Next time, I'm cooking you dinner at my place. Maybe then we can have a few seconds without interruptions."

"Sounds like a plan." I hid my smile. It was sort of funny seeing the calm, cool Dr. Underwood so discombobulated, but I understood his frustration.

We'd eaten most of our salads in silence before Noah flicked an uneasy glance at me and asked, "So what's Del Vecchio investigating?"

"A missing person," I said impassively. "Do you know Elliot and Gabriella Winston?"

"I don't believe so," Noah answered, then paused, tilted his head, and said, "Wait a minute. That's the third time I heard that name."

He stared at the ceiling as the server reappeared and replaced our empty salad plates with our entrées. Once she left, Noah said, "Now I remember. The first was when Chief Kincaid asked me if I had seen her anywhere near the

187

country club during the dance on Saturday night."

"I'm surprised he didn't ask me."

"I told him we were together the whole time," Noah explained.

A bit perturbed that Noah had spoken for me, I shoved away my irritation and asked, "How about the second time you heard the name?"

"When I stopped at home to walk Lucky before picking you up, a new neighbor approached me." Noah made a face. "As we were chatting, she mentioned that her best friend was named Gabriella."

"Would this woman be named Muffy?" I asked, recalling my conversation with Vivian Yager.

"Uh-huh." Noah forked a piece of lamb into his mouth, then took his time chewing and swallowing before he added, "She's living with Vaughn Yager and isn't finding our neighborhood too friendly."

"Then she's not a local." I guessed, taking a bite of my trout.

"No. Muffy was saying she wished that Yager would build a house over in Country Club Estates so she could be closer to her friend."

"I can't see him doing that." I patted my lips with my napkin.

"Me, either." Noah took a drink of water. "Yager loves living among old money."

"True."

I twirled the stem of my empty champagne

flute. In high school, Vaughn had been an outcast like me, and now that he'd made his fortune, he'd had several plastic surgeries and proven his hometown had been wrong when they called him a loser. Vaughn lived to one-up the people who had inherited their wealth rather than earned it.

"My impression is that Muffy hasn't quite figured out her new boyfriend yet." Noah glanced at me from the corner of his eye. "It takes a lot more work for a couple to really know each other if they didn't grow up together. They just don't have the same life experiences."

"But exploring those differences can be fun," I answered, still upset about Noah's narrow-minded view of me helping out on Jake's case.

"Oh." Noah's knuckles whitened as he gripped his fork and concentrated on finishing his entrée.

After I let him simmer for a while, I asked, "Did Muffy say anything more about her friend Gabriella? Anything about her being missing?"

"Let me see." Noah tapped his finger to his lip, clearly teasing me.

"What?" I prodded. "You have an amazing memory, so quit stalling."

"Okay. Okay." Noah held up his hands in mock surrender. "Muffy said something to the effect that getting Yager to build a house in Country Club Estates would be a waste of time, because she didn't think that Gabriella was planning on sticking around for long."

189

"Interesting." I pushed away my half-eaten plate. The food was great, but I was stuffed. "Did Muffy say if Gabriella was divorcing her husband?"

"That's what I thought she meant, but she never really said it." Noah frowned. "Why? Do you think Gabriella's missing because she left him?"

"Maybe." I didn't mention the ransom note, since Jake had cautioned me to keep quiet about it. "But if that was the case, surely her lawyer would have served him with the legal papers by now."

Something was bothering me, but before I could figure out what it was, the server came to our table, offered us dessert menus, and cleared the empty plates. I declined and asked for decaf cappuccino, but Noah studied the selections, then ordered the chocolate taster—a truffle, crêpe, soufflé, and pot de crème.

As we waited for Noah's goodies, I poked around in my subconscious, trying to pry loose whatever tidbit was nudging at me.

A few minutes later, as the server came through the curtains with Noah's dessert, I heard a burst of loud laughter and saw a group from the wildlife dinner staggering past our alcove. Staring at them, it dawned on me. If Elliot Winston was going to use the money he'd set aside for the wildlife park to pay the ransom, why was he still hosting this party? And wasn't it a little tacky to host a party when his wife was still missing?

CHAPTER 14

Noah and I were quiet as he ate his chocolate quartet and I drank my cappuccino. Once he settled the bill and we were in his car heading back to town, the silence grew. It appeared that neither of us was in the mood to make casual conversation, and I wasn't entirely sure what had gone wrong with our romantic dinner.

When Noah pulled into the dime store's tiny parking lot, I shoved aside my weird mood and said, "Thank you for a lovely evening."

"I'd give you the moon if you'd let me." Noah unbuckled his seat belt, leaned over, and cupped my cheek. "Don't make any hasty decisions."

"What? You're not tired of me trying to decide?" I asked, my breath hitched. The gut-wrenching tenderness of his expression closed my throat, and I struggled to continue. "This business of seeing both you and Jake has to end soon."

"Only if you're ready to choose me." Noah leaned closer and whispered into my hair, "We've always been destined for each other."

"I . . ." Confusion clouded my mind and I hesitated. Something was off.

"Not I, it should be us." Noah's sexy mouth was a millimeter from mine.

He closed the distance between our lips, his kiss soft and sweet. I didn't draw away, but I didn't exactly participate, either.

Noah pulled back, frowned, then tried again. This time, his kiss was hard and searching. Instead of the usual wonderful sensation, my stomach clenched. The strong pull of his hot, wet tongue didn't draw me in, and the darkness behind my closed eyes never lit up with fireworks.

Whether it was lack of sleep, preoccupation with Gabriella's disappearance, or something that I didn't want to think about, I just wasn't into making out with Noah. Not wanting to hurt his feelings or make him feel rejected, I waited for a good place to end the kiss.

Then using the center console as an excuse, I shifted out of his reach, and rubbing my thigh, I said, "Sorry, I've got a cramp in my leg."

Noah shoved a hand through his dark blond hair until it stuck out at odd angles and sighed. "Nothing about tonight went as I planned." He wound one of my curls around his finger. "Are we still on for Sunday?"

"Definitely!" I forced a note of excitement into my voice. "I've been looking forward to it." Opening the car door, I got out, then bent down so I could smile at him. "I'll be ready at eleven."

"Great." Noah's upbeat tone didn't match the unhappy lines around his eyes. "We'll have an early dinner afterward."

"Sounds fun."

I blew him a kiss and walked to my car. After digging the keys from my purse, I unlocked the BMW and slid behind the wheel. Noah waited for me to back out of the parking spot, then followed me down the alley.

But when we came to the main road, I turned left, and in the rearview mirror, I watched Noah's Jag head in the opposite direction. Was there some cosmic significance to that?

Noah was right. Nothing about the evening had been what I expected. Maybe it was Jake's invitation to go away for a weekend together. It felt like more of a challenge than a request, and perhaps I was reacting to the stress of making a decision.

A good night's sleep would probably put everything into perspective.

Wednesday was a long day at the dime store. We opened at nine a.m. and didn't close until Blood, Sweat, and Shears, a philanthropic sewing group, finished up that evening. In the past, I'd covered the twelve hours myself, but now that my father was working for me, he'd taken over the first shift, and I didn't have to be at the store until two.

Enjoying my morning off, I slept in, then had a leisurely late breakfast with Gran. While she made my favorite puffy French toast and Jimmy

Dean sausage, I told her about Jake's PI case and asked her if she knew Gabriella or Elliot Winston.

Gran wrinkled her brow, then said, "I don't think I've met either of them."

She adjusted the belt of her green and white polka-dot A-line swing dress and turned back to the stove. With her tiny waist and her hair in a French twist, she looked as if she'd just stepped out of a vintage nineteen fifties advertisement. Gran's clothing selection was always a surprise. One day she'd have on a flowered muumuu from the seventies and the next an authentic nineteen twenties flapper dress.

Evidently, our female ancestors had never thrown out a piece of apparel, and their entire wardrobes were packed in our attic. After Grandpa died and I'd moved in, Gran had taken all the outfits in her size, had them dry-cleaned, and now wore whichever era struck her fancy. Sadly, nothing had fit me. Apparently, my relatives had all been petite.

"Have you heard about the proposed wildlife park?" I asked as Gran slid a plate of steaming French toast and perfectly browned sausages in front of me. "It's supposed to go on those four hundred acres next to Vaughn Yager's factory."

"There was an article in the *Banner* about it." Gran poured two cups of coffee and put one next to my right hand. "And some guy from the Animal Safety Alliance came to the luncheon

Father Flagg had for the Marthas and told us how . . . uh . . . inh . . ."

The Marthas consisted of women from the church who provided hospitality for parish events and participated in fund-raising for certain charities. They were supposed to honor any requests from the priest, but Father Flagg was too smart to try to order them around.

"Inhumane?" I suggested. Gran's doctor had said it was best to supply the word she couldn't recall, rather than let her become stressed.

"Uh-huh. He was all wound up about God's critters needing to be free. He said that humans who were cruel to them needed to be gotten rid of."

Gran's black pumps clicked across the old linoleum as she went to a cupboard and took out the maple syrup. She thumped the jug on the table, then sat in the chair opposite mine.

"What did the ladies think of the Animal Safety Alliance guy?"

"Not much." Gran's pale blue eyes twinkled. "He spoke between the entrée and dessert, and most of them were more interested in getting a piece of my double chocolate rum cake than hearing about some zoo outside of town. Especially since the other choice of sweets was Myrtle Cormac's store-bought angel food cake with icing straight from a can of frosting."

"So no takers for his crusade against the

park?" I savored the perfect bite of French toast, sausage, and syrup, then asked, "Have you heard anything else about the park around town?"

"Not a word." Gran fingered her green button earrings. "So you're helping Jake with his case? Were you with him last night?"

Although she still wasn't a fan of Noah's, she had stopped plotting his demise, so I felt safe in mentioning my date with him.

Sniffing in disappointment, Gran immediately changed the subject, picked up the *Banner* from the tabletop, and said, "The editor needs to proof these articles better. Listen to this. 'Ben Irving and Carrie Justice were married on October first at the Methodist church. This ends a friendship that began in their school days.'"

It took me a second before I understood the problem. But once I did, Gran and I giggled like little kids. When I got up and hugged her, she gripped my back as if I were about to disappear.

As I resumed my seat, Gran said, "I love you to . . . uh . . ." She frowned, then completed her thought: "the fridge and back."

I was pretty sure she meant *moon*, but in keeping with the slightly offbeat tenor of our conversation, I responded, "And I love you with all my butt." Gran's eyebrows raised, and I explained, "I know it's supposed to be with all my heart, but my rear end is a lot bigger."

"Oh, you." Gran swatted my arm with the

folded newspaper and said, "Kern is going to drive me to Walmart this afternoon. Do you need anything?"

"I can't think of anything."

I was tempted to ask if Gran knew that Dad had shared his Monday-night chicken dinner with Catherine Bennet, but I didn't. He had a right to see someone without his mother's interference. And if my own experience was anything to judge by, Gran would definitely meddle in Dad's love life.

Once we were through with breakfast and had cleaned up the kitchen, I went to my room and called Jake. I needed to update him on what I'd learned about Gabriella from Noah.

When he answered, I could tell he was outside, and asked, "Did I catch you at a bad time?"

"No." Jake's sexy voice washed over me. "Now that I'm more certain Gabriella was actually kidnapped, I'm going door-to-door in the Winstons' neighborhood to see if someone noticed anything during the time she was abducted. So far, I'm not having much luck. Next, I'm going to check out the country club."

"Do you plan on speaking to the people opposed to the wildlife park?"

"They're on my list," Jake said. "Anyone I should move to the top?"

"The head of the Animal Safety Alliance," I suggested. "He spoke at the church ladies' luncheon and pretty much stated that that anyone who was cruel to our four-legged friends should be put down."

"Thanks for the intel." Jake's tone was a cross between amused and incredulous.

"Another thing." I repeated Muffy and Noah's conversation, then added, "It seems pretty clear that Gabriella was unhappy in her marriage."

"Maybe someone who knew she was fed up took advantage of the situation and lured her away," Jake suggested. "Of course that doesn't explain the way the crime scene was staged to look like a struggle, but that could have been the kidnapper trying to make it look more violent to scare Winston into paying."

"If it weren't for that ransom note, I'd say she left of her own free will." I flopped across my bed. "Speaking of that, is Elliot going to pay up? Tomorrow night is the deadline, right?"

"Winston says he's arranging to get the money and is ready to hand it over." Static hissed on the line and it was hard to make out Jake's words.

"That surprises me." I rolled over and propped myself up on one elbow. "Last night, Elliot hosted a huge party at the Manor for all the people he's trying to persuade to support the wildlife park. Wouldn't he have canceled that if he was spending his cash for ransom rather than going ahead with his pet project?"

"It's possible he'd prepaid for the event and

figured he might as well grease the wheels even if opening the park had to be delayed a year."

"I supposed that could be it." I frowned, not really happy with Jake's reasoning.

Whatever he said next was lost to the static, and after a few "huh's?" and "what did you say?" we gave up. I think Jake said he'd see me later at the store. But the connection had gotten so bad he could also have said he was bored or had just been gored.

I had just hit the END button when Mariah Carey's "Anytime You Need a Friend" started playing from my cell. I glanced at the time. What was Poppy doing calling at nine a.m.?

"Hey, girl," I greeted her. "What are you doing up so early?"

"I needed to let you know that Jesus will be at the dime store at two thirty." Poppy yawned. "After I talked to him, I forgot to let you know."

My mouth dropped open, and I stared at the phone as if it were a bomb. Had Poppy suddenly found religion? But even if she had, how would she know the precise moment and location of the second coming?

"Are you there?" Poppy's voice brought me back to my senses.

"Yes," I answered cautiously, wondering if I should dial 911 for her. I mean if she thought she'd talked to God, she might be having a psychotic break. Right?

"Did you hear me?" Poppy's tone was impatient. "My handyman said he could look at your wiring this afternoon. Is that okay?"

Ah. Not Jesus. *Hey-zoose.* I forgot that Poppy had flunked high school Spanish.

"That's fine," I quickly assured her." Why didn't you just text me?"

"Uh." Poppy hesitated, cleared her throat, then said, "The thing is . . . Are you really willing to referee between Dad and me?"

"Sure," I said quickly before my real feelings about the matter could surface.

While I wanted to help Poppy and her father improve their relationship, I wasn't sure I could. And if I failed, they both might hate me.

"Any possibility you could do it this morning?" Poppy asked.

"I guess so." I immediately started rescheduling things in my mind.

"Great." Poppy's voice was tentative. "Mom says that Dad is planning to do paperwork in his office until the noon city council meeting. Can you meet me at the police station in an hour?"

"Give me two." I had some phone calls to make first.

"Sure." Her voice sounded a little too happy at the delay.

"If we do this, just remember, two people can look at the exact same issue and see it totally differently. And neither of those people is wrong."

Poppy made a sound that could have been agreement, but then again it could also have been gas. We said good-bye, and, wondering what I was getting myself into, I rushed to my closet. What did one wear to mediate a truce between a bad girl and her police chief father?

I put on a pair of dark jeans and my black Devereaux's Dime Store polo shirt, then added a houndstooth blazer. I figured that Chief Kincaid would appreciate a more traditional appearance.

After making my calls, I took a long shower, and after using a blow-dryer on my hair, I twisted it into a chignon. I carefully applied my makeup, and when I was satisfied with my appearance, I slipped on a pair of black loafers.

I grabbed my tennis shoes for later, and, yelling to Gran that I was leaving, I headed outside. Hopping in my car, I drove to town, all the while doubting this was a good idea.

When I arrived at the police department, Poppy's Hummer was already parked in front of the building. As soon as I eased into the spot next to hers, my friend jumped out of the huge vehicle and met me at the PD's front door. Before my phobia could kick in, she pulled me inside and dragged me up the short staircase to the desk.

The dispatcher greeted Poppy and asked, "Did you want to see your father?"

"Unless he's busy." Poppy took a few steps back and I blocked her exit.

I could tell by Poppy's expression that she was regretting her decision and looking for any excuse not to talk to her dad, so I asked, "Is Chief Kincaid alone?" When the dispatcher nodded, I said, "Then please tell him his daughter and I are here."

A couple of seconds later we were sitting in the chief's office. He pushed aside the mountain of files and looked at us enquiringly.

Poppy's hand clung to mine, and when I glanced at her, I saw tiny beads of sweat on her top lip. Clearly, it was up to me to start the conversation.

"Thank you for seeing us on such short notice, Chief. I know you're a busy man." It never hurt to butter up the opposition in a negotiation. "Poppy would really like to repair the rift between you two, but feels that perhaps you don't always hear what she's trying to say."

"That's because half the time she doesn't make any sense," the chief snarled.

"Wrong," Poppy snapped. "I have a doctorate in sarcasm, a black belt in sass, and took first prize in bitching." She tilted her head and smiled sweetly at her father. "I'm an effing conversational ninja."

The chief's face reddened, and as Poppy opened her mouth to goad him, I dug my nails into her thigh.

"Okay, evidently we need some ground rules."

I took a deep breath. "The two of you have to listen to each other with an open mind, knowing that neither one of you is going to change your opinions."

They both scowled at me, but the chief gave a grudging nod and said, "Go on."

"First, Poppy is not going to close Gossip Central and attend grad school to obtain a psych degree." I figured I'd start with the easy stuff. "Not only is she happy running the business, she's extremely good at it."

"And I make a great living and it's fun," Poppy blurted out.

"Work isn't supposed to be fun." Chief Kincaid scowled. "It's supposed to be meaningful."

"Now, Chief"—I quickly intervened—"can you honestly say you don't relish being a policeman? That you only became an officer out of civic duty?"

There was a long pause before he said, "No. I do enjoy making sure everyone is safe."

"And Poppy likes helping them relax." I smiled. "I'm sure she uses a lot of the psychological skills she learned in college with her customers. I know they tell her their problems."

"Fine." The chief jerked his chin. "What I can't accept is where she got the funds to start the bar. It's tainted, and I can't get over that fact."

"Uncle Blackie is a good man," Poppy snarled over my comment. "Just because you—"

203

Cutting her off, I said to the chief, "Despite your aversion to how your brother earned his money, what he did wasn't illegal."

"But it was immoral." Chief Kincaid crossed his arms. "Using women like that is despicable, and Blackie should be horsewhipped."

"Actually," I said, keeping my tone even, "I did some research on him and his business. Yes, High Tail Inn is a brothel, but his employees receive a higher cut of their fees and have better health care and living conditions than any other sex workers in the state. If the women don't have a high school diploma, he pays for their GED, and he's sent a good handful to college. There's no rough stuff allowed, and each woman has an emergency button in her room. If the client does anything she's not okay with, she is told to press the button, and there is a security guard on each floor."

"So he's a humanitarian pimp?" Chief Kincaid sneered. "It's still wrong."

"Be that as it may"—I decided it was time to move on—"what's done is done, and Poppy is within months of repaying her uncle's loan."

"Really?" Chief Kincaid blinked. "How in the world is that possible?"

"Because I'm good at what I do, Dad." Poppy leaned forward. "I'm a good businesswoman. I run an excellent club. And my customers come back."

"I see." The chief rubbed his jaw. "Still, it's time to straighten up and settle down."

"Chief, think about it," I said. "Poppy has done just that. When's the last time she got into any trouble or you heard of any problem she caused?"

"Well . . ." He wrinkled his brow.

"It's been several years, hasn't it?" I asked.

"Dad, I'm not the wild child I was in high school and college." Poppy's breath hitched. "I may never be the daughter you hoped for, but I'm not a complete screw-up, either. At Christmas when you said to Mom you wished that all those years ago it had been the other one who was killed in the accident, not Iris, I . . ." She trailed off, then whispered, "I'm sorry, but I can't help that she died instead of me."

"What!" The chief jumped to his feet, rushed around the desk, and snatched Poppy from her chair. Clutching her to his chest he said, "I meant the driver of the other car, not you. I love you just as much as I loved your sister. Never think that I would have sacrificed you for her. All I ever wanted was for you to be happy. To fall in love with a good man and give me some grandchildren."

"I'm trying, Daddy," Poppy sobbed. "But he wants someone else."

That was my cue to leave. If I'd learned anything in my years as an investment consultant, I'd learned that finding out someone's secret can

205

change your life forever. And I wasn't ready for that to happen between me and Poppy.

I stood, slipped out the door, and headed to the dime store. I'd spend the time before my father went off duty making gift baskets and not thinking about which guy Poppy had meant. If my suspicion was true, things might never be the same between us.

CHAPTER 15

As Jake drove his pickup the short distance between the Winstons' subdivision and the country club, he considered what he'd learned during his door-to-door canvas. Although the police had already talked to Gabriella's neighbors and hadn't learned anything significant, Jake had considered it worth another try.

When he'd worked as a U.S. Marshal, he'd discovered that sometimes after the initial questioning, folks recalled additional details. However, for several reasons—not wanting to get involved or thinking whatever they remembered wasn't important or even just plain laziness—they failed to report the information. But sometimes if they were reinterviewed, they'd share those facts.

Jake had lucked out with a woman who lived across the street from the Winstons. Her house was at a diagonal from the vic's place, so her view from home was poor, but luckily she'd been walking her dog Saturday night. She'd told him that the motion sensor lights in the Winstons' side yard had turned on around nine thirty, and shortly afterward, she'd heard their kitchen door's distinctive squeak as it opened.

No one else in the area had noticed any sign of

life from Saturday evening until Elliot Winston's return Sunday morning. With that data and the arrival of the ransom note, Jake could now better focus his queries.

First on his list were the folks at the country club. The police had already spoken to the members who attended the dance and the employees, but Jake had questions that he doubted the officers had asked. Especially since they hadn't known about Gabriella's relationship with the golf pro.

After Jake turned between the two enormous brick columns, he followed the pristine blacktop to the club's lot, parked, and got out of his truck. Strolling around the perimeter of the club, perspiration trickled down his spine. Temperatures had soared into the eighties, and it was damn warm with the sun pounding down on him.

Stopping near the rear of the building, he squinted across the golf course and nodded to himself. In the distance, he could just make out the Winstons' backyard. As he'd suspected, it was a straight shot from their place to the clubhouse.

The dog-walking neighbor had said there weren't any vehicles in the Winstons' driveway and had been sure there were no boats on the lake. That meant the kidnapper had to have another means of transporting Gabriella. She might have been walked out of the neighborhood through the woods, but Jake's bet was that she'd been taken via golf cart.

Making his way back to the front entrance, Jake saw a guy in his late teens wearing a black sweater and a pair of black frayed denim jeans cleaning out the pool. Considering the heat, Jake thought the boy was rushing the fall season a little.

And as he watched, the kid wiped the sweat dripping into his eyes, thus proving Jake right. He hid a smile. Evidently, fashion was more important to the guy than comfort.

Jake moved closer and said, "Hey. Have you worked here long?"

The kid turned to look at him, and Jake saw that one side of the guy's hair was shaved and a swath of dyed black hair hung over the opposite eye, the ends catching in the studs on the sweater's shoulder. The boy stared at Jake, then shrugged silently and went back to digging out debris from the pool's filter.

"Son, I asked you a question." Jake kept his voice pleasant.

"Bugger off." The kid flung a mass of dripping leaves in Jake's general direction, but missed by a mile.

The little bastard's lame try at being a badass was annoying, and Jake wished he still had his tin to flash, although with this kind of kid it would probably result in less cooperation rather than more. Jake was tempted to walk away, but this jerk was the type who wouldn't have talked to the police. On the other hand, he probably knew all sorts of crap about the rich adults he was forced to serve.

Taking a calming breath, Jake said, "Fine. I just thought you might want to earn an easy twenty bucks. But I guess I was wrong."

The kid smirked, opened his mouth, then, after staring at Jake's unsmiling face, seemed to reconsider and said, "What do I gotta do?"

"Answer a few questions." Jake took his wallet out, selected a bill, and folded it in half lengthways. "Do you know Gabriella Winston?"

"Yeah." The kid fingered his earring. "I've seen her around."

"Who does she hang out with?" Jake ran the twenty between his fingers.

"Her and Muffy Morgan are tight." The boy reached for the money.

"Hold on, there." Jake stepped out of the kid's reach. "Anyone else?"

"She used to play tennis with the club president's wife, but that stopped a while ago." The boy sneered. "Heard they had some sort of catfight. The prez's wife must have found out about Mac and Ms. Winston."

"The golf pro?"

"Yep." The kid snickered. "The bitches around here have no idea how many women Mac

210

is sticking it into." The boy laughed. "The delusional old cougars think that a young guy like Mac actually finds them hot."

"Oh?" Jake encouraged. The kid was on a roll and Jake didn't want to interrupt.

"Yeah." The boy sneered. "What they don't realize is that any broad can have the body of a twenty-nine-year-old. At least, they can if they're willing to buy him expensive shit afterward."

"Interesting." Jake scratched his jaw. "So McGowan's for sale?"

"Yep. One even bought him a car. A fugly car, but still a brand-new car. All the old bags think they're his"—the kid nodded, then raised his voice to a falsetto and said—"one true love."

"Any chance that the thing between Mac and Gabriella was different than the rest?" Jake asked, trying to figure out if any of this was relevant to his case. "Could their relationship have been serious?"

"Doubtful." The boy twitched his shoulders. "I think they broke up after the hot tub incident a few months ago." The kid held out his palm. "Now hand over my money."

"One more question." Jake crossed his arms. "Were you working Saturday night?"

"Nope." The boy shook his head. "They don't let the likes of me indoors." He cracked up. "They know that I'm not housebroken."

Jake chuckled and gave the kid the cash, started

to go, then turned back and asked, "Is Mac around?"

"He didn't show up for work on Sunday and hasn't been here since."

As Jake headed to the front of the building, he considered the meaning of McGowan's absence. Had he kidnapped his lover and was holding her for ransom? He hadn't realized the guy was so young. Gabriella was forty-four. Fifteen years was a big age difference.

The clubhouse's ultramodern design wasn't to Jake's taste. The impressive entrance was cold and unwelcoming. And the overhead windows that appeared to hang unsuspended over the steps were just plain creepy.

When Jake stepped into the lobby, an elegantly dressed woman at the reception desk looked up from her computer and said, "May I help you?"

"I'd like to speak to the club manager." Jake smiled at the woman.

"Ms. Xiong is busy right now." The receptionist glanced back at her monitor, clicked on something, and asked, "Do you have an appointment?"

"No." Jake held out his hand. "My name is Jake Del Vecchio. I promise I only need a few minutes of her time." He leaned closer and lowered his voice. "It's about one of the club's employees."

"Well, Ms. Xiong told me not to disturb her, but for you . . ." The woman dimpled up at him. "Let me check with her." After murmuring into the phone, the receptionist pointed down a hallway and said, "Ms. Xiong's office is the last door on your right."

"Thanks, darlin'." Jake smiled, touched the brim of his Stetson, and strode through the corridor and into an open doorway.

The Asian-American woman sitting behind a massive desk was on the phone, but she nodded Jake to a wingback chair as she concluded the call.

While she was occupied, Jake took the opportunity to study the manager. It was hard to gauge her age, but he'd put her in the late forties to early fifties range. The skin on her cheeks and forehead was smooth, but there were a few lines around her dark eyes. And some strands of silver in her short, shiny black hair.

Once the manager hung up the receiver, Jake rose, stepped forward, offered his hand, and said, "Ms. Xiong, my name is Jake Del Vecchio and I'm a private investigator."

"Nice to meet you." The woman's handshake was firm, and when she nodded him back into his chair, her tone was businesslike. "The receptionist said you had a problem with one of our employees."

"Not exactly." Jake stretched out his long legs. There was no use beating around the bush. "I'm investigating the disappearance of one of your members, Gabriella Winston, and it's come to my attention that she was having an affair with your golf pro."

"I see." The manager's mouth tightened. "Mr. McGowan is no longer employed here."

"Because he hasn't shown up for work since Saturday?" Jake asked.

"I see you're well informed." Ms. Xiong raised a dark brow, evidently surprised at Jake's statement. "But that is only one of the reasons."

"And the other?"

"He also failed to show up for his monthly drug and alcohol screening on Monday." Ms. Xiong tapped a red-tipped nail on her desktop.

"Are you at all concerned that something might have happened to McGowan?" Jake pulled a notebook and pen from his pocket.

"I sent his assistant to check on him." Ms. Xiong crossed her arms. "He wasn't at his apartment and his neighbor said there been no sign of him since Saturday night."

"Did you report him missing?" Jake asked.

"I tried the emergency number on his application, but the woman who answered hung up on me." Ms. Xiong's lips twitched. "I suspect she was an old girlfriend, since he's proven himself such a ladies' man."

"Did you call the cops?"

"Mac lived over near the county seat, so I spoke to the sheriff's department, not the Shadow Bend

Police Department." Ms. Xiong straightened a pile of folders on her desktop. "The deputy took my information, but my impression was that little would be done. As the officer pointed out, Mac is a grown man with a history of drug use and few community ties."

"Did you know Gabriella Winston well?" Jake asked quickly, aware the manager's patience was wearing thin. "I've been told she was friendly with Muffy Morgan. Is there anyone else here that you can think of who might have information about her habits or plans?"

"With the exception of Mac, Ms. Winston didn't socialize with the help." Ms. Xiong narrowed her dark brown eyes. "But my impression was of a very unhappy woman."

"From my investigation, your impression seems to have been accurate."

Ms. Xiong stood. "Now, you'll have to excuse me, I have a meeting with the board in a few minutes. We need to discuss hiring a new golf pro."

Jake rose to his feet and handed the manager his card. "If you hear from McGowan, please give me a call."

"Certainly." Ms. Xiong herded him into the hallway. "I'm sure you can find your own way out." She gestured down the corridor. "Have a nice day."

Jake exited the clubhouse, walked to his

pickup, and slid behind the wheel. He stared out the windshield at the impossibly blue sky and considered his next step. He really should let Chief Kincaid know that Gabriella's lover was also missing.

Jake wasn't sure if, now that a ransom demand had been made, the chief still believed Elliot was behind his wife's disappearance and faking everything else. But whatever Chief Kincaid felt, Winston had agreed that Jake could share whatever he found with the police, and it felt like the right thing to do.

Digging out his cell, Jake punched in the nonemergency number for the police department and, once Chief Kincaid was on the line, said, "I've got an update for you on the Winston case."

"Did the kidnapper make contact regarding the drop-off spot for the money?"

"I spoke to Winston at approximately eight a.m. this morning, and he still hadn't heard anything," Jake reported. "But my investigation has turned up a couple of interesting leads. First, Gabriella was having an affair with a man named Donald 'Mac' McGowan. He's the golf pro at the country club. He's been involved with other female members and has a substance abuse problem."

"I'll send an officer to talk to him." The chief's voice was clipped.

"That's the second interesting detail," Jake said. "McGowan is missing, too." He flipped open his notebook and read the chief the transcript of his conversation with the country club manager. He concluded, "Which makes me wonder if the golf pro is our kidnapper."

"Or Elliot Winston caught McGowan in bed with his wife, killed them both, and made up this cock-and-bull story about her being abducted," Chief Kincaid snapped, then added, "And before you say it, Winston could have paid someone to slip the ransom note under his door. Either he lucked out that you were there when it arrived, or he sent the accomplice a message without you noticing."

"Then I take it the police are still investigating Gabriella's disappearance as a murder," Jake said slowly.

The chief's theory was entirely possible. Winston could have sent a text while he was dishing out the chili or grabbing the beers from the fridge.

"I have the forensic team rechecking everything they got from the scene," Chief Kincaid confirmed. Then, his tone a notch friendlier, he added, "I appreciate that you're looking into the other angle. With vacations and the flu, the PD's resources are even thinner than usual. It's helpful that I can pick the most likely theory of the crime and concentrate on it."

Jake blew out a breath that he hadn't realized he was holding. It was good that he and the chief could cooperate. Not every case would allow him that luxury. Still, it was nice starting his private investigator career out on the right foot with the local authorities.

"Next on my list of suspects is the animal rights guy that's opposing the opening of Winston's wildlife park," Jake said. "You wouldn't happen to know where I could find the man, would you?"

"Peregrine Pierce, president of the Animal Safety Alliance, has set up an office in Sparkville," the chief drawled, then chuckled. "It's at the intersection of Haven and Cyprus streets."

"Thanks." Jake ended the call, put his truck in gear, and headed for Sparkville.

Fifteen minutes later, Jake pulled his truck in front of a storefront with a faded sign reading: YOU PLUG 'EM, WE STUFF 'EM TAXIDERMY. A drooping banner that must have originally been covering the other sign read: ANIMAL SAFETY ALLIANCE.

Snickering, Jake exited his pickup, walked up to the door, and pushed it open.

A buzzer sounded and a few seconds later a voiced yelled, "Be right out."

While he waited, Jake rested a hip against the counter. He inhaled and caught the faint sent of what smelled like vinegar. He sniffed again and realized the odor must be from the taxidermy's pickling process. Probably acetic or formic acid.

Jake's uncle had tried his hand at mounting the heads of his trophy bucks, but Aunt Sabina had quickly put the kibosh on her husband's hobby when she saw, and smelled, all the chemicals involved. As a rancher's wife, she was okay with the hunting, just not the preserving.

A few minutes later, a tall, thin man with slicked-back black hair, a hooded brow, and a beaklike nose rushed out from the back. Jake glanced at the yellow tennis shoes on his feet. This had to be Peregrine Pierce. All the man needed were feathers and wings to look like his namesake falcon.

His dark eyes were full of anticipation, and he said, "Are you here to volunteer?"

"Sorry, no. Are you Peregrine Pierce?"

"Yes. I'm the founder of the Animal Safety Alliance."

Jake stuck out his hand and said, "I'm Jake Del Vecchio, a private investigator looking into the disappearance of Gabriella Winston."

"Winston as in Elliot Winston, the sicko trying to cage wild creatures who deserve to be free?" Peregrine stepped away as if Jake were contagious.

"She's his wife." Jake stared at the guy. "Do you have any idea where she might be?"

"No." Holding up his palms, Peregrine edged away. "I never met the woman."

Jake followed until the guy was backed up

against the rear wall, then leaned forward and said, "But you are protesting the opening of her husband's wildlife park."

"Yes." Peregrine crossed his arms. "But that doesn't mean I hurt his wife."

"It doesn't mean you didn't, either." Jake quirked a brow. "What better way to get revenge for all the suffering animals than to snatch the woman Winston loves?"

"I respect all life-forms," Peregrine squawked. "You have no right to accuse me of anything."

"Which I haven't done." Jake pursed his lips. "You flew to that conclusion."

"Why else would you be here asking about a missing woman who is married to a man with whom I'm at war?" Peregrine demanded, jabbing a clawlike finger at Jake's face.

"Just gathering information." Jake's tone was cool.

"Well, think about this." Peregrine's voice oozed contempt. "Maybe Mrs. Winston left on her own accord. Maybe she was tired of living with a man who had no respect for the freedom of others."

"Something to consider," Jake agreed. "When did she tell you that?"

"Saturday," Peregrine said, then covered his mouth.

"I thought you said you never met her." Jake narrowed his eyes.

"I called Saturday evening to talk to Elliot Winston, but he wasn't home." Peregrine swallowed. "I thought if I could sway Mrs. Winston to my point of view, she could talk Mr. Winston out of opening the park. But she told me she had already tried that and was damn tired of her husband ignoring her." He hurriedly added, "We only talked for a few minutes."

"The police can check the Winstons' phone records," Jake warned.

"Then you'll see that I'm telling the truth," Peregrine chirped. "Someone knocked while we were chatting, and Mrs. Winston hung up to answer the door."

"When was that?" Jake asked.

"Around nine thirty."

"Thank you for your time." Jake nodded and left the building.

He sat in his truck and ran his hands through his hair. Had Peregrine Pierce heard Gabriella's kidnapper arrive?

CHAPTER 16

My workbench, an old kitchen table that I'd rescued from the trash, held everything I needed to create a fantastic gift basket. As I organized my materials, I watched Dad charm a trio of middle-aged women seated at the soda fountain. They were eating our October special—apple cider ice cream tarts—and flirting with my father.

While some Shadow Benders felt my dad should still be in prison, the single ladies between forty-five and sixty-five were glad he was out and available to pursue. I'd noticed that whenever my father was behind the soda fountain, a lot more middle-aged women developed a taste for sundaes.

Contemplating the two baskets that I was working on, I tuned out the feminine voices vying for my dad's attention. The baskets each appealed to a different demographic. The one on my left was aimed at encouraging a child's imagination, while the one on my right was intended to inflame adult desires.

I examined the Halloween basket, the one for Clark Garrison's tenth birthday party. The green treat pail that I had chosen to use for the container had a decal of a cartoonish zombie, and I had painted the boy's name on the front below that sticker. The bucket's lining was a child-size black T-shirt with ZOMBIE HUNTER printed on the front in red.

Clark's mother had assured me that her son was a huge *Walking Dead* fan, but she wanted the basket to reflect the more innocent side of Halloween as well. Endeavoring to please her, I'd found lighthearted toys to tuck inside the pail. Zombie finger puppets, temporary tattoos, and, of course, gummy zombies.

Now I was ready to place my trademark—the one perfect book—in the center. Steve Mockus's *How to Speak Zombie* had been the clear choice.

Happy with the Garrison basket, I turned my attention to the one for my friend Veronica Ksiazak. Ronni and her hot boyfriend, Fire Chief Cooper McCall, were spending the weekend in St. Louis.

At first it didn't look as if there was much chemistry between them, but after a couple of months of dating, things were heating up. For the first time since I met her, Ronni was closing her bed-and-breakfast. And Coop had arranged for three days off work. Things were definitely getting more serious, and I wanted my basket to be the match that ultimately started the fire.

I studied my handiwork. It needed something to be truly amazing. Ronni had asked for flames and passion, so, which would sizzle more, a French maid's costume or a pair of black thigh-high fishnets?

Already nestled in the folds of red satin lounge pants for Coop were a bottle of vanilla musk oil, a box of cream-center cocoa truffles, and a copy of *Tantric Massage for Beginners*.

Closing my eyes, I thought about the couple receiving the gift. A firefighter and a B & B owner. What else might appeal to them?

My deliberation was interrupted by the sound of Mariah Carey's "Anytime You Need a Friend" playing. I snatched up my cell phone. Hoping Poppy and the chief hadn't had a reversal of their ceasefire once I left the police station, I crossed my fingers and swept my thumb over the screen.

"I can never thank you enough for helping me talk to my dad." Poppy's voice sounded rough, like she'd had a good long cry. "How did you know exactly what I needed to happen?"

"You've been my best friend since kindergarten." I swallowed the lump in my throat. "How could I not know the tune that was in your heart? Even if you forgot the words, I knew the song you needed to sing."

"That almost put me into a diabetic coma. Did you read that off some greeting card?" Poppy sniffed, then said, "But seriously, thanks. If you ever need me to do something like that . . ."

"I'll hold you to that," I warned. "However, right now, I'm good."

We chatted a few more minutes, and as I hung up I noticed that the trio of women from the soda fountain was now in front of the candy case. They had their heads together and were pondering the selection.

When one of the threesome giggled, my father looked up from clearing the dirty dishes off the soda fountain counter and asked, "Can I help you ladies with anything?"

"No, Kern," the ringleader answered. "We're just admiring your nuts."

There was a dead silence, then the women's cheeks turned as red as the fake Halloween blood that I'd put in the zombie basket. Finally, among titters and snorts, Dad's admirers waved their good-byes and fled. Glancing at my father, I saw that his ears were pink, but there was an amused expression on his face. I smiled fondly and checked the time.

Shoot! According to the Ingraham schoolhouse regulator hanging on the wall behind the cash register, it was already a few minutes after two. Dad's shift was over, and only one basket was completed.

Where had the hours gone? As if coming out of a fog, I gazed around. The store was spotless, the shelves were fully stocked, and Dad had set up the craft alcove for the sewing group. Thank goodness I wouldn't have to wrestle the four long tables and the folding chairs out of the back. The only thing he'd forgotten to put out was the serger that the club president had dropped off earlier in the week, which would take me less than five minutes to retrieve from the storeroom.

Dad came over to where I was standing and said, "Unless you want me to stick around to help with the after-school crowd, I'm going to take off."

"Thanks, Dad. Taryn is coming over after his last class to staff the teen lounge, so we're all set." I kissed his cheek, then teased, "Are you seeing Catherine again tonight? Or one of those other women?"

"What other ladies?" Dad wrinkled his brow. "Catherine's making me dinner." Red creeped up his neck and he explained, "As a thank-you for the other night."

"Have fun." I wondered if the fried chicken was all she was thanking him for. Wiggling my brows, I suggested, "You might want to bring her some flowers."

"I've got it covered." Dad winked back at me and strolled out the door.

Jesus arrived at two thirty. He performed a miracle worthy of his namesake on the electrical issue in the employee bathroom and departed twenty minutes later with a check and my thanks.

As the handyman left, I hastily popped the last bite of my boiled ham, cheese, and mustard on rye into my mouth and tucked Ronni's and Coop's baskets out of sight. I stationed myself behind the soda fountain a few seconds before a torrent of adolescents cascaded through the front door.

The kids who wanted ice cream crowded the counter while the others, led by Taryn, headed upstairs to the lounge. I had already set up the drink and snack bar, along with a portable cash register, so my clerk should have everything he needed until the kids departed for home around five.

In between my frequent checks on the teens in the lounge, I pulled out fabric and notions that I hoped would tantalize the sewing group into an impulse purchase, or two or three. Once the temptations were enticingly displayed, I readied the refreshments I intended to sell to the Blood, Sweat, and Shears members.

I was cleaning up the soda fountain when Jake walked out of the storage room. Evidently, he'd complied with my request that he park in the rear lot and come in through the back entrance. His chin was stubbled with a day's growth of beard and his eyes were deeply shadowed with fatigue. He looked frustrated as hell.

"Hi, sugar." He took off his Stetson, fingered the brim for a moment, then put it on a stool. "Uncle Tony and Ulysses are going to the all-night poker party at the American Legion." Jake stared at me. "So I was thinking, if you aren't busy, you could come over and I'd cook you dinner."

I flashed back to the last time we managed to find some privacy and exchange some steamy kisses and felt my cheeks get hot and other parts of me tingle. Quickly, almost afraid he could read my thoughts, and because I definitely did not want him to ask if I'd made up my mind about a weekend away together, I said, "The store's open until nine, and it's my turn to work."

"That's a damn shame." His blue eyes were as bright as the Hope diamond, and he took my hand. "Any chance Kern would fill in for you?"

"Nope." I smiled. "Dad has plans." After I told Jake about catching Catherine leaving my father's apartment, I said, "Looks like you'll just have to be patient and wait until our Saturday-night date."

"Seems as if I have no choice in the matter," Jake grumbled. "Of course, Saturday, Tony will be at my place and Birdie will be at yours, so there's no possibility for us to be alone anywhere but my truck."

"Sorry." I really was. And I wasn't. Jake was too tempting, and I still wasn't any closer than before in making up my mind between him and Noah. "Maybe we could find a movie that isn't too crowded."

"Right," Jake grunted. "Like every horny teenager in the area."

He didn't appear appeased, but before I could say something soothing, I noticed a huge hairy creature crawling on Jake's hat. I pointed at the monster arachnid and screamed. Jake's gaze followed my finger and he quickly dispatched the fiend.

Returning from disposing of the body, he grinned. "I'll never understand you."

"Really?"

He snickered and said, "You can handle boiling hot wax smeared on your privates and still be afraid of a tiny little spider?"

I blinked. How did he know that I waxed? *Oh. Yeah.* That time in the hotel when we were investigating Joelle's murder. We had gotten nearly naked before we were interrupted.

Not wanting to remind him of our failed tryst, I asked, "Any luck with the Winston case?"

He summarized the result of his door-to-door canvass, visit to the country club, and chat with Peregrine Pierce, then added, "Elliot Winston called when I was driving back here from Sparkville."

"Oh?"

"He got another note from the kidnapper." Jake stepped closer and lowered his voice. "Winston is supposed to bring the money to the bandstand in the town square tonight at eleven forty-five."

"That's an odd time." I poured us both a cup of coffee, and Jake and I took seats on adjoining stools. "Any clue why the kidnapper would choose it?"

"My best guess is that it's late enough that there will be very few folks out and around, but early enough that the cops wouldn't be suspicious of the people who are still walking in the square."

"Smart." I took a sip of coffee. "Does Elliot plan to pay the ransom?"

"He said he is." Jake frowned. "He refuses to tell Chief Kincaid about this note, and I don't feel like I can overrule his decision, which means if things go south during the drop-off, I'm his only backup."

"Will the kidnapper release Gabriella?" I asked with my own frown.

"The note said that she'll be set free after the money has been counted."

"What are the odds of her being okay?" My knowledge of criminals all came from books and television, and I doubted they were a hundred percent reliable. "Do you think she might already be dead?"

"It depends if she's seen the guy or not." Jake blew out a long breath. "If she knows her abductor's identity, I doubt he'll let her go."

I shivered at the image of poor Gabriella tied up and blindfolded for the past four days. Jake scooted closer and put an arm around me. His lips brushed mine, but before he could do anything else, the sound of thundering feet echoed down the steps.

"Shit!" Jake jerked away from me as if a cattle

prod had been shoved into his groin. "I forgot about all the little buggers upstairs."

My heart racing, I nodded. What was it about Jake that made me lose my common sense? Getting to my feet, I walked to the register and flipped open the counter. I stepped behind it and quickly closed up the opening. Putting some distance, not to mention a physical barrier, between Jake and me seemed like a prudent move.

"Which of your groups is tonight?" Jake asked. "Is it the book club or the bird-watchers or the calligraphers? I can't keep 'em all straight."

"Winnie and Zizi Todd's sewing circle is on Wednesdays," I answered, pulling out an old rag and rubbing the brass on the cash register.

While I polished, I watched the teenagers pour out the front door. As they passed me, most waved and yelled good-bye. They were a good group of kids and were grateful for a place to hang out.

Once the register gleamed, I started working on another gift basket.

Jake stared at me for a while, then said, "Did you ever find out why your grandmother got married so quickly after Tony went MIA?"

"What? No!"

I nearly dropped the bottle of wine that I was placing in a basket that I was creating for my best customer to give to one of his clients. He was big deal real estate agent who sold high-end properties in Kansas City and ordered upward of twenty baskets a week—a number of them were thank-you gifts after a purchase, but many were intended to woo someone into signing with his firm.

"What makes you ask about Gran and Tony right now?" I asked.

"I think it's something we should clear up." Jake's expression was a mixture of stubborn and sheepish. "I don't want to be sandbagged with the information and have it cause trouble between us. You need to sit Birdie down and make her tell you the whole story."

"Okay." I drew out the word. While I agreed with Jake in theory, getting Gran to talk would not be an easy task. "Any suggestions on how I force someone as stubborn as a grease stain to confess?"

"I'm sure if you explain why we want to know, Birdie will cooperate." Jake rubbed the back of his neck. "She wants us to be together."

"While that's true"—I made sure he didn't see me roll my eyes—"I don't want to get her hopes up. If I do, she'll have the invitations to our wedding in the mail the next day."

"And that's a problem why?" Jake ran his knuckles over my cheek.

My pulse thudded in my ears and I could barely breathe. Was he proposing?

Jake went on as if he hadn't just about given me a heart attack, "Maybe the four of us should have a sit-down—you, me, Tony, and Birdie."

"Any possibility that Tony already knows?" I tilted my head. "Have you asked him?"

"I did and he doesn't." Jake fingered the brim of his Stetson.

"Oh. I'm surprised you never mentioned it." I digested that tidbit, then said, "Do you think he'd be willing to confront Gran with us?"

"He could be persuaded." Jake smiled widely. "Birdie isn't the only one of our elderly relatives who wants to see us together."

Although I knew it would be best if we got whatever Gran was hiding out of the way, I didn't want to accept what had to be done. Facing my grandmother and demanding to know a secret from her past would be awkward at best and very possibly downright excruciating.

However, since I had been thinking about talking to Gran myself about this issue, I embraced the idea of help and said, "How about we do it Saturday before we go out?" I warmed to the idea. "You can bring Tony with you, and I'll make sure that Birdie is home."

"That's fine, as long as it doesn't turn into a double date." Jake gave me a firm stare, then he put a hand in his jeans pocket and asked, "What time will you be finished here tonight?"

"The meeting ends at nine, but it'll take me

fifteen or twenty minutes to clean up and get the store ready for tomorrow."

"How about we grab a quick bite to eat afterward?" Jake asked.

"That sounds good." I rubbed the bridge of my nose, unsure how he'd react to what I was about to suggest. Finally, I just bit the bullet and said, "Because I think I should help you with the ransom stakeout."

Jake wrinkled his brow, then seemed to make a decision and nodded. "That's not a bad suggestion." He narrowed his eyes and added, "However, you only observe. If there's trouble, you call nine-one-one and remain concealed. Under no circumstances do you interact with the perp."

"Got it," I agreed. "In that case, I'll see you around nine fifteen."

"Until then." Jake leaned across the counter to kiss my temple, then headed upstairs.

I was shocked that Jake had accepted my offer of assistance so easily. And I couldn't help compare his attitude to Noah's. Noah hated the idea of me investigating a crime. Jake was protective, but understood that it was better to show me the safe way to help rather than try to wrap me in cotton and tuck me away in some pretty box.

The difference between the two men was becoming more and more clear. Now I just had to figure out which of them suited my personality best.

CHAPTER 17

Thirty minutes later, I was still weighing Noah's and Jake's pros and cons when the first of the sewing circle members arrived. Zizi Todd skyrocketed her vehicle into the best front-of-store parking spot and leaped out of the old muscle car.

Zizi drove a scratched-up GTO with a smashed-in front grille and a series of cracks fanning up the windshield. Between the duct tape and the corrosion, it was hard to determine the Pontiac's original color, but my guess was red. Or maybe silver. Possibly black.

Zizi's carrot-colored hair and long-limbed lean body made me think of a grown-up Pippi Longstocking. Her bright blue jumper and striped tights only added to the impression. Did she choose her outfits for that purpose?

Zizi might dress like a nine-year-old, but in fact, she was studying to become a clinical social worker and was in the top of her class. I'd heard her recite complex passages from the *Diagnostic and Statistical Manual of Mental Disorders* without hesitation. A feat I doubted many of her fellow students could match.

I opened my mouth to greet Zizi, but wasn't surprised when she ignored me. As usual her focus was on getting to the bathroom in the rear of the store. She generally drove to Shadow Bend straight from her part-time job in Kansas City. Since traffic was usually horrendous this time of day, she'd probably been trapped in her car for over an hour and a half, and she never remembered to use the restroom before leaving work.

When Zizi joined me in the craft corner a few minutes later, she blew her bangs out of her eyes and said, "That was a close one. I thought I wouldn't make it this time. For future reference, what aisle is the underwear? Or maybe I should just get a box of Depends."

"Or you could remember to go before getting into the car," I teased.

We were still giggling when Zizi's mother, Winnie, arrived. Winnie was the original hippie. Her long gray hair was a froth of frizzy curls, and the fringe on her leather vest reached past her knees.

A teenager during the sixties, Winnie had run away and lived in San Francisco for twenty years. Then in the late eighties she had returned to Shadow Bend visibly pregnant. Although several of the townspeople had expressed concern that she was not only a single mother, but also in her forties, she'd laughed off the worrywarts and as always did as she pleased.

Due to a sizable estate Winnie had inherited

from her grandparents, she was set for cash. And since her doctor hadn't been bothered about her age, neither was she. Zizi was the proof that Winnie had been right.

I gave Winnie a hug and asked, "What's on tonight's agenda?"

"With the cool weather coming, we're back to making blankets," Winnie explained.

Both Winnie and Zizi were true humanitarians, and together they had cofounded Blood, Sweat, and Shears in order to support the county's homeless shelter. The group had grown from half a dozen women to over twenty. They ranged from seventeen to eighty-four, but all had one thing in common—compassion for others.

Each member paid for her own materials and donated most of the finished products either directly to the shelter or to the shelter's resale shop. Their generosity and true desire to help was an example of the best part of living in a small town.

While Zizi and Winnie chatted, I slipped into the storage room and phoned my grandmother. With Dad occupied for the evening with Catherine, I wanted to check in on Gran and let her know I wouldn't be home right after work. I liked to keep tabs on her, and she felt the same way about me.

Birdie assured me she was fine, and she was happy that I was seeing Jake after work. She'd have probably been okay with the fact that our "date" was to assist in a ransom drop-off, but I didn't tell her. I was never one for sharing gratuitous information. Especially if said info had even a chance of resulting in a lecture from my grandmother.

When I returned to the craft area, most of the other seamstresses had arrived. Some were still milling around the tables, but others were already cutting fleece into two-and-a-half-yard lengths and measuring out the satin binding.

As I moved closer to the group, I noticed an unusually high volume of whispering and tutting. Had I missed an especially good bit of gossip?

Joining the ladies, I listened to the discussion.

Cyndi Barrows, a woman who had started out as a part of the country club clique but astonishingly had transformed almost into a local said, "I really wasn't at all surprised to hear that Mac had disappeared."

Zizi paused in midcut, her shears half open. "Who is that?"

Cyndi pushed her dark brown hair behind her ear, concentrating on the line of stitches she was sewing, then without looking up, she said, "He *was* the golf pro at the country club."

Zizi raised a brow. "I thought you didn't spend much time at the club anymore."

"I don't." Cyndi shrugged her slim shoulders. "But my boyfriend likes to golf, so we do go

240

there for that, and then sometimes we have lunch and I hear people talking."

Cyndi had been engaged to Frazer Wren, but when after five years he claimed that he was afraid of commitment, she'd broken up with him. We were all glad she'd found a nice man to date. At least I assumed he was nice from her comments—I had never heard his name.

"Why weren't you surprised that this Mac person had gone missing?" Winnie asked.

"Well." Cyndi's hazel eyes sparkled and her voice sank to a whisper and she said, "The poor man was like . . . like catnip to those cougars at the club."

I hid my smile. Funny that Cyndi used the term since Boone had long since nicknamed the ladies out there Country Club Cougars.

"He didn't enjoy the attention?" Zizi frowned. "Did he run away from them?"

"Not exactly" After a predictable show of reluctance, Cyndi continued, "The thing is, the poor guy didn't have a lick of common sense. He let those women talk him into doing some really stupid things."

"Like what?" Zizi stopped cutting material and cocked her head.

"Drugs and booze and public sex." Cyndi wrinkled her button nose. "I knew that before long, he'd end up in real trouble and have to leave town." She sighed. "I just hope he's okay. He wasn't a bad guy, but he was immature and just couldn't seem to say no to anyone. Especially a woman."

After that exchange, talk turned to the more mundane topics like the weather. I wandered away and got to work. I could use the time to finish up some bookkeeping and complete a couple more of my real estate tycoon's baskets. He was a stickler for deadlines.

At seven thirty, the sewers took a fifteen-minute break. For five dollars each, I provided coffee, tea, and a selection of baked goods that I purchased at a quantity discount from the bakery. Payment was on the honor system, with the women putting their money in an old cigar box.

After making sure there were plenty of cups, plates, utensils, and napkins, I went back to my spreadsheet. Have you ever noticed that if you run *the* and *IRS* together it looks like the word *theirs?*

Disgusted with the amount of taxes I had to pay, I shut off my computer and started on the baskets. As I stood behind my workbench, my attention was jerked away from the Chocolate to Die For basket when Winnie and Zizi paused a few feet away from me.

"Why are you rubbing your arm?" Zizi asked her mother.

"I went to the clinic for my annual physical today, and Dr. Underwood insisted that I have a tetanus shot," Winnie complained. "I swear, every time I go in for one thing, he finds something else that I need."

"You just don't like going to the doctor." Zizi juggled her cup and plate in one hand in order to massage her mom's biceps.

"True." Winnie shrugged, then, her lips twitching in amusement, she said, "You'll never guess who's working at the clinic."

Winnie took a sip from her mug, then a bite of shortbread cookie. When her daughter didn't answer she urged, "Go ahead and guess."

"The Easter bunny." Zizi licked the icing off a chocolate cupcake.

"Smartass." Winnie made a face, spreading wrinkles across her cheeks like waves in an ocean. "It's the weirdest thing ever."

She glanced at me, and although she lowered her voice I could still hear her when she said, "Jake Del Vecchio's crazy ex-wife is Dr. Underwood's new receptionist. How strange is that?"

"Why is that odd?" Zizi crumpled the cupcake wrapper and tossed it into a nearby trash can. "The poor woman had a horrible experience, and now that she's recovering, she needs a job to keep her mind occupied. Hiring her sounds just like something he would do." Zizi had a dreamy expression on her face. "He's such a good man."

She was right. Noah was a good man. Maybe too good. Was that even possible?

"I suppose." Winnie pursed her lips. "But it

probably doesn't hurt that Mrs. Del Vecchio's really a gorgeous woman. It was hard to tell when she first moved here, but now that she's put on a little weight and has started to curl her hair and wear some makeup, she's a knockout."

Whoa! I hadn't seen Meg in a while. I might have to drop by the clinic and take a look.

"What are you saying, Mom?" Zizi asked, narrowing her eyes to slits. "Do you think Dr. Underwood is interested in Mrs. Del Vecchio?"

"All I can say is, they were having a passionate discussion the whole time I was in the waiting room." Winnie chuckled. "But I couldn't tell if it was the good kind of passion or the dark kind."

I scowled. What in the hell had Noah and Meg been talking about?

At eight fifty, I announced that the sewing circle had ten minutes to finish up, and returned to the register to handle any final purchases.

Winnie was the last to leave, and when she came over to say good-bye, I casually asked, "I heard you and Zizi discussing Noah and Meg. Wasn't it nice of him to give her a job?"

"Of course." Winnie nodded, then with a shrewd look said, "Unless Dr. Underwood thinks keeping her around will give her an opportunity to get her ex back."

"I'm sure that's not it." I shook my head so vehemently, I felt my eyes cross. "Noah isn't that devious of a person. Now, his mother . . ."

"That's true." Winnie's expression softened. "But Nadine would be trying to get rid of Jake's ex and seal the deal between you two, not the other way around. Anything that gets your claws out of her son."

"Yep," I agreed, then corrected, "But I do not have my 'claws' in Noah."

"Of course not." Winnie must have seen through my bland expression to the annoyed one that I was trying to hide, because she said, "That's just how Nadine would see it, not me." She reached out and patted my hand. "Although some of Shadow Bend's single women might agree more with the good doctor's mother than with us."

"And that's part of the problem," I muttered to myself as I escorted Winnie out of the door and locked it behind her. If I chose Noah, our relationship would be under constant scrutiny. And I doubt anyone would ever take my side if he and I had a disagreement.

"What's the frown for?" Jake's voice made me jump. He was staring at me with a look of concern. "If you're having second thoughts about tonight's stakeout—"

"Nope." I gave him a smile and said, "Let me finish closing, then we can go to the Dairy Queen and you can go over the plan while we eat."

CHAPTER 18

Like most every other small Midwestern town, Shadow Bend had a Dairy Queen. However, we were one up on many of the surrounding communities, because ours was a Brazier. In addition to ice cream, it served hamburgers, hot dogs, chicken strips, and the like.

DQ did a brisk business for lunch, after school, and during the dinner hour. But since it was nearly nine thirty on a Wednesday night, there were only two other vehicles in the parking lot when Jake pulled his truck into a spot near the entrance. And from the appearance of those cars, they probably belonged to the employees stuck working the weekday graveyard shift.

Jake helped me down from the pickup's cab and held open the Dairy Queen door. A chime sound signaled our entrance, and the teenage girl perched on a stool behind the counter looked up from her cell phone. She heaved a sigh, slowly got to her feet, and made a show of reluctantly slipping the bright pink rectangle into her pocket before sauntering toward us.

The girl recited, "Welcome to Dairy Queen. How may I create an unbelievable moment for you tonight?"

Both Jake and I ate here often enough to know

what we wanted without consulting the posted menu, and when Jake nodded for me to go first, I said, "Chicken bruschetta combo with minimal lettuce and a diet soda, please."

The girl frowned and said, "I'm sorry. We only have regular lettuce, and I don't think it's that minimal kind."

Swallowing my amusement, I said, "Okay, just don't put too much of it on the sandwich."

Jake's voice sounded like he was holding back a laugh when he told the girl he wanted a cheeseburger combo and a chocolate shake, but she didn't seem to notice as she laboriously entered our selection into the cash register.

Holding out her hand, the teenager said, "That will be nineteen dollars and fifty-nine cents."

After Jake paid, the girl gave him a receipt and said, "I'll call the number on the bottom when your food is ready."

Jake stuffed the change from his twenty, plus a couple of singles in the tip jar on the counter, then led the way through the dining area. He glanced back to make sure that I was following him, then headed toward a booth in the back.

As we walked by all the empty tables, I snickered. "You better listen hard for our number. You don't want to get the wrong order. I'd hate for someone else to get my minimal-lettuce chicken."

"I'm all ears, darlin'." Jake chuckled, then

waited for me to choose a bench before sliding into the opposite one. "I won't let anyone steal your fancy sandwich, but I can't guarantee the safety of your fries."

"From you." I poked his forearm. "Last time I barely got any."

"Hey," Jake protested. "They were just sitting there getting cold." His cheek creased. "I figured you were finished with them."

"I like to eat my food together," I explained. "Not scarf all my fries at once like you."

Before Jake could respond to my accusation, our number was called, and he teased, "I better go fetch our supper before someone else gobbles your precious fries and you go all crazy lady on them."

When Jake returned with our order, my mouth watered. It had been more than seven hours since my lunch, and this smelled heavenly. We spent the next few minutes opening cardboard containers, squeezing ketchup into the lids, and unwrapping straws.

Once we had taken care of the important stuff, I asked, "What's the plan for tonight's operation? Are we picking up Elliot?"

"No." Jake lifted his bacon cheeseburger to his mouth. "The note specified that Winston had to be the one who brought the money and he had to be alone. He'll drive by himself and park as close to the bandstand as he can. Surprisingly, a million in hundreds only weighs a little over twenty pounds, so he'll have no problem carrying it."

"I was imaging it would be much bulkier." I swirled a fry through a pool of ketchup and savored the salty goodness, before I resumed our conversation. "Where did Elliot get the million bucks?"

Jake took a drink of his chocolate shake, swallowed, and said, "He had it messengered from his bank in California."

"It's good he could do it so quickly." I paused to take sip of my diet soda, then said thoughtfully, "Two days has to be cutting it pretty close."

"That's an understatement." Jake shook his head. "The bank needed twenty-four hours to get the money, and once they had it, the security guard Winston hired had to fly from Los Angeles to Kansas City. Winston met him at the airport this afternoon and had to drive back to Shadow Bend."

"Why didn't Elliot just have the funds wired to Shadow Bend's Savings and Guaranty?"

"Either the local bank wasn't able to get that much cash in such a short time," Jake said, "or Winston didn't trust them to do it right."

"So Elliot arranged for the money before he got the message telling him where to deliver it." I picked up my chicken bruschetta. It oozed mozzarella and Italian herb–seasoned diced tomatoes. The basil cheese focaccia roll had a satisfying crunch as I bit into it.

"Uh-huh." Jake polished off his burger and wiped his fingers. "The note was waiting under Winston's door when he returned from the city."

"Convenient." Something was bothering me about the timing, but I shrugged it off. "Where are we going to be stationed in the park?"

"I'll be behind the bench on the path leading to the bandstand." Jake threw an arm across the back of the booth. "It gives me the best view of the front and sides of the structure."

"And where do you want me?" I asked before popping another fry into my mouth.

"I've got the perfect spot for you." Jake's lips quirked up.

"Where?" I asked, not at all liking the expression on his face.

"Did you know that the chamber of commerce put up their Halloween decorations over the weekend?" Jake asked, his blue eyes twinkling.

"I heard about it, but haven't been out to see them," I answered cautiously.

"Their big display is at the rear of the bandstand," Jake informed me.

"Okay." I drew out the word, then lifted a brow and asked, "I take it that my hiding place is among the witches and goblins?"

"Not so much among the decorations"—Jake chuckled—"as inside one."

"What in the hell does that mean?" I asked, pursing my lips.

"They have these giant fiberglass pumpkins," Jake explained. "When I did recon this afternoon, I noticed that they were hollow."

"Shit!" I glared at him. "You want me to sit in a jack-o'-lantern like Peter, Peter, the pumpkin eater's wife? Will I even fit?"

"Yep, and there's eyeholes so you can see out." Jake grinned. "You'll be able to watch the back of the bandstand. If the kidnapper leaves that way, you can text me so that I can tail him."

"Shouldn't I follow him after I text you?" I tapped my fingernails. "What if he disappears before you get there and we lose him?"

"Under no circumstances are you to leave your pumpkin," Jake snapped, then evidently heard what he'd said and fought a smile.

"Yes, sir." I saluted, then, as he reached for one of my remaining fries, I moved them a safe distance away. "No leaving the jack-o'-lantern."

"I've got a pair of night vision binoculars for you." Jake got up, slid in next to me, and snatched a fry before I could react. "There shouldn't be any problem keeping the perp in sight until I can get there."

"Okeydokey."

Jake had a point. It would be silly to go running after a dangerous criminal. I would just wait in my pumpkin for the big strong man.

Stifling the giggle that bubbled up from *that* thought, Jake and I finished my dinner. As we ate, the conversation turned to my father's new girlfriend and my mother, who was back in Texas hunting for husband number five or maybe six— I had trouble keeping track.

Jake didn't like talking about his parents, and as usual when I brought up the subject of his folks, he tried to appease me with generalities. But determined that this time he wouldn't evade the subject, I kept asking questions until Jake abruptly stood up.

Oops! I must have gone too far. I knew Jake's parents had practiced benign neglect during his childhood. They had sent him to boarding and military schools, then to his great-uncle's ranch during vacations. However, Jake was aware of all my family's warts, and I wanted to know more about his early years.

"We'd better get going so we can get into position well before the perp arrives," Jake said. "Do you want to use the restroom before we leave?"

"Probably a good idea." I put my trash on the red plastic tray and slid out of the booth. "I'll meet you in the parking lot."

After finishing my business in the ladies' room, I found Jake waiting by the passenger door of his pickup. He opened it, helped me inside, and drove to the dime store, where he parked his truck in one of the empty spaces in front of the window.

When we got out, Jake handed me the night vision binoculars and asked, "Do you have your pepper spray?"

I nodded, and we walked across the street to the town square. Early on in our relationship Jake had given me a pepper spray gun, which he had instructed me to keep with me at all times. And I had to admit, not too long ago, the bright blue revolver *had* come in handy.

Although it was close to eleven o'clock, there were still a few cars parked along the street and a smattering of folks on the sidewalks. However, most of the people were filing in to the movie theater's Art Deco entrance. Recently, the theater's owner had moved the five dollar bargain midnight movie up an hour in hopes of attracting the earlier-to-bed Gen Xers as well as the Millennial night owls.

Jake ignored the others and silently guided us into the town square. The dimness of the pole lights that lined the footpaths made it a challenge to navigate the cobblestone paths without tripping on the attractive, but not necessarily smooth, walkway.

Evidently, the lack of illumination wasn't as much of a problem for Jake as it was for me, and I had to hustle to keep up with him. As I lengthened my stride, I fished inside my shoulder bag until I located my keys and the flashlight attached to the ring.

Switching it on, I aimed it at the path in front of me. Now that I wasn't afraid of face-planting on the uneven stones, I hurried to Jake's side.

I was just congratulating myself on my preparedness, when he turned and in a low voice ordered, "Douse the light. The perp might be watching."

"Sorry." I clicked off the tiny Maglite and tucked it in my pocket. Jake took my hand, and we continued to the center of the square.

Jake led me to the stone benches along the sidewalk leading to the bandstand and whispered, "Get your pepper spray out and stay behind these while I do recon."

I sat cross-legged on the ground with my purse between my legs and dug out the pepper spray gun. It seemed like Jake was gone a long while, and I wiggled, trying to find a comfortable spot.

Did I dare turn on my phone to see the time? I reached for the cell, then, recalling Jake's negative reaction to my flashlight, I decided against it. Why ask for trouble on my first stakeout?

"Are you asleep?" Jake whispered as he crouched down next to me.

Crap! I must have zoned out. I pasted an innocent expression on my face and said, "Of course not. Just trying to be quiet."

"I didn't see anyone else in the area, so let's get you in your pumpkin before that changes." Jake took my hand and helped me stand.

"Can't wait," I muttered.

"Are you sure you want to do this?" Jake halted and peered into my eyes. "I won't think any less of you if you're scared and would rather wait in the truck."

"I definitely want to do this and I'm not frightened." I lifted my chin. "But you'll have to take my word for it, because my Wonder Woman cape is at the dry cleaners."

Jake chuckled, and we continued to the other side of the bandstand. As we rounded the corner, I was momentarily distracted by the elaborate Halloween decorations. The chamber of commerce had outdone themselves.

An enormous inflatable witch stirred a cauldron, and next to her a black cat bristled at a scarecrow. A vampire bent to pet a huge spider. And fake cobwebs were draped dramatically over tree limbs.

Jake pointed to the jack-o'-lantern he had selected for me, which was one of several among large bales of hay. The tops were all open, as if a giant had sliced off the lids in order to carve them. I wished he'd have cut a door leading inside of the darn thing instead. Biting my lip, I plotted my climb into the oversize pumpkin. Did I need a running start? Maybe I could use the hay bales like steps.

As I visualized my asÇent, I moved closer to my objective. It had to be four feet tall. Could I do some sort of chin-up on the edge?

Before I could decide the best approach, I felt hands on my waist, and as I achieved liftoff, Jake whispered, "In you go, sugar."

I barely stopped a scream from escaping my throat, and even though I knew he couldn't see me, I shot him a dirty look. He could have at least warned me before taking me airborne. And where was my pack of peanuts? Most flights included a snack.

As my feet touched the bottom of the jack-o'-lantern, I realized that Jake had lifted my considerable poundage as if I weighed no more than a sack of feed. That man's muscles were nothing less than amazing.

I looked around my new home, jumping when Jake's face appeared in one of the eyeholes, and he said, "Make sure you have your phone ready and on mute. Keep your pepper spray in your hand." He stopped and stared hard at me. "Do not leave this pumpkin."

"Got it," I agreed, unsure I could get out of the thing without help anyway. "Phone, gun, stay put. Anything else I should know?"

Jake gave me a suspicious glance, then said, "Just one thing." He beckoned me closer to the opening, and when I complied he leaned in and gave me a quick, but intense kiss. "Don't make me regret involving the woman I love in something dangerous."

All the air left my lungs, and I could only nod. Had Jake really just said he loved me? He'd told me he cared for me before, but he'd never used the L-word. Come to think of it, Noah had declared his love for me when we were teenagers, but I couldn't remember him saying it since we'd been dating again.

That could mean that Noah was waiting for my decision. Or it was entirely possible that although we had feelings for each other from the past, that's all they were. A sort of ancient echo of our youthful infatuation.

Shaking my head, I pushed my romantic issues aside and readied myself for surveillance. According to my cell, which I gripped in my right hand, it was eleven thirty. Fifteen minutes until the drop-off.

I glanced at the sky. The moon illuminated the immediate area, but even with the night vision binoculars, it was tough to see much beyond the bandstand's perimeter. If the perp made his escape this way, I'd have only a few seconds to alert Jake before the bad guy was lost in the darkness and the trees.

I concentrated all my attention on scanning the space. Although the pavilion was round with no ostensible back or front, the way the columns were placed and the walkway on the other side, made the part that I was facing seem more like the rear. So if I were the kidnapper, I'd approach it from this angle.

A few seconds later, my theory was proven true. A figure dressed in black pants and a black hoodie darted past my pumpkin, ran up to the bandstand, and slipped behind one of the pillars.

From my viewpoint, it was hard to tell anything about the perp. All I could see was his back. I couldn't even tell his height or build, since he was hunkered down.

I texted Jake the info, and he replied that as instructed, Winston had put the money on the bench inside the bandstand and left. I saw from the cell's display that it was eleven forty-five.

A minute went by, then another three. Finally, the kidnapper stepped into the pavilion and I lost sight of him. Again, I texted Jake, then settled in to watch for the kidnapper's exit. I didn't have long to wait.

Seconds later, the guy darted out of the bandstand, clutching a large duffel bag to his chest. I texted Jake for the third time and kept my binoculars trained on the dark figure. He was peering over his shoulder as he ran, so all I could see was the back of his head, and as I watched, he plowed right into the witch.

I flinched as he bounced off the inflated decoration and hit the ground. The bad guy immediately jumped to his feet, but he failed to look behind him and hurtled backward into my jack-o'-lantern.

Unfortunately, due to my weight on the opposite side of the pumpkin, the resin shell tilted. Before I could adjust my position to keep the jack-o'-lantern upright, I felt it lose its battle with gravity. As it tipped to its side, my head hit the inner wall, and for a nanosecond, everything went dark.

As I blinked back to reality, I felt myself being pulled out of the cracked shell. Jake was frantically running his hands over me, demanding to know if I was okay, and the kidnapper was nowhere in sight.

CHAPTER 19

After Jake made sure that I was all right, we checked the town square, but found no sign of the kidnapper. The sidewalks in front of the buildings on the outer perimeter of the square were deserted, and because the movie theater had its own lot, the only vehicle that remained parked along the street was Jake's pickup.

After placing the duffel bag full of hundred-dollar bills in the bandstand, Elliot had returned to his car and driven out of the downtown area. He was waiting a few streets over.

Jake texted him to meet us at the truck, and a couple of minutes later, Elliot's metallic white Land Rover pulled into the spot next to Jake's Ford. Elliot leaped out of the driver's seat and rushed up to where Jake and I were leaning against the side of the pickup.

"What happened?" Elliot's breathing was as ragged as if he'd run the entire distance instead of driven it. "Do you have Gabriella?"

"No." Jake put a hand on the other man's shoulder. "Remember the note said she wouldn't be released until the money was counted."

"Since you're here, I assume you were unable to follow him." Elliot wiped at a tear. "I was hoping he'd lead you to her."

I was a little surprised to see him show such emotion. When he'd first hired Jake, I wasn't sure he even cared about his wife. Then, with her still missing, when he held the party at the Manor, I was convinced he was totally heartless. I guess Jake's explanation of the man's personality had been true. It made me wonder if Gabriella knew how much her husband truly loved her.

"I told you that was a long shot." Jake squeezed the guy's arm.

"Yeah. But I still hoped it would happen." Elliot glanced at me. "Were you able to see anything that might help identify the guy?"

"Not really." I shrugged. "It was dark and he was moving fast. He had his hood up and the drawstring was pulled so tight only his eyes were uncovered. He wore gloves so I never saw his skin."

"Tall? Short? Skinny? Fat?" Elliot was nearly screaming. "Nothing?"

"Sorry." I screwed up my face. "From my perspective I couldn't tell his height, and as to his build, he seemed average or maybe a little on the slim side."

Jake glanced over at me and asked, "What does McGowan look like?"

"Maybe five-ten and a hundred and sixty pounds," I answered slowly.

"Could he have been the person you saw?" Elliot asked, grabbing my hand.

"It's possible." I eased my fingers from Elliot's crushing grip. "All I can say for sure is the guy wasn't super tall or overly bulky."

Elliot asked the same questions again and again until Jake interrupted and said, "Now that the money has been delivered, it's time we brought the police up to speed. And be prepared, the chief won't be happy to hear we kept this payoff information from him."

"Let's wait to see if Gabriella is released." Elliot crossed his arms. "I don't want the cops doing something stupid and getting her killed."

"Like what?" I asked. "It's not as if any of us know where she's at."

"If Gabriella hasn't been returned by tomorrow afternoon, I'm calling the chief." Jake's voice was firm and he stared hard at Elliot.

"Fine," Elliot muttered, then brightened. "Hey, maybe Gabriella is waiting for me at home right now." He rushed toward his Land Rover and flung open the door. "I'll let you know if she's there."

"She won't be, will she?" I asked Jake as we watched Elliot speed away.

"Doubtful." Jake scowled as he ran his fingers over the bump on my forehead. "How are you feeling? Any headache, nausea, or blurry vision?"

"Don't worry." I smiled at him. "I'm a lot tougher than I look."

"I know, sweetheart." Jake pulled me against

his chest and smoothed my hair. "But it scared me shitless when I saw you out cold."

"It was only for half a minute," I protested, cuddling closer.

"The longest thirty seconds of my life." Jake tilted my chin up.

"Uh . . . That's nice . . ." I stuttered. "Not nice you were worried, but . . ."

I wasn't used to this kind of intense concern. No one had ever fussed over me that much. The people in my life all saw me as the strong one. As someone who could take care of herself. Even Gran never fretted if I was sick or injured. It wasn't that she didn't care; it was more that she assumed I wouldn't want her to make a big deal about it. So why was I enjoying Jake's concern so much?

"It's hard for me to see you in danger." Jake's mouth hovered over mine. "But I know that you wouldn't be happy waiting off on the sidelines."

"True." I could feel his warm breath against my face and had trouble forming my thoughts into words. "I never wanted to be the cheerleader. I always wanted to be battling it out with the team."

"I would have never guessed." Jake chuckled as he closed the gap between us.

Jake's kiss was slow and unhurried. He leisurely explored my lips, and when he moved on to nibble at my earlobe, I whimpered my disappointment.

I'm not sure how long we stood in front of my store kissing, but finally Jake leaned his forehead against mine and said, "If I don't stop now, we're going to get arrested for public nudity."

"Right." I reluctantly stepped back, putting a few inches between us. "And I need to go home and get some sleep since I'm alone at the store tomorrow."

"But you're off at noon?" Jake took my hand. "How about lunch?"

"I better not." I led Jake down the alley to the parking lot behind the store. "There's a ton of baskets ordered and I need to get them done."

"I'll bring you your favorites from Little's Tea Room," Jake coaxed.

"You've got a deal. But I need to work while we eat." I retrieved my keys from my purse, unlocked my car, and slid behind the wheel. "See you at twelve thirty, and don't forget the homemade potato chips."

"Wouldn't dream of it." Jake leaned into the open door and gave me a quick kiss.

Without any craft groups, Thursday was usually a slow day at the store, which is why we were open only for the morning. A few folks wandered in to buy this and that, but for the most part, I had the place to myself until I locked up at noon.

I was finishing up the last of my real estate mogul's monthly basket order when Jake strolled

265

out from the backroom, and I jumped. I was still getting used to him having a key to the rear door and coming and going that way, since no else did. Even my dad usually used the front entrance.

Jake slid two white cardboard boxes onto the soda fountain counter, reached over to the dispenser, and grabbed napkins, then sat on the end stool.

Tying the final bow, I said, "Great timing." I left the finished basket on my workbench, along with the mess I had made creating it, and let myself out from behind the register. I plucked two bottles of water from the soda fountain's cooler and said, "I'm starved."

"Then let's dig in." Jake's smile was so warm my heart did a little flip.

I handed him one of the waters and dropped tiredly on the stool next to him. Without any help in the store, I'd been on my feet for the past four hours, and I was pooped. The place might not have been busy with customers, but I'd been hard at work on the baskets.

Jake opened the carton flaps and handed me a chicken salad croissant wrapped in waxed paper, a foam tub of fruit salad, a paper envelope of chips, and a fork.

"Hmm." My mouth was already too full to form a sentence of appreciation.

We munched in silence for several minutes until the edge was off our appetites, then I turned away from the food on the counter, looked at Jake, and asked, "Have you heard from Elliot today?"

"No." Jake wiped his mouth with a napkin, opened his water bottle, and took a long drink. "As soon as we're done eating, I'll go call him. If he hasn't heard from Gabriella, then I'm heading to the police station to confess our sins to the chief."

"You better bring your rosary beads and prepare for a stiff penance," I said, snickering. I might be a lapsed Catholic, but I knew the drill.

As Jake chuckled, I casually glanced out the front window and frowned. There was a barefoot woman wearing an extremely short red nightgown staggering down the middle of the street. Leaping to my feet, I rushed to the door, fumbled with the lock, and finally flung it open.

Jake had followed close behind me, and just as I said, "Isn't that Gabriella Winston?" the woman stumbled and collapsed on the asphalt.

Jake and I sprinted toward her. Luckily, there was no traffic, and Jake swung her into his arms and carried her back to the dime store.

"Are you hurt?" Jake asked as he laid Gabriella on the old blanket that I hastily grabbed from the storage room and spread on the floor.

"I don't think so," Gabriella rasped. "But I'm really, really thirsty."

"Here you go." I snatched my untouched bottle

of water from the counter, screwed off the cap, and handed it to the poor woman.

"Take small sips," Jake cautioned, then turned to me and said, "Call nine-one-one."

"On it." I glanced around. Where had I left my cell? While I searched my workbench, I asked, "Should I request an ambulance?"

"Do you need to go to the hospital?" Jake was busily examining Gabriella. He ran his hands up her legs, torso, and down her shoulders. When he reached her forearms, he frowned and asked, "Are you bleeding anywhere?"

"I . . . I don't think so." Gabriella's voice was still husky, but she sounded better.

Seizing my phone from where it had been hiding under a cashmere throw, I said, "Ambulance or police?"

"Neither. The chief's cell," Jake instructed as he dug his own phone from his pocket and tapped the screen. "I'm calling Winston."

While Jake and I made our calls, I watched as Gabriella sat up. Something was nagging at me about this situation, but I had no idea what.

After I told Chief Kincaid that we had Gabriella and that the ransom had been paid the night before, I made sure he was on his way and hung up before he could yell at me.

Kneeling down near the shaking woman, I introduced myself and Jake, then asked, "Can I get you anything?"

She shivered and said, "Do you have something I could put on?"

"Absolutely."

Shit! I was a moron. I hadn't even thought to tell Jake to have her husband bring her some clothes, and doubtlessly Elliot was already in the car on his way.

I got up and walked to the rack that held Scumble River High School insignia athletic wear. I found Gabriella a pair of sweatpants and a T-shirt. When I brought them to her, I glanced down. She needed shoes.

I hurried to the clearance bin and rummaged until I located a pair of flip-flops. They'd been a part of my cupcake contest display and had brightly colored cupcakes painted on the straps. They looked like they'd be a little small for her— Gabriella was a tall woman with long, slender feet—but they'd have to do.

When I gave the sandals to her, she asked if there was a restroom. I escorted her to the rear of the store and left her there with instructions to call me if she needed anything.

By the time Chief Kincaid strode through the door, Gabriella had already returned from the bathroom. She and I were sitting on stools at the soda fountain, and she was nibbling on a cookie. I wondered what took the chief so long to arrive. The police station was only a short walk away. He must not have been in his office when I called him.

The chief's shrewd gaze swept over Gabriella, and I had to give the man credit. Instead of marching right up to her, he approached the traumatized woman slowly.

His hands were loose at his side and his voice was soft when the chief introduced himself and said, "Mrs. Winston, it's a relief to see you."

I had told him she seemed physically fine, but added that we hadn't asked her if she'd been sexually assaulted. That was a subject for the police to broach, not us.

"Thank you." Gabriella gave him a tiny smile. "It's a relief to be here."

"I'd like you to come to the PD and tell me what happened to you," Chief Kincaid said, stepping closer and holding out his palm for her hand.

"I was on my way to the police station when I collapsed." Gabriella cowered against me and grabbed my fingers in a death grip. "But now I'd rather stay here."

"Okay." The chief moved back, then shot me a hard look and said, "Devereaux, did you give Mrs. Winston those clothes she's wearing?"

"Yes." I frowned at his critical tone. Defending myself, I said, "She was barefoot and all she had on was a flimsy nightgown. She was cold." Then I realized the problem and said, "*Hell!* You're saying that Gabriella might have had forensic evidence on her."

"Precisely." A nerve ticked in the chief's cheek, and he turned to Gabriella. "Mrs. Winston, did you put the pants and shirt on over your nightdress?"

"No." Gabriella shrank away from him. "I'd been wearing it since Saturday night. It stank. When I used the restroom, I threw it away."

"I suppose you washed up, too?" Chief Kincaid's jaw tightened.

"As best I could, but I need a shower." Gabriella's forehead wrinkled, then her corn-flower blue eyes widened. "I wasn't raped, if that's what you're thinking. There's no evidence to collect."

"Even without a sexual assault, your abductor might have left DNA that we could use to find him," Chief Kincaid explained.

"You don't need DNA." Gabriella crossed her arms. "Mac McGowan is the one who kidnapped me."

I doubt any of us were surprised at her statement. I knew that I sure wasn't. Still, before Chief Kincaid or Jake could respond, Elliot arrived. He rushed up to Gabriella, pulled her into his arms, and held her tight. I could see the tears in his eyes as he smoothed his hand over her hair and pressed kisses all over her face.

While the couple embraced, the chief keyed the radio clipped to his shoulder and issued an all-points bulletin for the golf pro. He also instructed the officers on duty to start looking for the man, and called a female crime scene tech to come to the store.

As soon as the crime scene tech showed up, she led Gabriella to the bathroom to process her. When they returned, the tech had a case full of samples and a bag with the nightgown that she'd recovered from the trash can.

Once Gabriella was sitting next to her husband on a soda fountain stool, Chief Kincaid asked, "Mrs. Winston, where were you held?"

"I don't know." Gabriella shuddered, burrowing closer to her husband. "Mac put me in some sort of rolling suitcase when he took me from my house. I couldn't see anything, but it felt like he had me in the back of a golf cart, then in a car. After a while he brought the suitcase inside somewhere. He let me out and tied me to a chair, but it was dark and I couldn't see much. I think we were in a basement or a cellar." She took a deep breath and added, "I asked him why he'd taken me, and he said that he was sick of the drug screening and the two-faced old bitches at the country club. He was broke and needed money to get out of town."

"Were you expecting McGowan the evening you were kidnapped?" Chief Kincaid had taken a notepad from his pocked and was jotting down Gabriella's answers. When she didn't respond right away, he looked up and said, "It's my understanding that you had a prior intimate relationship with Mr. McGowan. Is that information correct?"

Gabriella glanced at her husband, then her shoulders slumped and she nodded. "Yes. I had had an affair with Mac, but I'd ended it a few months ago, and I was surprised to see him Saturday night. He'd never come to the house before. But when I opened the door, he pushed his way inside." She turned to Elliot. "I'm so sorry. The kids were gone and you were so tied up with that stupid wildlife park. Mac made me feel beautiful, but I knew it was nothing compared to what we have. I was weak."

"It's my fault." Elliot tightened the arm he had around his wife. "We'll start over. I'll be more attentive. I'll never neglect you again."

Studying Elliot, I wondered how long he'd be able to keep that promise. If Jake's explanation about his obsessive-like personality was correct, in a few months or maybe sooner, something else would catch his interest and Gabriella would be right where she had started. He might love her, but he just didn't seem like he'd ever be able to put all his energy into a relationship with his wife. I hoped I was wrong, but I doubted it.

"Were you kept in the same place the whole time you were missing?" Chief Kincaid refocused Gabriella's attention to his questions.

"Yes." Gabriella trembled. "At first it seemed

that I was alone. Mac only interacted with me to feed me and let me use a bucket in the corner for a bathroom. But the past couple of days I think he was there all the time."

"How did you get away?" Chief Kincaid asked. "Did he let you go?"

"No." Gabriella shook her head. "When he came back last night with the money, he said he'd release me in the morning just before he took off. It was late and he wanted to get some sleep before hitting the road." She took a quivering breath and continued, "But when he woke up and untied me, I saw that he had a gun in his jeans. I knew then that because I could identify him, he wasn't going to free me."

"He planned to kill you." Chief Kincaid made a note. "How did you get away?"

"I . . . I . . ." Gabriella dropped her gaze to her lap. "I suggested we have sex before he left. For old times' sake. And when I got close, I grabbed the gun. I started to edge toward the door, but he rushed me and the gun went off. When he staggered back, I ran outside and into the fields behind the house. And I continued running until I came out on a road that I recognized, then I headed to town."

"Can you lead us to where you were held?" Chief Kincaid asked.

"I got lost and turned around several times before I found a familiar road." Gabriella shook her head. "And I'm not too good with directions to begin with."

"Did McGowan come after you?" The chief asked.

"I never saw him." Gabriella buried her face in her hands. "Do you think I might have killed him?"

"If you did, it was self-defense." Elliot glared at the chief.

Gabriella tugged her husband's head down and whispered in his ear.

He nodded several times, then looked at the chief and said, "Gabriella's been through enough. I'm taking her home." As he led his wife away, he added, "If you have any further questions, contact my lawyer."

CHAPTER 20

I stared at the Winstons' backs as they walked out of the dime store. That had been odd. What had Gabriella said to her husband to make him decide to end the interview? Was she hiding something?

Jake and Chief Kincaid had been silent as the couple made their exit, but now the chief grabbed his radio and instructed the dispatcher to advise the officers searching for Mac that they might be looking for a body instead of a suspect. He also directed the dispatcher to call the county sheriff's office to ask if any recent gunshot wounds had been reported by the hospital or the local doctors.

Once he was finished giving his staff orders, he turned to Jake and me and informed us of his displeasure in our actions—past and present. Among the litany of our transgressions were Jake's failure to inform the chief about the ransom drop and our stupidity in bringing Gabriella to the dime store instead of the police station when we'd found her on the street.

Jake and I waited until Chief Kincaid wound down, then Jake said, "You know that I had to honor my client's wishes. I've only been able to share the results of my earlier investigation with you because Winston gave me permission to do so."

Chief Kincaid grunted, then demanded, "Why didn't you call nine-one-one when you saw Gabriella on the street? Bringing her to the store was foolish."

"She collapsed a few feet from my door," I explained. "She was nearly nude. It seemed best to get her inside and then call for help."

"Why didn't you ask for an ambulance?" Chief Kincaid crossed his arms.

"When she said she was unharmed, I assumed you'd want to talk to her sooner rather than later." Jake raised a brow. "And if she went to the hospital, it could be hours before the doctors allowed you to speak to her."

"I see. You're certainly correct about that." Chief Kincaid's disapproving expression relaxed. "Tell me about the ransom drop."

Jake and I went over last night's comedy of errors, which seemed to put the chief in a better mood. He actually chuckled when we described where I'd been hiding and what had happened to the pumpkin.

When Jake finished his account of the evening, he looked at the chief and asked, "So what's your plan? Do you believe Gabriella's story?"

"I did until she suddenly clammed up and Winston whisked her out of here quicker than my hound dog trees a squirrel." Chief Kincaid rubbed his jaw. "Now I'm wondering what I missed."

"Maybe Gabriella just panicked when she

realized she might have killed a man," I offered. "Up until you asked her about Mac following her, it's possible she never thought about why he didn't come after her."

"Could be." The chief headed for the door. "We won't know a damn thing until we find the place she was being held. I was hoping she could retrace her steps with one of my officers and lead us there."

"Let's give the Winstons some time to calm down, then I'll go over and see if Gabriella would be willing to show me as much as she remembers," Jake said. When the chief frowned, Jake, as if to stop the other man's protest, held up his palms and said, "It may not be ideal, but I think it's our best shot."

"Well . . ." Chief Kincaid exhaled unhappily.

The chief was clearly in a quandary. It was obvious he hated the idea of Jake doing what he considered the police's job. But he was a practical guy and he knew that Jake was right.

"And if Devereaux will go with me, that might be the tipping point for Gabriella," Jake added. "Because Dev was here to take care of her when we first found her, she probably feels some bond with her."

"I don't know about that." The chief studied me and shook his head.

Jake explained, "After her experience with McGowan, Gabriella probably wouldn't be

279

comfortable alone with me or one of your officers. However, if Devereaux is with her, the poor woman might feel safe enough to at least try to find the building."

"Fine." Chief Kincaid's steely gaze zeroed in on me. "But since you aren't employed by the Winstons, even if Jake's clients tell him that he can't give me a full account, I expect you to report back to me."

I glanced between the two men. Did I want to do this? Gabriella was safe. Either her kidnapper was dead or would soon be found by the cops. There was really no good reason for me to get involved.

Except, there had been something off about Gabriella's story. And there was no way my OCD mind would allow me to forget about it until I'd figured out what didn't add up.

Heck. The baskets were finished. My store was closed for the day. Why not spend the afternoon with Jake? Even if that meant tracking down a kidnapper's lair. It was better than getting the oil changed on my Z4, which was the only other item on my to-do list.

And the last time I'd taken my BMW to the local service station, an overgrown hamster with tobacco wads in both cheeks had greeted me as I stepped out of the car. I'd asked the guy to check for a fuel leak.

An hour later when he came back with my

keys, he said the vent line had been goobered up, but they'd fixed it. I'd asked the meaning of *goobered up*. After chewing his cud for a moment, he shrugged and said *goobered up* was just *goobered up*. But it was okay now.

Resisting the urge to slap him until he spoke in a language I understood, I'd paid and left. I wasn't looking forward to another round of trying to translate Redneck into English.

Once I had reassured the chief that I'd give him the full rundown and he left, Jake and I finished our nearly forgotten lunch, and I locked up the store. As we drove to Country Club Estates, I kept replaying our rescue of Gabriella and all that came afterward, but I couldn't figure out what was bothering me.

Jake had texted Elliot that we were coming over, and he was on the front step when we pulled into the driveway. Jake helped me out of the truck, and we made our way up the sidewalk toward Elliot.

"I want to speak to you before we go inside," Elliot said, looking over his shoulder. "Please don't share this with Gabriella."

"Okay," Jake drawled, and I nodded. "What do you want to talk about?"

"Your suggestion that perhaps Gabriella could retrace her path to where she'd been held got me thinking," Elliot said slowly. "If McGowan was killed when he and my wife struggled for possession of his gun, the ransom money might still be there with him."

"True," Jake said with a patient expression on his face.

"If Gabriella is able to lead you to the building where she was held, I want you to look for the money before you notify the cops."

"I can't do that." Jake's lips thinned.

"Who knows how long the cops will keep it as evidence, and I need it back right away." Elliot lifted his chin. "Now that Gabriella is home safe, I still have a chance to get the wildlife park opened on time. But only if I have that million back."

"In most instances, since you're my client, I'd do what you ask regarding the police." Jake scowled. "But I can't remove evidence."

"Let me take you for a ride through the wildlife park." Elliot tugged on Jake's arm. "I'll show you why it's so vital that it opens."

"Sorry." Jake freed himself from Elliot's grasp. "I can't do anything illegal."

"Then you might as well leave." Elliot turned to go. "Gabriella won't cooperate with either you or the police department."

"She might if I tell her why you want the ransom back," I snapped, then could have bitten my tongue. I needed to keep my mouth shut. This was Jake's case, but Elliot's pigheadedness bugged me.

"Wrong." Elliot smirked. "If you tell her what I'm going to do with the money, she'll never show you or the cops where she was kept."

Damn! He had a point. I glanced at Jake, whose expression should have scared the crap out of Elliot. At least if the man had any sense.

Apparently, Elliot lacked even the most basic of survival instincts, because his posture remained defiant. Scowling, Jake took my hand and led me back to his truck.

Once we were out of earshot, Jake said, "Winston has us in a bind."

"He does," I agreed, not sure where we were headed with this conversation.

"I'm going to let him show us the park and agree to recover the ransom for him," Jake said, surprising me. Then he added, "But if we find the place Gabriella was held, I'll call the police."

"You have no choice." I could see how much Jake hated having to lie, so I tried to lighten the mood. "You'd better get a check from him for the rest of your fee before we leave."

Jake looked at me like I'd gone crazy. Then I winked, and he smiled.

We walked back to where Elliot was waiting, and Jake said, "I'll look at your park."

Fifteen minutes later, I was riding in the back of Elliot's Land Rover admiring how much he'd accomplished in his preparations for the refuge. There was already a massive fence surrounding the acreage, insuring that the neighboring properties were completely safe.

Elliot pointed out the expansive grasslands where bison, deer, llamas, and camels would roam, as well as various shelters for the animals. He also showed us where an administrative building and information center would be located. And the spot reserved for the nursery where any animals born on the property would be boarded.

As Elliot continued down the road, heading toward the back, I assumed we would see more pastures. Instead, we came to another heavily fenced area, but this one was electrified. He got out of the SUV, opened a gate with a key, drove through, got out, and locked it behind us.

"This location has been designed for the large predators," Elliot said, gesturing to the enclosed acreage. "They'll be free to roam the grasslands. And although you can't see them, dens have been dug forty feet underground for the animals to take shelter from extreme temperatures. It's not exactly living in the wild, but it's close."

"Nice," I said. "But wouldn't putting them back in the wild be better?"

"Definitely," Elliot said, then his tone regretful, he explained, "However, that's not always feasible. Or even the best choice for certain creatures born in captivity. Our animals will be rescues from illegal or inhumane confinements.

Many will have reached the point where, if a spot can't be found for them, they are too ill to be released and would have to be euthanatized. Here, we'll provide medical treatment and, when possible, integrate them into social groups."

"But you'll still allow people to view them," I said, trying to recall the article that I'd read that had listed all the negatives about wildlife parks. "Won't that cause undue stress?"

"We will allow visitors," Elliot said, then pointed to the left. "But see that? We're building elevated walkways that will wind throughout the sanctuary." He beamed. "The boardwalk will ease the trauma of having humans at eye level. This way, the animals' territory won't feel as if it's being invaded."

"Are there really enough animals to fill a place like this?" Jake asked. "It seems like a lot of property for a few homeless critters."

"A thousand times over." Elliot's expression turned grim. "I've already received more than fifty messages from various zoos attempting to locate a good home for their overflow of wild animals."

"How in the world will you fund the park once it's up and running?" I asked. "The food and staff will cost several million a year, and there's no way you'll have enough visitors to run in the black."

"That's certainly true." Elliot nodded. "That's

why most of the costs of the refuge will be covered by donations, both money and food, and a lot of our staff positions will be filled by academics volunteering to care for the animals in order to study them."

As Elliot showed us the rest of the park, I had to admit, I wished there was a way for Jake to rescue the ransom money in time for the park to go forward. This sanctuary was clearly Elliot's dream. Something he'd been envisioning and working on for a long time.

The wildlife refuge was almost in his grasp, but he'd sacrificed his life's ambition to save his wife. And he'd done it even after he'd been told about her infidelity. Elliot's devotion, despite Gabriella's betrayal, was what true love was really all about. He might get obsessed with a project and not always show his feelings, but he did love her.

Suddenly, it felt as if one of Elliot's future tigers landed on my chest and settled in for a nap. I stared at the back of Jake's head. He had done the same for me that Elliot had done for Gabriella.

First, Jake had taken an early retirement from the U.S. Marshals so he could live in Shadow Bend. Yes, he'd said it was because he feared his injured leg would compromise the safety of his team, but he could have stayed on in a support or training position.

Second, even though I had denied being bothered by it, when he realized how much having his mentally ill ex-wife living at his uncle's ranch upset me, he'd figured out a way to both help her and make things okay for me. He'd put my feelings first, assuring me that he'd send her back to St. Louis if that was what I wanted. If that's what I needed.

Third, he'd worked out a way for us to spend more time together. He hadn't asked me to carve a window in my already busy life, he'd made the change. He obtained his private investigator's license and rented the office space above my store.

And to top it all off, although he clearly didn't enjoy seeing me in danger, he'd welcomed me as a part of his PI firm. It was unofficial for now, but he'd talked about me getting my license.

I wasn't sure when or how it had happened, but I loved him. Maybe it was when he'd refused to give up on us all through my vacillating between him and Noah. I realized that Jake's love made me feel free rather than trapped. Even more than that, it gave me a sense of security that I hadn't felt since my world exploded when my dad went to prison. Not only did I love Jake, I trusted him.

I tested the word in my mind. Yes, I truly did trust him. Up until Jake, the only person I had ever completely trusted was my grandmother. I was still gradually learning to trust my dad. Definitely not my mother.

Searching my heart, I realized that no matter what Noah said or did, I would never truly believe that he wouldn't hurt me again. I might as well stop ignoring the truth, because when all was said and done, I'd never be first in his life. That position was already taken by his mother, and no matter how many buckets of water I threw at Nadine, she wouldn't melt away.

Hell! I wouldn't even come second to Noah— that spot was reserved for his patients. And being number three wasn't good enough for me.

Noah was just an old high school flame that I had always imagined rekindling. He was the boyfriend who showed me how far I'd come, not how far I could go. I still loved him, but not the way I needed to love the man whom I wanted as a husband.

Leaning forward, I traced Jake's jaw with my finger, enjoying the slight prickle of the stubble on his face. He turned and raised an eyebrow, but I just smiled and sat back. I couldn't wait to let him know how I felt about him, but we weren't alone and I really needed to talk to Noah first. It was only fair that I tell Noah my decision before Jake and I started to make plans for our future.

CHAPTER 21

Noah tossed the phone into its base and frowned. Dev had asked him if he'd meet her at Gossip Central. Ordinarily, he'd be ecstatic that she had reached out to him, but something felt off. It was odd for her to want to see him on a weeknight. Even stranger for her to be so spontaneous.

He drew his brows together, contemplating the various possibilities. He could only come up with two reasons for their impromptu date. In one scenario, tomorrow morning he would be in Kansas City at the best jewelry store in town. In the second, he would be too hungover to go to work. Either way, it was a good thing he was scheduled for the afternoon shift at the clinic.

Unsure whether he should be whistling or moaning, Noah strode from kitchen into the den. He wasn't meeting Dev until seven, so he had some time to kill. Flopping down on the sofa, he grabbed the remote and turned on the TV. After several minutes with no idea of what he was watching, he switched it off.

Gazing around the room for something to do, it occurred to him once again that this was the only spot in his house that felt like home. He really needed to make some changes in the rest of the place.

When he'd bought it nearly three years ago, he'd told the decorator to do whatever she wanted. Then, after she'd finished and he'd written her an obscenely large check, he'd been sorry that he hadn't participated more in the process. The only reason that he'd hired an interior decorator in the first place was because it had been easier than fighting his mother.

Nadine had insisted someone of his background needed a showplace, not a comfortable bachelor pad. And because he had never liked conflict, his mother always got her way. He scowled. How could he have been so weak? It was almost as if he took the course of least resistance.

Was that true in his pursuit of Dev? Did he truly love her, or had they just drifted back together when the obstacles in their path had been cleared? Yes, his mother had been opposed to their relationship, but nearly everyone else in Shadow Bend was happy to see them reunited. Folks liked the idea of first love winning out over all roadblocks.

He certainly cared for Dev and was attracted to her, but was that enough?

Checking his watch, Noah saw that he had an hour before he had to leave for the club. He jumped to his feet, strode down the hall, and into his home gym. Stripping down to his shorts, he pushed the play button on his CD player and Puff Daddy's "Victory" blared from the speakers. The slow intensity suited his current mood.

Noah pulled on fingerless leather gloves, lay down on the bench, and started his routine. He couldn't seem to get past two hundred pounds, and the muscles in his arms strained to raise the heavy barbells again and again. A few minutes later, sweat was pouring off his face.

He was surprised that he enjoyed the monotonous activity, but it was oddly soothing. He'd never been the athletic type, but on a dare he'd enrolled in a weight lifting class in college and discovered that he liked it. It was good to do something that required brawn instead of brains. Something primitive.

Once Noah got into his rhythm, his mind wandered. Shoving away thoughts of Dev and their upcoming date, he thought about Mac McGowan. He'd heard that the golf pro had kidnapped Gabriella Winston and was now missing.

Despite his heinous crime, Noah felt sorry for the guy. The man had been working hard on resisting his addictions. He'd joined NA and talked about going to meetings several times a week.

Mac had mentioned that he had fallen in love and was trying to straighten himself out for that woman. Noah had been fairly sure the lady in question had been a country club member and already married. It wasn't as if Mac had admitted any of that, but he had said that he needed to get his act together and be more than she already had at home.

Wait a minute. Noah stopped in midlift. Could Mac have meant Gabriella? But if that were true, would he have kidnapped her? Maybe he thought that once he had the money, she'd forgive him.

Completing the upward thrust of the barbell, Noah considered that explanation. Mac had seemed like such a gentle guy. More of a follower than a leader. Certainly not someone capable of planning a complicated kidnapping scheme and carrying it out.

Still thinking about Mac, Noah finished his workout, wiped his face and neck with a towel, and rose from his prone position. Grabbing a bottle of water from the mini fridge, he took a long swallow and wondered if he should tell Dev about his impression of the golf pro. It wasn't as if his opinion of the man's personality were covered by doctor-patient confidentiality.

Noah smiled. Dev would like that Noah was willing to help with Deputy Dawg's case, and the information would be harmless. She wouldn't be in any danger, because Gabriella was home and Mac was missing. And best of all, Noah would look good in her eyes.

Turning off the music, Noah strolled into the master bath and turned on the shower. Lucky was asleep in the sink, but the Chihuahua barely opened one eye before returning to his dreams.

Sometimes Noah wondered if the little animal realized he was a dog and not a cat.

Occasionally, Noah thought he should swear off women altogether and stick with dogs. Dogs never ask about the previous dogs in your life. They don't get upset if you pet another dog. And the later you get home, the happier they are to see you.

Grinning at the notion, Noah showered, dried off, and shaved. After splashing on cologne, he walked into his closet. Pulling on freshly pressed jeans and a blue and white striped Oxford shirt, he rolled up the sleeves, shoved his feet into loafers, and grabbed his car keys and wallet from the top of the dresser.

It was time to head to Gossip Central and find out what his future would be.

Walking into Gossip Central, Noah heard shouting. He tensed, then saw the table full of men in the Sports Pen, an area corralled on three sides and facing the front of the club. The guys were watching the TV over the bar and cheering for the Kansas City Royals.

Gossip Central had originally been a cattle barn, and when Poppy purchased the property, she had kept that theme. A stage, dance floor, and curved mahogany bar occupied the center of the barn, and what had once been the hayloft was now a space that could be rented for private parties. The stalls had been transformed into secluded little spots with comfortable seating and themed decorations.

Secluded, that is, except for the concealed listening devices. Poppy had confided in Noah that she liked to know what was being said in her establishment. She never shared the information with anyone, except occasionally Boone and Dev, but she enjoyed the power.

Poppy glanced up from the pitcher of beer she was drawing, gave Noah a warm smile, and said, "Dev's waiting for you in the Drive-In."

The Drive-In was the smallest of the converted stalls, and the only one with a door that could be closed. Its theme was a drive-in theater. It was intended as a romantic hideaway for two, and the booth was the front half a Chevy Bel Air. The table was a tray that was originally designed to hook to the car's side window, but was now on a stand in front of the driver and passenger seats. Coming attraction posters on the wall featured ads for *Some Like It Hot* and *A Streetcar Named Desire.*

When Noah entered, he saw Dev staring into her wineglass. The expression on her face wasn't one of a woman about to declare her undying love and devotion.

When Noah drew in a pained breath, Dev glanced up at him and said, "Could you close the door?"

"Sure." Noah's chest tightened.

Noah slid into the passenger seat. Dev opened her mouth, but seemed at a loss as to what to say. Finally, she poured him a glass of wine and pushed it toward him.

"It's that Bordeaux you like." Dev watched him as he picked up the glass.

"Thanks." Noah had a feeling that he would need something stronger than wine. They sipped in silence until he said, "I was surprised when you called. You're not usually so spur-of-the-moment."

"True." Dev toyed with the stem of her glass. "The thing is—"

Wanting to put off what he was afraid she was about to tell him, Noah said, "Before I forget, I heard about Gabriella Winston's return and that she claims that Mac McGowan was the one that kidnapped her." He raised a brow. "That had to be a shock."

"Yep."

"For me, too," Noah said. "I know Mac, and he seems like a really gentle guy. He never struck me as someone who thought for himself. And definitely not a guy who was capable of planning a complicated kidnapping scheme and carrying it out."

"Really?"

"He told me that he had fallen in love and was trying to straighten out for the woman," Noah continued. "He said that he had to get his act

295

together and be more than she already had at home."

"Well, that's interesting," Dev murmured, then snickered. "I wonder if he was involved with a modern-day Bonnie and he had to outdo Clyde."

"Maybe." Noah shrugged. "But my impression was that she was already married and her husband was wealthy."

"That would fit a lot of the country club crowd." Dev wrinkled her brow, then shook her head. "Anyway, I asked you to meet me to talk about us."

"Oh." Noah took her hand and asked, "Is there going to be an us?"

"Noah." Dev eased her fingers from his and cupped his cheek. "I'm so, so sorry. Although I know it's as painful for you to hear as it is for me to say, what we have is affection and friendship, not the kind of love we'd need to sustain a forever marriage. I never want to hurt you, and sooner or later that's what would happen if we were to get married. One or both of us would feel that something was missing from our relationship and look elsewhere. Or if we didn't actually cheat, we'd want to do it."

"So you've decided on Del Vecchio." Noah fought to keep his voice from cracking. "He's all sizzle and no substance. We have more than just chemistry. We have a common past and the same kind of goals."

"See"—Dev's tone was gentle—"that's what I mean. You love me, but you aren't in love with me. Your reasons for us to be together are all sensible ones, but you would never give up everything to be with me. You would never be able to put me ahead of your mother or your patients. Jake has proved that I'll always be first for him."

"You weren't first when he brought his ex-wife back here to live with him," Noah snapped.

"But when he realized how much that bothered me, he made it right." Dev stroked Noah's jaw with her thumb. "I know that there is someone somewhere who can be *more* for you than I am. A woman who will fill your heart and your dreams. She's out there right now waiting for you. And when you find her, you'll see that I'm not that *more* that you deserve."

"Is there anything I can say or do that will change your mind?" Noah's throat had closed and he had trouble pushing the words out.

"I'm sorry, no." Dev scooted out of the booth and stood. "I will always treasure your love and our friendship, but I've made up my mind."

Noah watched Dev open the door, then, without glancing back, she walked away.

"Son of a bitch!" Noah roared as he slammed his fist onto the table. When the wine bottle wobbled, he grabbed it and filled his glass to the brim.

He blinked back the tears that threatened to leak down his face. Where was his famous cool demeanor? He refused to sit there and cry over a woman who didn't want him. Instead, he gulped down the contents of his glass, then refilled it again and again.

Noah wasn't sure how long he sat drinking, but the wine bottle was empty and his mind was fuzzy. He knew he should get up and leave, but he couldn't find the energy to stand, let alone walk out of the bar. Not to mention that he shouldn't get behind the wheel.

This was all Del Vecchio's fault. Picturing the asshole's face on the wall next to the booth, Noah drew back his fist, but before he could swing, he heard a soft voice say his name.

Poppy stood in the open doorway, her platinum blond hair like a halo of light around her beautiful face. Her gorgeous amethyst eyes were full of sympathy and something else. Something he might be able to name if he were sober.

Without a word, Poppy slid in next to him and put her arms around him. He leaned against her, buried his face in her neck, and let his tears fall.

CHAPTER 22

Although I should have stopped to talk to Poppy on my way out of Gossip Central, I'd been afraid that if I opened my mouth to speak the tears clogging my throat would escape, and I hated crying. She knew that something was up because I had asked her to reserve the Drive-In for me and Noah. But my guess was that she thought I was telling him that he was the one for me, not breaking up with him.

I had a restless night and felt like crap the next morning, but I had to open the dime store. Friday was Dad's day to work the afternoon shift and I couldn't justify asking him to switch just because I didn't sleep well. Especially since I wasn't sure if he was alone in his bed or if Catherine had stayed over.

He'd mentioned that Wednesday dinner at her house had been so nice, he'd invited her out again on Thursday, so she might be in his apartment right now. She seemed nice and I was happy that Dad was dating, but that was about as much as I wanted to know. Seeing her behind him, possibly only wearing one of his T-shirts wasn't on my top ten list of father/daughter experiences. I'm sure Dad felt the same way about my love life.

Lucky for me and my customers, a pot of

coffee and a half-dozen leftover pecan cookie bars improved my mood. Between the caffeine and sugar, I could almost forget the dejected look on Noah's face.

However, I still wasn't ready to talk to Jake about my decision. It just seemed too coldhearted to go from Noah's misery to what I hoped would be Jake's happiness. Also, I wasn't sure how to tell him or what I expected him to say or do when I did.

If it were the other way around, I was confident that Noah would be buying me an engagement ring before the sun set. But Jake hadn't said anything about marriage. Well, that wasn't entirely true. He hadn't seemed upset with the idea of Gran sending out invitations to our wedding, but he hadn't exactly gotten down on one knee, either. I thought that was what he wanted, but we'd never discussed it, or really anything, about the future.

As I waited on shoppers and stocked shelves, I worked myself up into such an emotional state that I didn't want to be around when Jake got back to his office. I was safe for a while. He'd texted me that he'd be out all morning trying to find where Gabriella had been held hostage. But I wanted to be gone before he returned.

Yesterday afternoon after we'd seen the wildlife park and Elliot had driven us back to his house, Gabriella had reluctantly agreed to show us what she remembered. But none of the country roads she'd led us up and down had panned out, and eventually we'd admitted defeat. At least, Elliot, Gabriella, and I had. Apparently Jake was made of more patient and sterner stuff than the rest of us.

The store was empty when my cell started playing "Sue Me." Since I wasn't busy, I answered it. I'd been expecting Poppy to call, but the *Guys and Dolls* tune was Boone's ringtone, not hers.

With Poppy's hours at the bar it was possible she wasn't out of bed yet, which was my excuse for not phoning her. But I still thought it odd she hadn't contacted me last night to find out what had happened with Noah. Unless he'd told her and she was mad at me.

Poppy had always had a soft spot for the good doctor, and if my suspicions were true, she might have even deeper feelings for him. Would it upset me if the two of them ended up in a relationship? It would certainly be awkward at first, but if they could handle it, so could I.

Before I could consider that possibility further, Boone demanded, "Dev, are you there?"

"Yes. Sorry." Apparently, he'd been talking to me while my minded wandered. "I just lost my train of thought for a second. What did you say?"

"I wanted to know if you were busy this after-noon," Boone repeated. "I'm going over to talk to Riyad Oberkircher about the Malone house, and I need you to go with me."

"For the ghost tour?" I asked. "The Halloween activities are starting next weekend. Isn't it too late to include it now?"

"There's still time if we can get permission in the next day or two. I have an inspector on standby."

"Why do you want me along?" I'd known Boone for too long to think he wasn't up to something. "I'm not on the chamber committee."

"Riyad has a proposition for you," Boone answered. "He wouldn't say what it was, only that if you agreed, he could tell me the name of the owner."

"Fine." I'd wanted to be out of the store when Jake got back. Now I had a good reason. "What time?"

"Can you leave in half an hour?"

"Sure. Dad's coming into take over at two, so that's perfect."

"I'll pick you up." Boone paused, then added, "Put on some lipstick."

"Why?" I frowned. I'd just gotten rid of one extra boyfriend and didn't need a replacement. "It better not be that kind of proposition."

"I don't think you're his type." Boone chuckled. "Riyad likes his women tiny and blond."

With that reassurance, I hung up. As usual, Dad was a few minutes early, so I had time to comb my hair and put on a little mascara and lip gloss. Boone was pulling into a space out front when I walked out the door, and when I slid inside his car, he instantly reversed out onto the street.

We chatted about the upcoming holiday events as he drove to Riyad's office. I didn't want to tell him about my breakup with Noah until I'd talked to Jake. It had just dawned on me that it wouldn't be fair to tell my BFFs before him, which meant, if Poppy ever did telephone, I'd have to avoid her call. If I picked up, she'd get the whole story out of me before I could stop myself.

As I was thinking, Boone pulled into the large lot behind the building that housed Riyad's law practice. It was in one of the newer structures a few streets over from the town square, and although the tan brick and boxy construction lacked charm, it did have plenty of parking.

We left Boone's Mercedes safely ensconced in the rear of the lot, away from any possible dings. As we entered the lobby, Riyad's name was on a door to the left. Boone opened it, gesturing for me to precede him. The petite blond secretary knew Boone and immediately showed us into the attorney's office.

Riyad Oberkircher was sitting behind his desk, busily typing on his keyboard. A large photo of a beautiful saluki was encased in an elaborate silver frame and held pride of place on the desktop. When we stepped into the room, the lawyer looked up, smiled, and straightened the picture.

"Good afternoon, Boone, Dev." Riyad's slight Southern accent always threw me for a loop.

The attorney was a curious mixture. His mother had been from Saudi Arabia and his father was German. How the couple ended up together, let alone living in Cape Girardeau, Missouri, was a story that Riyad had never shared. But the combination of cultures resulted in his exotic appearance and his unusual drawl.

Boone and I returned the lawyer's greeting, then sat in the two chairs facing him.

After a bit of chitchat, Boone said, "I really need to know how to contact the owner of the Malone house." He crossed his legs, straightening the crease on his gray suit pants. "Dev's here, so what do you need from her to in order to tell me who owns the place?"

"Here's the deal." Riyad shoved his fingers through his short black hair. "The owner of the Malone house has always insisted on strict anonymity. Boy howdy, did she insist." He grimaced. "However, when I took over as her attorney a few years back, I was given an envelope with the instructions to open it if she didn't communicate with me at least every four months. Generally, I get a note and a check every quarter, but when it didn't arrive on the first of the month, I waited a few days, then opened the letter this morning."

"I see," Boone said, seeming as confused as I was about my presence.

"Coincidently, you called as I was reading the note." Riyad grinned. "Not to look a gift horse in the mouth, I asked you to bring Dev. You said you were on retainer as her attorney, right?"

"I am." Boone nodded.

"You both agree to keep what I'm about to reveal confidential?"

"Sure." I shrugged, then winked at Boone. "I'm pretty good at keeping secrets, and Boone is if he has to. What's my involvement?"

"The letter stated that I was to contact Devereaux Sinclair, give her the key to the house, and ask her to check the place out," Riyad explained.

"Check it out for what?" I asked. Every word Riyad spoke left me more confused.

"I don't know." The tall, spare man shrugged. "But considering the owner is Roberta Malone, I'm guessing she may have passed away."

"I thought Roberta Malone died in the first fire," Boone said, wrinkling his brow. "That was over ten years ago. If she was still alive, why hasn't anyone seen her since then?"

"My understanding from her previous attorney is that Roberta was a vain woman, and when her face was scarred in that fire she became a hermit," Riyad explained. "She got more and more paranoid as the years passed and has been living almost entirely off the grid."

"How old would she be?" I asked. She'd seemed ancient to me as a teenager, but thinking back, she'd probably only been in her fifties.

Riyad consulted the folder in front of him and said, "Sixty-six."

"But why me?" I shook my head. "The police should be the ones to search the house."

My stomach clenched and I tasted bile. I wasn't eager to find a body. Especially one that might have been there a long time.

"The problem is"—Riyad grimaced—"ethically, I can only turn over the key to you. I don't know for a fact Roberta is dead, so her instructions take precedence over my own inclinations."

"I don't want to do it." I scooted my chair back. "I barely knew Ms. Malone. Why would she choose me, of all people, to find her?"

"Her letter said you were dependable and had grit." Riyad shrugged again. "She didn't think many other people around here did."

"What if I refuse?" I asked.

"I am to wait another three months, then ask the next person on her list."

"Which means there would be no hope of using the house for the ghost tour," Boone whined.

Riyad pointed a finger at Boone and said, "Bingo."

"If we find her body, you won't be able to use the house anyhow," I grumbled. "And if we don't, you still won't have permission for the second inspector, so this whole thing is an exercise in futility."

"Still"—Boone's expression became more somber—"you can't in good conscience ignore the fact that if you don't do as Roberta asked in her letter, she might be lying there dead for over half a year."

"And although it's highly unlikely," Riyad said, joining in the conversation, "Ms. Malone could be ill or injured and waiting for help."

"Highly unlikely, my butt," I snapped. "Try bloody miraculous."

"I'll go with you," Boone offered. "We can do it right now and be done with it."

"Fine." I crossed my arms. "But let me go on record as saying this is a bad idea."

The men were right. There was no way I could sleep at night if I didn't go check out that house. Best-case scenario, we'd discover that Roberta was fine and had just forgotten to contact her lawyer. Which meant we'd probably be greeted with a shotgun. Worst-case scenario, we'd find her body. Even worse, she'd turned into a vampire.

Okay, that last probably wouldn't happen, but it was almost Halloween, so you never know. Maybe we should stop somewhere and pick up some garlic or a cross. And a nice solid wooden stake might be good, too.

While my mind wandered, Boone and Riyad

had stood and were shaking hands. The men were now looking at me as if I'd missed something.

Boone poked my shoulder and Riyad said, "Here's the key. Please let me know after you've finished at the house."

"Of course," I murmured, biting my tongue to stop any of the hundred snarky comments in my brain from spilling out of my mouth.

Once Boone and I were back in his car and he was driving toward the Malone house, I said, "You know there isn't a chance in hell the chamber of commerce will be able to use Roberta's place on the ghost tour."

"I guess." Boone sighed, then after a long moment of thoughtful silence, he brightened. "We can use the library. We just got the reward money a few weeks ago and renovations haven't been started yet."

"Perfect."

Just a few months ago, Boone, Poppy, Noah, and I had uncovered a fortune in hidden Civil War treasure. The federal government had claimed it, but given Shadow Bend a hefty reward. A good chunk of it was being used to reopen our town library, which had been sitting empty for many years. The old building was pretty spooky and would be a good stop on the ghost tour. Especially the creepy basement.

"I hope no one has cleared out all the cobwebs," Boone mumbled.

Ignoring his muttering, I said, "Now that we have the key and Riyad is off the hook, why don't we just call Chief Kincaid and ask him to send an officer for a wellness check?"

"Oberkircher may have fulfilled his ethical duties, but we haven't." Boone frowned at me, then grinned. "Besides, this will be an adventure."

"Famous last words," I sneered. "This is a bad decision."

"Bad decisions make good stories," Boone teased as he pulled into Roberta Malone's dandelion-covered driveway.

Pointing to the tire tracks in the weeds, I said, "Someone else has been here."

"Probably just teenagers looking for a good spot to drink or make out."

"Uh-huh." I twisted my lips. "I don't have a good feeling about this."

"Then let's get this show on the road before you chicken out." Boone parked the car.

As I made my way up the cracked sidewalk, I noticed a well and the generator hooked up to the huge propane tank that Vivian had mentioned. It was a lot easier living off the grid when you could avoid utility bills by producing your own electricity and water.

When I approached the front entrance, I saw that it looked brand-new and realized that it must have been replaced after the latest fire. The firefighters would have needed to break into the house to put out the flames.

Inserting the key, I closed my eyes and turned the knob. The door swung open on well-oiled hinges, and we crossed the threshold. We stood in the French Colonial's large vestibule, and I gazed at the mural on the staircase wall. It was peeling and so faded I couldn't decipher its original image. There was a thin layer of dust everywhere, but no indication of the recent fire.

"I don't smell any decomposition," I said. "That's a good sign."

"Maybe." Boone shrugged. "We've had a pretty dry summer. If she's been dead awhile, she could be nearly mummified."

"Oh." I swallowed the bile rising in my throat from that thought, then said, "It just occurred to me, wouldn't the firefighters have found Roberta when they put out the fire in the basement?"

"Unless she was okay at the time of the fire and hid."

"True," I agreed, then asked, "Where should we start looking?"

"Let's clear this floor first," Boone said. "Then check the second story."

Boone was a big fan of the various *Law & Order* television shows and viewed himself as attorney Jack McCoy or Detective Nick Amaro, depending on the day.

There was nothing amiss in the dining room

or parlor, but as we moved past the staircase and into the study, it was evident that someone had recently been living in the place. Crumpled potato chip bags were strewn around the old leather couch, and the nineteenth-century Regency-style library table was littered with abandoned beer cans and wine bottles. Liquid had leaked out of the containers, marring the tabletop's finish.

I cringed at the mistreatment of the beautiful antique. The mahogany with satinwood banding and gorgeous down-swept legs that ended in brass casters made me drool. It would bring close to three thousand dollars if the owner could bear to part with it.

The room across the hall probably had been originally designed for another use, but someone had transformed it into a makeshift boudoir. A queen-size air mattress, featuring a built-in air pump, and even an attached headboard took up most of the floor.

Stepping closer, I rubbed the sheet between my fingers. It was Egyptian cotton and had to have at least a four hundred thread count. I examined the pillows. They were goose down and enclosed in satin cases. I had never seen such a luxurious inflatable bed.

Turning to Boone, who had been conducting his own investigation, I said, "Whoever has been sleeping here has expensive tastes."

Boone handed me a bottle of cologne and

winked. "I would say so—this is Virgin Island Water by Creed, and it runs close to two hundred bucks an ounce."

"Wow." I looked at the label, sniffed the cap, and asked, "Is this a men's or a women's fragrance?"

"Both." Boone shook his head. "I just read an article about it, and it's unisex." He grinned and pulled a suitcase into view. "But these are definitely men's clothes."

"Was Roberta seeing someone?" I frowned, then shook my head. "That sure doesn't seem like the recluse that Riyad described."

I led Boone back to the hallway and into the kitchen. It, too, showed signs of recent occupancy. There was a half-full carafe in the Mr. Coffee, dirty dishes were piled in the sink, and foam take-out containers overflowed the trash.

I felt a slight breeze and glanced toward the back door. A corner of the cardboard taped over its broken window had come loose. Why would Roberta need to break into her own house?

As I thought about it, something caught my eye, and I looked down. A tennis shoe–clad foot was sticking out from behind the kitchen table.

I moved slightly forward for a better view, then recoiled. We had found a body, all right. But it wasn't Roberta Malone. Instead, lying there with the bullet hole in his chest and a gun beside him was Mac McGowan.

Evidently, Boone and I had discovered where Gabriella had been held during her kidnapping. And it seemed clear that she *had* killed her captor. Did that mean the ransom money was somewhere in the house, too?

CHAPTER 23

"Can you repeat that?" Jake asked, certain he'd heard Deveraux wrong. "I think we must have a bad connection or something."

"Boone and I found Mac McGowan's body at the Malone house." Dev's voice sounded shaky. "Chief Kincaid is on the way, but I thought you might want to come here as well." She paused, and her voice was steadier when she said, "You know, as Elliot Winston's representative."

"Not as your boyfriend?" Jake teased. He loved Dev's independence, but he sure as hell wished she'd lean on him a little more.

"That would be good, too." Dev's exhale was audible. "I am sort of freaked out, and Boone is nearly catatonic. Evidently, playing detective isn't as fun as he expected it to be."

"Where did you say you were?" Jake asked. He'd never heard of the Malone house. After Dev described the place and gave him directions, he recalled seeing it on the road behind the Sinclair property. Grabbing his hat, he said, "I'm on my way."

Jake had just gotten to his office when Deveraux had called. He hadn't had any luck finding where Gabriella had been held. A lot of the country roads looked alike and were unmarked, so he could understand how she'd gotten turned around, but he'd hoped that if he drove up and down them, he'd spot something.

Now, as he returned to his pickup, hopped inside, and headed toward the crime scene, he realized that Devereaux had solved the mystery for him. She hadn't said if the ransom had been found, but if it had, the police already had it, and Winston couldn't blame him that the cops had the money in custody.

Jake rubbed his chin. He still wasn't entirely clear about why Deveraux and Boone had been the ones checking on the owner rather than law enforcement or Roberta Malone's attorney.

Maybe he should have one of his friends from the marshal service run Riyad Oberkircher's name through the system and see if anything popped on him. Jake was furious that the man had sent Deveraux into what could have been a dangerous situation. Had Oberkircher even considered that she might need more backup than Boone?

A long ten minutes later, Jake slowed as he approached the driveway. There wasn't a house number on the rickety mailbox, but the multitude of police vehicles was a damn good indication that he was at the right place.

Pulling his truck onto the side of the road, Jake jumped out of the cab and hurried toward the door. Although Dev had said she was fine,

316

she'd sounded rattled. He was anxious to see for himself that she was okay.

Before Jake reached the front step, an officer with a prominent paunch blocked his path and ordered, "You need to return to your pickup, sir. This is a crime scene and no one is allowed inside."

"Is Chief Kincaid here?" Jake asked. No way was this guy keeping him from Devereaux.

"The chief is busy." The officer puffed out his chest, which was hard to do, considering the size of his belly. "I'm in charge."

"I understand that." Jake had run into men like this guy before. Full of their own importance and on the downward slide to retirement. He glanced at the man's name tag and said, "Officer Krefeld, I've been consulting with Chief Kincaid on this case. Please tell him that Jake Del Vecchio would like to speak to him."

"This ain't my first rodeo, cowboy," Krefeld sneered, cocking an eyebrow at Jake's Stetson. "The chief told me not to let anyone inside, and that's what I'm doin'." He fingered his gun. "You march your ass off this property before I accidently discharge my weapon."

The longer Jake stood arguing with this dickwad, the more he felt the need to see Devereaux. He could doubtlessly disarm this jerk before the idiot knew what had hit him, but Chief Kincaid wouldn't be happy if Jake made one of his officers look like an incompetent buffoon.

Holding up his hands, Jake backed away and headed for his truck. Behind the wheel, he sent Dev, Boone, and the chief a text, hoping one of them would get him inside. After several minutes with no responses, he turned on the engine, slammed the gearshift into drive, and pulled onto the road.

Once he was out of sight, he parked and considered his options. There was nothing on this stretch but fields. The next house was several miles away. Except . . . he paused . . . the Sinclair acreage was across the field from the Malone property. Could he come in that way? Maybe the officer guarding the rear of the house would be more reasonable than the one out front.

He sent another trio of texts explaining his plan, then drove to Dev's place and parked on the concrete apron beside the garage. He marched to the rear of the Sinclairs' land and stood next to their old barn. Getting his bearings, Jake realized that it was less than half a mile between the two properties. In fact, he could see people moving around near the Malone back door.

As he started across the empty pasture, a sign nailed to a fence post caught his eye: PRAYER MAY BE THE BEST WAY TO FIND JESUS, BUT TRESPASSING IS FASTER.

Chuckling, he noticed that there was a path of flattened grass in the direction that he was headed. If this was the route that Gabriella had taken during her escape, why hadn't she recognized the area yesterday when they'd driven past the Sinclair land?

Still, someone had recently used this shortcut, and he doubted it was Deveraux, her father, or grandmother. Could it have been McGowan?

Tucking that idea into the back of his mind, Jake walked the last few feet and paused at the Malone property line. The man and woman dressed in white Tyvek coveralls, booties, and rubber gloves stopped what they were doing and stared at him in silence.

Raising his voice, Jake said, "Could you please tell Chief Kincaid that Jake Del Vecchio is here and would like to speak to him?"

"Sure." The woman stepped through the open door and yelled, "Chief, Jake Del Vecchio here to see you." There was an indistinguishable reply, then the woman moved back out and said, "Go ahead. They're in the parlor."

"Thanks." Jake touched the brim of his Stetson, then walked across the lawn.

As he neared the door, the male tech stopped him and handed him disposable covers for his boots, then said, "You need to put these on before you go inside." After Jake complied, the man offered him a pair of gloves and added, "Wear these if you need to touch anything."

Putting the gloves in his shirt pocket, Jake

entered the kitchen and glanced at the man crouching near the body. He was wearing a black vest with the words MEDICAL EXAMINER stenciled in white. It looked as if he was taking a liver temp to get time of death. Jake nodded to the ME and then hurried down the hall.

When he found the parlor, he scanned the room for Devereaux. She was seated on a threadbare settee, staring out the window. Boone and Chief Kincaid were on the matching chairs. The chief was writing in a notebook, and Boone, after a brief glance at Jake, leaned back and closed his eyes as if he were trying to pretend he wasn't a part of what was going on.

When Dev saw Jake she shot him a dazed look, and he hurried over to her. "Sorry it took me so long to get here. Are you sure you're okay?"

"I'm fine." Devereaux took his hand, and he sat next to her. She tightened her grip on his fingers and asked, "Why the delay?"

Jake explained the situation with the jerk out front, then said, "So I parked at your house and walked through the field."

"Smart." Dev gave him a tiny smile. "Sorry I didn't get your text, but I noticed that there are quite a few dead zones in this place."

"More than you'd ever guess," the chief murmured, his lips quirking upward.

"Oh?" Jake rubbed his thumb over Dev's knuckles and glanced at the chief.

320

"When my officers searched the house, they found Roberta Malone's body."

"Was she murdered, too?" Jake asked. "Gabriella didn't mention anyone else being held captive."

"Hard to say for certain before the autopsy, but she was found in her bed, so it's doubtful." Chief Kincaid shrugged. "Although, if her death was a result of homicide, from what Dev's told me about the letter she left with her attorney and the state of decomposition, it was at least a couple of months ago."

"Any indication of why McGowan picked this place to hold Gabriella?" Jake asked.

"Most likely he saw the article in the paper about the fire and thought it was an abandoned house." Chief Kincaid studied his notes. "Evidently, the only one aware that Miss Malone was still residing here was her attorney. I called the fire chief and he checked his reports. There was no mention of the place being occupied. I surmise that while the firefighters inspected the place, Miss Malone holed up somewhere else. She probably came out of hiding once they were gone and passed away at some later date."

"So McGowan broke in through the back door and set up camp," Dev said slowly. "Do you think he knew Roberta's body was upstairs?"

"The techs said the only footprints in the dust on the stairway were the officer's that found her." The chief rubbed the back of his head. "So the evidence suggests that he was unaware of the deceased's presence."

Before Chief Kincaid could go on, the ME came into the parlor and said, "Could I see you in the kitchen for a moment, Chief?"

Once both men had left the parlor, Dev lowered her voice and said, "Gabriella told us she was held in a basement, right?"

"Yes." Jake studied Devereaux. Where was she going with this line of inquiry?

"I overheard an officer say that the basement had a foot of standing water." Dev wrinkled her brow. "I can't see Mac keeping her down there."

"You're right." Jake glanced at Boone, who still appeared to be in his own little world. "Gabriella would have been in a lot worse shape physically if she'd been in the water for four or five days."

"That was what I thought, too." Dev frowned, then said, "I wonder why she lied."

"I don't know." Jake scratched his jaw. "But something doesn't feel right about this whole thing."

Devereaux opened her mouth, but the chief returned before she spoke and said, "You all can go ahead and leave. Stop by the station tomorrow morning to give your statements."

"Any sign of the ransom money?" Jake asked the chief as they all walked into the vestibule.

"Not so far." The chief shook his head. "But

this place has a lot of hidey-holes. It'll take us several hours to process the entire house."

When Jake, Dev, and Boone got to Boone's car, Dev took the keys from Boone and said to Jake, "Want a ride to your truck?"

"No. When I walked over here, I noticed a path of flattened grass. I want to take another look at it." Jake kissed Devereaux on the forehead. "How about you drop off Boone and I'll come get you at his place? We can go to the Golden Dragon for an early dinner. We need to compare notes and figure out what's hinky about this case."

"Definitely." Dev turned on the car. "Give me an hour to make sure Boone is okay."

"Deal." Jake waited until Dev drove out of the driveway before heading to the backyard. There was something he was missing in this situation, and it would gnaw at him until he figured it out.

As he slowly retraced his steps through the meadow, carefully examining the ground, Jake was more and more convinced that someone had recently taken this shortcut between the Malone and Sinclair properties, and more than once. But if Roberta Malone had been dead for a couple of months, it couldn't have been her.

Then again, why would Mac McGowan use this route instead of driving straight to the Malone place? The house was isolated enough that it was unlikely anyone would notice his comings and goings, and even if there was no garage, he could have pulled his car behind the house to keep it out of sight.

Once Jake reached the Sinclairs' yard, there was no further evidence of a path. The grass looked as if it had been freshly mowed that morning. Deveraux had mentioned that her father was a little fanatical with keeping the lawn looking nice. Unfortunately, Kern's obsession meant any trace evidence was long gone.

Sighing, Jake walked to his pickup and climbed inside the cab. He turned the truck around to face the lane, then braked. If McGowan had used this means to access the Malone property, where had he parked his vehicle? He certainly couldn't leave it in the Sinclairs' driveway.

Glancing at his watch, he saw that he had forty-five minutes before he was supposed to pick up Devereaux. He'd check out the main road on either side of the Sinclairs' land. Maybe he could figure out where McGowan had stashed his car. And if it was still there, there was a chance he'd left the ransom money somewhere inside of it.

After half an hour Jake admitted defeat. There really wasn't anywhere within a five-mile perimeter where McGowan could have concealed his car. Parking it alongside the road for very long would have been too noticeable, and the police that patrolled the area would have investigated.

So if it had been McGowan who hiked back

and forth between the Sinclair and the Malone property, what was the reason? Jake didn't have a clue. Maybe Deveraux would have an idea.

After picking her up at Boone's, Jake summarized what he'd discovered. As he drove them to the restaurant, Dev grew quieter and quieter. It was clear that she was taking in all the information and trying to fit the pieces together.

Pulling into the Golden Dragon's parking lot, Jake recalled his uncle telling him that a year or so ago, after the Methodists put up a new church near the highway, they'd sold their old building to the couple who opened the place. Tony hadn't believed that the citizens of Shadow Bend would support a Chinese restaurant. But if the crowded lot was any indication, the townspeople had embraced it wholeheartedly.

When Jake escorted Dev inside, the smells of ginger, soy sauce, and garlic reminded him that he'd skipped lunch, and his stomach growled. They gave their name to the man at the podium and took a seat on a bench against the wall.

As they waited, Jake's cell buzzed, indicating he had a text. Swiping the icon, he saw Elliot Winston's name on the screen: ANY CHANCE YOU CAN COME OVER AROUND SEVEN TO REPORT ON YOUR EFFORTS AT RECOVERING THE RANSOM? GABRIELLA IS GETTING REST-LESS SITTING AROUND THE HOUSE AND IS LEAVING AT SIX THIRTY TO MEET HER FRIEND

MUFFY FOR A DRINK AT THE CLUB SO I'LL BE ALONE.

Jake ignored the message. He wasn't ready to discuss the situation with his client yet.

He was returning his phone to his pocket when a stunning Asian woman in her early twenties approached and asked, "Del Vecchio?"

"Yes, ma'am." Jake smiled.

The hostess smoothed her tight-fitting dress over her nonexistent hips and seemed to notice Devereaux for the first time. Her brow wrinkled as she gazed uncertainly between Jake and Dev.

Finally, the woman asked, "Is Dr. Underwood joining you? Would you like his customary booth?"

Jake was pleasantly surprised when he saw a flicker of irritation in Devereaux's eyes, and hid his grin when she snapped, "Noah and I aren't attached at the hip. Whatever table you have available is fine."

What was that all about? Jake mentally shrugged, then took Dev's hand and followed the hostess. Maybe everyone's adoration of Dr. Dolittle was starting to bug Deveraux, and if that were the case, Jake couldn't be happier.

They were seated at a table for two tucked into a far corner, which suited Jake to a T. The location provided them with some privacy, and they wouldn't have to worry about being overheard as they discussed the murder.

Once the hostess handed them menus and disappeared, Jake said, "I'm starving. Let's order and then see what we can figure out about the case."

"You read my mind."

Devereaux's smile made Jake's pulse speed up. She was just so damn adorable. And the fact that she was totally unaware of her appeal made her that much more attractive.

When their server appeared, they asked for pot stickers to share, two hot and sour soups, a kung pao chicken for Devereaux, and a moo shu pork for Jake. He requested a beer, and Dev said she was fine with the hot tea and water.

While they waited for their food, Devereaux asked, "Ready to compare notes?"

"Sounds good." Jake poured tea in their cups, and as Dev added half a packet of fake sugar to hers, he said, "Here's what we have. Saturday night, McGowan, who is Gabriella's ex-lover, kidnaps her and takes her to the Malone house. Either before he snatches her or once they're there, he breaks a window in the back door to get inside. Because of the newspaper article about the fire, he assumes that the place is empty."

"So far, I'm with you." Devereaux nodded, using a chopstick to stir her tea. "Go on."

"McGowan holds Gabriella at the Malone place from Saturday night until Thursday morning when she escapes." Jake paused while his beer and their soup were served. Once the waitress left, he continued, "Monday night, Elliot Winston receives a ransom note. The kidnapper doesn't get back in touch with him until Wednesday and then demands the money be delivered that night."

"Which brings us to my first group of problems." Dev took a long drink of water and held up one finger. "Why did it take so long for the ransom note to show up?" She put up a second finger. "How is it that McGowan knew the exact the amount of time it would take Elliot to get the money?" A third finger joined the other two. "And was Mac McGowan really Gabriella's *ex*-lover?"

"My guess is that the note wasn't sent immediately in order to ratchet up Winston's apprehension." Jake ate a couple of spoonfuls of soup before continuing. "And McGowan could have made Gabriella tell him how long it would take for her husband to access the cash." Jake frowned. "But why do you doubt that the affair was over?"

After Dev relayed what Noah had told her, she said, "I know Mac was a player, but it sounds as if he'd found the woman he wanted to settle down with, and despite the incident in the hot tub and their so-called breakup, I think that woman was Gabriella."

CHAPTER 24

I watched Jake's face after I made my pronounce-
ment, absurdly happy that he was thinking it over
before responding. The fact that he always took
me seriously and never tried to brush off my
intuition made me love him that much more. I
couldn't wait to tell him that I had chosen him,
but now was not the time.

"Okay." Jake nodded slowly, took out a memo
pad, and jotted down some notes. "Let's put
Gabriella and McGowan's relationship aside for
a minute and keep going with what we know."

"Sure." I gestured for him to go on while I
finished my soup.

"The ransom was picked up Wednesday night."
Jake paused while the server deposited our pot
stickers in front of him, and after thanking her, he
continued, "Then, sometime Thursday morning,
Gabriella shot McGowan and escaped, running
until she got to town."

"Which brings up even more questions."

I nabbed two pot stickers with my fork and
put them on my plate before Jake scarfed down
the whole order. He ate a lot faster than I did, so
sharing with him was always a challenge.

"Go on." Jake's lips tilted upward, clearly
amused by my attempt to safeguard my dinner.

"Where was Mac's car? Roberta Malone's house didn't have a garage, and it wasn't in the driveway."

"I thought maybe he had parked his vehicle a little ways from your family's property and walked through the pasture. But I examined the area for five miles in either direction, and there just isn't anywhere he could have left it without someone noticing and finding it odd. And if it had been towed and impounded, the chief would have been informed and mentioned it."

"I do think Mac was on our land at some point," I said, then told Jake about the incident with Banshee and the "apparition" in our backyard. After I finished, I said, "That ghost could have been Mac."

"True. Although it could have been someone else, too." Jake polished off the remaining four dumplings on the serving platter, and I was glad that I'd grabbed a couple before he got to them.

"Maybe. Anyway, I think Mac's car was at the Malone house at least some of the time, because there were tire tracks already in the driveway when Boone and I arrived." I ate my first pot sticker before asking, "What's your opinion?"

"Right now, I'm keeping an open mind," Jake said. "Anything else?"

"Well, it certainly looked as if someone was having a good old time staying at the Malone house," I mused. "There were empty beer cans and wine bottles in the study and a comfy queen-size luxury air bed in the room across the hall." I bit my lip. "The more I think about it, the more it looked as if it was a couple staying there. We agree that Gabriella wasn't kept in the basement like she claimed, right?"

"Uh-huh." Jake took a swig of beer. "And from what you described, your hunch that McGowan and Gabriella were still having an affair might be true."

"The only clothes we saw were men's." I wrinkled my nose. "And from what little I know of Gabriella, she wouldn't be happy wearing the same nightgown for so many days."

"Maybe McGowan really did abduct her, but she pretended to go along to keep him from hurting her," Jake suggested.

"I don't think that's what happened. Remember the scene at the Winston house was set up to look like a kidnapping. Since Elliot received the ransom note and Gabriella showed up, we've all been forgetting that. But there's something else. I just can't put my finger on it." I closed my eyes and tried to catch the elusive notion floating around in my head. Finally, my lids popped open and I blurted, "I don't think Gabriella was the victim at all. I think she was the mastermind."

"Explain."

"The soles of her feet," I clarified. "Thursday, when you carried her into the store and she was lying on the blanket, I looked at her feet to figure out what size flip-flops to give her."

"And?"

"And the soles of her feet were dirty, but they weren't scraped or bleeding." I frowned. "If she had run all the way from the Malone place to town without any shoes, they should have been a bloody mess."

"And that's why McGowan's car wasn't at the house," Jake said thoughtfully. "Gabriella drove it and parked it somewhere close to the town square."

"And I bet the clothes she wore all week are in the trunk." I sipped my now cold tea. "She probably changed just before pathetically staggering down the main drag."

"That sounds about right. I did notice Gabriella smelled more like some tropical drink than perspiration when I carried her inside," Jake said.

"Boone found a bottle of cologne called Virgin Island Water, and its scent was sort of like a rummy coconut and lime."

"And the only blood on Gabriella anywhere was a smudge on her forearm, which was probably McGowan's." Jake chugged the last of his beer. "If she wasn't the one who planned the kidnapping, she would have just told us she took the keys from McGowan after she shot him and drove herself to freedom. Why claim she had to run?"

"Which leads us to the million-dollar question,"

I said slowly. "Was the shooting an accident or was it her plan all along to kill Mac? But why would Gabriella do any of it? Why fake her own kidnapping?" I asked, then answered myself. "Because she wanted to prevent her husband from spending all his money on the wildlife park, and as Elliot mentioned and the letter he found from her attorney confirmed, Gabriella had no legal recourse to stop her husband from using his trust fund anyway he chose."

"We need to find McGowan's vehicle before she has a chance to move it." Jake waved over the server, asked for our entrées to be packaged to go, and requested the check. "I doubt she tried for it yesterday, and Winston probably hasn't left her side today, but he texted me that she was getting restless and going out for a drink with her friend Muffy tonight at six thirty. It's six fifteen now. I bet she isn't really meeting her pal. That's just the excuse she gave her husband to get away from him. I bet that she's going to move McGowan's car. Maybe dump it in a lake somewhere."

"And my guess is the ransom money is in that car. We need to catch her in the act, because once she has the cash, we'll never prove she was behind the whole kidnapping scheme." I snatched the remaining pot sticker on my plate and stuffed it into my mouth as Jake paid the bill.

He and I raced to his truck, threw ourselves

inside, and he hit the gas. I held on to the grab handle above the door as he squealed out of the parking lot.

Eyes on the road, he said, "Our best option is to follow her from her house to wherever she's got McGowan's vehicle stashed."

"Won't she notice a huge pickup on her tail?" I asked as Jake took a corner without braking and I tightened my grip on the handle.

"She won't be expecting anyone to be following her." Jake grinned, then winked at me. "And I was a deputy U.S. Marshall, so I damn well should be able to keep her in sight without her noticing."

I nodded, but wasn't as confident as Jake that Gabriella would be as careless as he expected. I sure hoped there were at least a little traffic to conceal our presence.

It was six twenty-nine when we got to Country Club Estates. There was only one way in or out of the development, so Jake tucked his pickup behind a billboard that advertised lots for sale starting at a hundred and fifty thousand dollars. He turned off the lights and the ignition, grabbed his phone, and his thumbs flew over the device's screen.

"What if she left early?" I was worried we'd somehow missed her.

"I just texted Winston to see if the coast was clear for me to stop by." Jake paused when his cell buzzed, read the message, and smiled.

"Gabriella is leaving right now. He advises that I wait thirty minutes."

"Shouldn't we call Chief Kincaid?" I asked, knowing the chief was going to be ticked we hadn't notified him of our suspicions and were following a suspect on our own.

"Probably." Jake grabbed two pairs of compact binoculars from the glove box and gave one to me. "But we really don't have time for the police to get here and take over." He arched a brow. "And do you really think anyone on the Shadow Bend force would be able to follow her undetected?"

"Probably not," I admitted. "But shouldn't we at least let him know what we're doing?"

"We'll notify him as soon as Gabriella leads us to McGowan's car." Jake tensed, then said, "There she is."

He pointed to a red Lexus that was pulling out onto the main road from between the development's pillars. I watched through the binoculars as her taillights faded in the distance, then, at the last possible second, Jake eased the truck into the road and drove after her.

When Gabriella headed toward the country club, it looked as if we were on a wild-goose chase. But then she made an abrupt U-turn and took the route into Shadow Bend. At first it seemed as if she were just aimlessly driving around, but finally she turned into an old Sinclair gas station. And no, my family had no connection with the Sinclair Oil Corporation.

The station was a few blocks over from the town square and had been closed for at least twenty years. No one wanted the property because of the prohibitive cost of removing the underground storage tanks, which meant it was now a derelict eyesore.

Jake parked in front of a dance studio a couple of businesses down. We quickly got out of the truck, and, keeping in the shadows, we crept toward the station. Concealing ourselves behind a huge fiberglass dinosaur statue, we watched Gabriella's movements through our binoculars. She was at the far side of the building, tugging off a tarp from what looked like a compact car.

I stared as she loosened the canvas cover, then whispered to Jake, "Did you say that path between the Malone land and ours led to our old barn?" When he nodded, I said, "Gran stored Dad's Jeep in that barn while he was in prison, and she had it covered with a tarp." I pointed to Gabriella. "I think that that's the same one. I bet if we could see the inside, there would be SINCLAIR printed in red marker."

"Well, that would explain why Gabriella walked between the two properties," Jake said softly. "She must have been trying to find something to conceal the vehicle. Maybe it took her a couple of field trips before she found something."

"I wonder if she forgot that she'd need to hide the car when she plotted the fake kidnapping or if originally Mac was supposed to drop her off." I kept my gaze on Gabriella. The vehicle was nearly uncovered. "Maybe killing her lover wasn't in her original plans."

As the tarp slid to the ground, I whispered, "That's the car I saw Mac driving." As Gabriella walked to the rear of the vehicle, I tensed and tugged on Jake's sleeve. "Shouldn't we call the chief now?"

We watched while she lifted the duffel containing the ransom out of the trunk.

As she dragged the bag toward her Lexus and hoisted it into the back seat, Jake said, "Now we call the cops."

While Jake dialed Chief Kincaid's cell, gave him our location, and explained the situation, I kept an eye on Gabriella. Carrying a black plastic garbage sack, she returned to Mac's car, and, using a flashlight, she began to examine the interior, occasionally tossing things into the trash bag.

I nudged Jake and pointed. He nodded and said into the phone, "She's making sure there's nothing with her prints in the car. I need to stop her before she wipes down the interior." He thrust his phone at me and ordered, "Stay here and talk to the chief."

As Jake sprinted toward Gabriella, I could hear the chief speaking into his radio, instructing all officers to report to our location. We were so close to the police station that sirens immediately filled the air.

My heart thudded louder and louder as I watched Jake and Gabriella arguing. Cold sweat trickled down my sides. The woman had killed once before. What would stop her from doing it again?

I wiped my damp palms on my jeans and sucked in a ragged breath. The cops were close, but I was closer. There was no question; I needed to get to Jake.

Rushing forward, I saw Gabriella nod and drop the garbage bag. Jake took a step toward her, but she darted to the rear of the car and reached into the trunk. I tried to swallow the fear clogging my throat and tell Jake not to follow her, but before I could speak, Jake ran around the fender, and she swung a tire iron at his head.

Jake crumpled to the ground, and I launched myself at Gabriella. Apparently, the surprise that there was another person around caused her to freeze, and as I grabbed her by throat, she fell backward onto the dirty asphalt. I landed on top of her and used the fact that I outweighed her by twenty, or forty, pounds to keep her down.

I risked a glance at Jake and saw that his eyes were closed and he wasn't moving. Tightening my fingers on Gabriella's neck, I snarled, "If Jake's dead, so are you."

CHAPTER 25

When my cell trilled late Saturday morning, I glanced toward my bed. Jake's eyes were closed and an occasional soft snore puffed from his slightly parted lips. I had been sitting in a chair watching him sleep for the past eight hours, all the while fighting the urge to wake him just to see if he was really okay.

Lucky for Gabriella, Jake had regained consciousness a few seconds after being knocked out, and the police had arrived before I could beat the crap out of her for injuring the man I loved. The cops took the pseudo kidnap victim into custody, and, despite Jake's protest, I drove him to County Hospital.

After hours sitting around the ER while Jake was given a variety of tests, we were finally sent home. The doctor prescribed Tylenol, ice, and rest, then instructed us to come back immediately if Jake experienced headaches, short-term memory loss, dizziness, sensitivity to light or noise, fatigue, change in personality, or sleep difficulties.

Still shaken from seeing Jake unconscious even for only a few seconds, I brought him home with me, stripped him down to his boxer briefs, and put him in my bed. Then, after Gran helped me drag the lounger into my room for me to sleep on, Jake and I spent our first night together. It wasn't exactly as I'd pictured it, but just hearing him breathe was better than any sensation I'd imagined.

When my cell *ding*ed for the second time, I cursed myself for not silencing the ringer.

By the time I fumbled the damn device from the pocket of my sweatpants, Jake's eyes had popped opened and he said, "Good morning, sugar."

"Any symptoms?" I asked, ignoring the phone, which chimed again.

"Nope." Jake nodded to my cell and said, "You'd better get that."

Noticing that it was the chief, I agreed and put it on speaker.

"How's Del Vecchio?" Chief Kincaid asked.

"So far, so good," Jake answered.

Pleasantries over, Chief Kincaid said, "The forensics are back, and we're going to begin questioning Gabriella Winston as soon as her lawyer gets here. I thought you two might want to watch."

Jake said, "We'll be there in fifteen minutes."

Happy that I had showered last night, I changed from my sweatpants into jeans, scraped my hair into a ponytail, and washed my face. While Jake cleaned up and dressed, I wrote Gran a note telling her where we were going—she and her friend Frieda were hitting up the garage sales today.

Gran had been a trouper last night when Jake and I showed up and told her what had happened. She'd called Tony to let him know where Jake was and that he was okay. And she hadn't blinked an eye when I led Jake into my bedroom. In fact, I think she was disappointed that I was spending the night in her chair rather than sleeping with Jake.

We took my car to the PD, and Jake was not happy squished into the Z4's compact interior. It was all I could do not to dissolve in a fit of giggles seeing his knees up around his ears and the adorably grumpy look on his face. Considering I hadn't even had a cup of coffee yet, I was in a pretty good mood.

When we reached the station, the dispatcher told us that Gabriella's attorney had just arrived, and he and his client were in the interrogation room. Jake and I were directed to the area behind the one-way glass, where Elliot Winston stood with a thirtysomething brunette.

Elliot was deathly white and barely acknowledged our presence. The woman next to him was the county prosecutor. I'd met her before, but couldn't recall her name. Evidently, Chief Kincaid had told her that he'd invited Jake and me to watch and she wasn't happy, because she scowled at us before silently turning her attention back to the scene in the next room.

The chief was seated across from Gabriella,

and he tapped the file in front of him. "It's all here. You might as well confess."

"I'm the victim." Gabriella fluttered her lashes. "I have nothing to confess to."

"You assaulted Jake Del Vecchio." Chief Kincaid crossed his arms.

"I was defending myself." Gabriella cringed theatrically. "He came at me out of nowhere."

"He wasn't armed, and he was working for your husband." The chief raised a brow.

"It was dark and I didn't recognize him," Gabriella explained.

"Right." Chief Kincaid's tone was disbelieving. "Moving on." He pulled out a piece of paper and put it in front of Gabriella. "We have your prints on the steering wheel of McGowan's car and on the handle of the duffel bag containing the ransom money."

"I drove the car to escape my kidnapper." Gabriella's voice was breathy.

"If you drove, why did you originally state that you ran all the way?" Chief Kincaid's expression was impassive. "And why did you tell your husband you were going for drinks with a friend?"

"You're confusing me." Gabriella frowned at the chief's first question, then to his second said, "I wasn't sure the money would be there until I opened the trunk, and I didn't want to disappoint Elliot if I didn't find it."

"I see." Chief Kincaid selected another page from the folder. "Although you claimed to have been kept in the basement, we found your prints all over the Malone house, and the lab is checking the sheets for your fluids."

Her lawyer whispered furiously into her ear, but Gabriella waved him off. "Mac forced me to have sex with him. We had been lovers, and he wanted to resume that relationship. I felt it was safer to go along with him."

I heard the prosecutor murmur under her breath, "That's right, sweet cheeks, ignore your attorney and keep talking."

"Which brings us to this." Chief Kincaid took a third sheet from the file and showed it to her. "This is your credit card statement. You, not McGowan, purchased the inflatable bed, pillows, and sheets."

"Elliot and I were going camping." Gabriella widened her eyes. "Mac stole them out of our garage when he kidnapped me."

"We'll ask Mr. Winston about this so-called camping trip, so you might want to reconsider your answer," Chief Kincaid warned.

I glanced at Elliot, who shook his head and whispered, "There was no camping trip. Gabriella considered an unheated pool roughing it."

"I . . ." Gabriella bit her lip. "The stuff might not have been for camping."

"So you admit you lied about that and running

from the scene rather than driving the car?" Chief Kincaid pounced.

The prosecutor muttered, "Strike one."

"But let's get back to my other questions." The chief glanced at his notes. "Why did you conceal the vehicle and why steal the tarp from the Sinclairs' barn?"

"Uh." Gabriella seemed belatedly to realize she was being backed into a corner, but again waved off her attorney's urgent whispers. "I told you. I was confused. I think I have PTSD."

"Don't worry, the prisons have counselors you can talk to about that," Chief Kincaid assured her. "However, let's put that all aside for a minute and talk about you killing McGowan."

"That was self-defense!" Gabriella cried. "I had to shoot him to get away."

My stomach clenched as she whispered to her lawyer. *Damn!* That couldn't be a good sign.

Gabriella's attorney abruptly stood and said, "We're done here. My client has nothing more to say."

Was Gabriella about to wiggle out of everything? I looked at Elliot. He was expressionless and made no move to go to his wife.

"You better sit down," the chief said in a conversational voice. "Did you know that the angle and distance of a gunshot can be determined from the crime scene?"

"No." Gabriella shrugged, sweat glistening on

her forehead. "How would I know something like that?"

"I guess you don't watch any police dramas on TV." Chief Kincaid smiled grimly.

"I only watch educational television." Gabriella wrinkled her nose. "Not that trash."

"For which the Shadow Bend Police Department is eternally grateful."

"Why is that?" Gabriella's beautiful eyes held a flicker of unease.

"Because, according to the forensics, there is no way in hell you and McGowan were fighting over the gun when he was shot," Chief Kincaid thundered. "And while you wiped your prints from the weapon, you were too much of an ignoranus to wipe them from the bullets."

"I was not," Gabriella snapped, as her lawyer tried to shut her up. "And don't you mean ignoramus?"

"Strike two." The prosecutor's smile was fierce.

"No. An ignoranus is someone who's both stupid and an asshole."

"Are you going to let him speak to me that way?" Gabriella whacked her lawyer on the shoulder.

The man shrugged.

"You're just a shallow woman who should have been happy with what she had." Chief Kincaid's face was red. "Were your wedding vows 'I will love you forever or until I get bored'? 'Whichever comes first'?"

"Marriage is like a game of cards. You start out with two hearts and a diamond." Gabriella giggled, and I wondered if she were just a touch crazy. "But to win the game, you really need a club and a spade."

"Shut the hell up!" Gabriella's attorney tried to put his hand across her mouth, and she pried it off.

"Instead of appreciating that your husband was trying to do something noble, you were worried that he wouldn't have enough money left to buy you all the *things* you wanted," Chief Kincaid said, quickly continuing his attack.

I was impressed. The chief was really skilled at this. Every word he uttered was like a razor shaving away another layer of Gabriella's deceit.

"That's not true!" Gabriella's expression turned petulant. "Elliot is a do-gooder who has no concept of the value of money." Her voice was sullen, and she pushed away her lawyer, who had resumed begging her to shut up. "I wasn't born with a trust fund. I know what it's like to be poor, and I wasn't going to let that happen again. My husband is an idiot, and I wasn't about to allow him to ruin us."

I looked at Elliot. A single tear rolled down his cheek, and he stood frozen, staring at his wife.

"And you were willing to do anything to stop

your husband from squandering his money?" Chief Kincaid gripped the table edge. "Even commit murder?"

"It was self-defense." Gabriella grew more composed and her words held utter conviction. "I had no choice. I had to protect the money. Mac wanted me to run away with him, but I couldn't do that. He'd never amount to anything. Then after we got the ransom, he refused to go without me."

"So you killed him," Chief Kincaid thundered.

"I had to." Gabriella twitched her shoulders. "Mac just couldn't understand that we were through. It was as if I wasn't speaking English. He stood in the kitchen, staring at me and scratching his head." She snickered. "At least it was a vacation for his balls."

Gabriella's attorney moaned.

"So you never intended to leave your husband?" Chief Kincaid asked.

"Of course not." Gabriella frowned. "Since Elliot wouldn't be able to touch his trust fund for another year, I'd have time to distract him from that stupid wildlife park. Meanwhile, I'd have the million safely tucked away for a rainy day."

"Strike three," the prosecutor crowed.

The chief gathered his papers and tapped them into a neat pile before inserting them into the folder, then stood up. "I hope you enjoy all the luxuries in prison. We have enough evidence to put you away for a long, long time."

"What?" Gabriella blinked as if coming out of a trance. Suddenly, she seemed to realize how truly screwed she was and grabbed the chief's hand. "How about a deal?"

"I can't imagine what you have to trade, but that will be up to the prosecutor." Chief Kincaid shook off Gabriella's fingers, then opened the door to the interrogation room and said to the officer standing on the other side, "Lock her up. I've had enough of this superficial woman's selfishness to last a lifetime."

EPILOGUE

The past week had been surreal. I couldn't believe it was already Saturday again. It seemed that everyone from Elliot Winston to the county prosecutor had wanted to talk to me. Some, like the attorney, I couldn't avoid. Although to be fair, the woman had never handled a fake kidnapping turned murder before, and even with what Gabriella had said to Chief Kincaid, it wasn't quite the confession that would ensure a slam dunk conviction.

The prosecutor had questioned me for several hours and told me that although I might have to testify in court, it was more likely that Gabriella would accept a plea. An offer of second-degree murder was on the table, which, unlike first degree, where the punishment was either death or life without parole, second degree meant only a ten-to-thirty-year sentence.

Evidently, Gabriella's lawyer was trying to get the prosecutor to reduce the charge to voluntary manslaughter or murder in the heat of passion, which would cut his client's time behind bars in half. However, the prosecutor was holding firm. But one way or another, Gabriella was going to prison.

In contrast to my interview with the prosecutor, my conversation with Elliot was brief, but confusing. I still wasn't sure why he'd wanted to speak to me. There was nothing that I could tell him that he didn't already know. And even less, that would make him feel any better. He'd lost both his wife and the wildlife park.

Yes. Once the ransom money was released from evidence, he might be able to get the park back on track. But I wasn't sure his heart was in the project anymore. Elliot was a broken man who seemed lost in his cold gigantic house. I wondered if, after all that had happened, he'd even stick around Shadow Bend.

If my heart-to-heart with the prosecutor and Elliot hadn't been strange enough, there was the meeting with Roberta Malone's attorney. Riyad had informed me that Roberta had named me executor of her will and director of the charity she had established. Her house was to be turned into a shelter for women who had lost their homes due to divorce or widowhood. Roberta had left an enormous trust fund to supply the money to run Malone House and pay me a stipend for my time.

While I was still reeling from that little bombshell, the *Banner* had run an article on the role that Jake's private investigation firm had in solving the kidnapping/murder. Thank goodness, as per my wishes, Jake and the chief had managed to leave out my part in cracking the case. And luckily, very few people knew just how much I had been involved in the process.

Boone had, of course, wanted to hear every detail, and when he and I met Poppy for a drink at Gossip Central so that I could tell them both at once, she had been strangely distant. My first inclination was to ignore the problem between us, but she and I had been friends for too long, so I'd insisted that we get together to talk. Just the two of us. I'd asked her to come to the dime store after it closed at four, and she was due any second.

While I waited for Poppy, I thought about Jake. We'd never gotten together with Gran and Tony to find out what Birdie was hiding. And I still hadn't told him that I'd broken up with Noah, although I'm sure he suspected it when I told him that I would go away this weekend with him.

There just had never been a good time to tell him that I loved him. I wanted it to be a special moment. Somewhere nice with some privacy. An impossible combination to come by, since we both lived with our elderly relatives, and I didn't want to tell him in the store or his office.

But Jake was picking me up at six, and we were heading to Kansas City. We were booked for two nights at the Ambassador Hotel, and no one expected us back until noon on Monday. This was it. I had new lingerie and had made Jake one of my erotic baskets. I would tell him I loved him and then . . .

My thoughts trailed off as Poppy pushed

through the dime store's entrance. I locked the door behind her, and we settled in our usual stools at the soda fountain. I poured us each a cup of coffee and nudged a plate of peanut butter brownies toward her. I figured this conversation would require more than plain chocolate.

Poppy avoided my gaze and said, "I'm not sure why you thought we needed to talk."

"Yes. You do." I narrowed my eyes. "Let's get it out in the open and deal with it."

"I don't know what you mean." Poppy glanced at the brownies, then shuddered and pushed the plate away.

"Yes. You do," I repeated, patting her hand. "We've been friends for nearly twenty-five years. You can't shut me out just because there are things you don't want to face."

"Fine," Poppy snapped. She poked my shoulder with her index finger and said, "How could you hurt Noah so badly? He's such a kind, sweet man. He didn't deserve how you treated him. Do you know he got so drunk after you left him at Gossip Central that I had to drive him home? What if he'd gotten into a car accident and been killed because of you?"

She was right about Noah being a nice guy. But I hadn't had a choice. In our situation, someone was bound to get hurt. Although I was sorry it was Noah, I'd never lied to him, and he knew the risks when we'd started dating. And I knew, no matter what, he'd never drive drunk, so that accusation was baseless.

Taking my friend's hands, I said, "What I did or didn't do to Noah isn't the problem." I grabbed her chin when she tried to turn away from me. "The real issue between us is that you're in love with him."

"I am not." Poppy's beautiful face paled and she blinked back tears. "He's too good for someone like me. He needs someone clean and pure."

"Just because you've sown some wild oats—" I paused when Poppy snorted, then I grinned and said, "Okay, a whole field of wild oats—doesn't make you dirty or unworthy. Noah would never judge you on your past."

"It doesn't matter." Poppy shrugged. "He's too wrapped up in you to ever see me."

"Give him a while. He'll soon realize that although he loves me, he isn't in love with me." I scooted over and put my arm around her slender shoulders. "Once he's had a chance to process things, you need to ask him out. Right now he thinks of you as a friend, but I bet it wouldn't take much to change that to something more."

"Wouldn't it be weird?" Poppy asked, a tiny line between her brows. "Me dating your ex? I don't want to ruin our friendship."

"It will probably be uncomfortable at first," I conceded. "But all I want is for all of us to be happy. If you and Noah become a couple, I think we can get past the initial awkwardness."

Poppy and I talked for another hour, polishing off the plate of brownies and finishing the pot of coffee. When I walked her to the door, I was confident that our friendship could withstand the discomfort of her being with my ex-boyfriend. Thank goodness Noah and I had never slept together. Even as teens we'd never gone all the way.

As Poppy stepped over the threshold, I warned, "Make sure you don't wait too long to ask Noah out. Half the unattached females under thirty-five were probably waiting for him to dump me and go on the market again. And Meg is working for him now, so she'll see him every day."

Poppy ran her hands over her tight-fitting black jeans and smiled. "I don't think that will be a problem."

Tossing her platinum curls, she waved and headed to her Hummer. I hoped she was right. Poppy was stunning, but I'd caught sight of Meg the other day, and she was pretty damn beautiful, too. If she were interested in Noah, Meg might give Poppy some competition.

When Jake picked me up, I noticed that he'd had running boards installed on his truck. I pointed to them and asked, "Are these for me?"

"They sure are, sugar." Jake brushed a kiss

across my lips. "I still plan on helping you in and out most of the time, because I love the feeling of your gorgeous ass in my hands, but this way you won't feel so helpless."

"Thank you so much." I gave him a kiss, handed him the erotic gift basket, and climbed into the cab. "That's the sweetest thing anyone has ever done for me." Certainly, no had ever called my round bottom *gorgeous* before.

Jake and I kept the conversation light on our drive from Shadow Bend into the city, but as we checked into the hotel, we both grew quiet. And when he opened the door to our room and I walked into the elegant living room, I silently gawked at the staircase leading up to the loft bedroom. Jake had apparently booked us a suite.

Jake threw his Stetson on the chair and carried our overnight bags and the gift basket upstairs. Watching him, butterflies took flight in my stomach and my mind went blank. Should I unpack? Strip? Turn on the TV?

I was still standing frozen staring out the window when Jake returned. He drew me into his arms, rested his chin on the top of my head, and stroked my back. All the stress and tension oozed out of me, and I laid my cheek against his chest.

"Darlin'." Jake's rich voice swept over me. "We can do as much or as little as you're comfortable with. Just because we're in a hotel room doesn't mean we have to have sex." Using his thumb, he tilted my face up to his and grinned. "But that's not saying that I'm not hoping we do."

"Can we talk first?" I hated that my voice was so shaky, but this was a big moment in my life. I'd never told a man that I loved him before. "I need to say some things before we go any further."

"How about some wine?" Jake let me go and walked to the wet bar. "I had them put that moscato you like on ice, and I could use a beer."

"Great."

We settled on the sofa with our drinks, and I shifted so that I could see his face while we talked. "I guess the first thing I need to tell you is that last Thursday night I told Noah that I wasn't going to date him anymore."

"Are you telling me the same thing?" Jake's jaw tightened, and he thumped his beer bottle on the coffee table.

"No!" I put my glass next to his bottle and took both his hands in mine. "I'm telling you that I . . ." Drawing in a deep breath, I went for broke. "I love you."

"I feel the same way about you." Jake smiled widely. "I've loved you since our first kiss. Hell! Maybe since that day we met when you tripped and I got to hold you in my arms."

"It seems as if I've spent my entire life searching for pieces that would make my world whole. Even when I found one, I had no idea how it was supposed to fit with the others." I released his hands so that I could cup his cheeks. "Then you appeared and it took me a while, but I finally put the puzzle together. I saw how my life was supposed to be lived. It's supposed to be lived in your arms."

"That's exactly where you should be." Jake scooped me into his lap and whispered, "Because that's the picture I see for my life, too."

I wrapped my arms around his neck, savoring his words and the warmth of his embrace. Jake pulled the elastic band from my hair and ran his fingers through the heavy mass of ringlets, massaging my scalp. I sighed in bliss as he arranged the curls around my shoulders.

I turned to kiss him, but Jake took my chin between his fingers before our lips met and said, "If we start this now, I won't be able to stop with a kiss. Are you ready for that?"

"More than ready," I murmured.

My last thought before Jake's mouth claimed mine was that I was glad no one knew where we were. For once, we weren't in the pickup truck. There wouldn't be any cops flashing their bright lights at us and threatening to arrest us for indecent exposure. I could enjoy this moment without worrying about an interruption.

At that exact moment, Jake's cell buzzed. He frowned, then shrugged and said, "That's not Tony's ringtone." He shut the phone off without looking at the screen and went back to nibbling my throat.

When a few seconds later my cell rang, hearing that it wasn't Dad or Gran's ringtone, I followed Jake's example and silenced it. This was our private time. And I planned to enjoy every second of it.

Still. Wasn't it odd that someone was trying to reach both of us?